The
Cornbread
Killer

Also by Lou Jane Temple

Bread on Arrival
A Stiff Risotto
Death by Rhubarb
Revenge of the Barbeque Queens

The Cornbread Killer

LOU JANE TEMPLE

ST. MARTIN'S MINOTAUR ≈ NEW YORK

ISBN 0-312-20605-4

M
TEM
CI
7/03

For my grandson, Ramsey Wilson Walker,
with special thanks to his mother, Kelly

Acknowledgments

I hope you can all visit the revitalized Eighteenth and Vine district in Kansas City. I know you can all read Buck O'Neil's fascinating book, *I Was Right on Time: My Journey from the Negro Leagues to the Majors* (Fireside Press, 1996). Buck is the president of the board for the Negro Baseball League Museum on Eighteenth and Vine and has done so much to tell their story. Thanks to Pam Whiting, then of the mayor's office, now of the Chamber of Commerce, for providing vital information about the Eighteenth and Vine project. Thanks to Steve Westheimer for providing vital information about jazz and Charlie Parker lore. Art Kent, lighting designer, electrified the subject of theater power for me.

Kansas City Star reporter James Fussell wrote an interesting article about the Kansas City African-America social clubs. *Crisis* magazine, the magazine of the NAACP, ran a great piece about jazz as a Cold War weapon. Both of these pieces helped me very much, as did reading *The Carolina Rice Kitchen: The African Connection*, by Karen Hess (University of South Carolina Press, 1992).

A special thanks to writer Cort Sinnes for looking at my pages with his editor's hat on.

With the writing of every book, my friends seem to take turns nurturing me when I need it in a dozen different ways. Special thanks this time to Lennie and Jerry Berkowitz, Sally Uhlmann, and Bonnie Winston.

Very special thanks to my editor, Joe Veltre, who has the patience of Job.

The
Cornbread
Killer

Cornbread

1 10" cast-iron skillet
1 egg
2 cups buttermilk
1½ cups stone-ground yellow or white cornmeal
½ cup coarse ground yellow cornmeal
2 T. melted butter
1 tsp. each kosher salt, baking powder, baking soda
Optional: 3 strips bacon, cooked and crumbled, and 2 T.
   melted bacon fat

After testing dozens of versions of this batter bread, I've come to the conclusion that a cast-iron skillet or cast-iron cornbread molds are the key to delicious cornbread. I also rejected the recipes with wheat flour and sugar. Using the two kinds of cornmeal gives the bread wonderful texture, but you could make cornbread with just stone-ground meal and it would be fine. You can also add a ¼ cup of sugar for a sweeter taste or ¼ cup of all-purpose flour for a lighter crumb. If you don't have a 10" cast-iron skillet, use an 8" skillet and only use two thirds of the batter, baking the rest in muffin tins.

   Spray the skillet with Pam or another non stick spray. Place in a preheated 400 degree oven and let heat while you make the cornbread batter. Combine the dry ingredients, then add the egg, buttermilk, and melted

1

butter and mix. Put batter in the hot skillet and bake at 400 degrees for 20 minutes. For a more soulful version, replace the butter with the bacon fat and add the crumbled bacon. Cracklings of duck skin or pork fat are good in this, too. To make cracklings, put strips of duck or pork skin with fat attached on a baking sheet with a rim and roast at 350 degrees until the skin is crisp, stirring occasionally so the strips in the middle of the pan get moved.

One

The street had ghosts. Every once in a while she would see the tail end of one, just a wisp of someone's leftover spirit, out of the corner of her eye. She always recognized them; the apparitions looked like the hepcats who used to play on the street, Bennie Moten or the Count, sometimes Charlie Parker with so much sadness in his eyes. One day she saw a young Duke Ellington, elegant in white tie and tails, stop and look up, then tip his silk top hat at her before disappearing around the corner of 18th and Vine. Sometimes the ghosts brought a sound track with them, short snatches of laughter and music that filled the room and then were gone.

Evelyn Edwards stared out the window of her cramped office. The city had found this space for her to use while she was putting together the big dedication weekend. It was on the second story of a building not yet officially restored; a dusty, old-fashioned billiard hall was still open on the first floor. Next weekend, the Eighteenth and Vine Historical District would be up and running. Where would she go then? Sooner or later someone would ask her when she would have her belongings moved out. If Nolan Wilkins had anything to do with it, it would be sooner.

Why had she burned so many bridges to get here? She was filled with such urgency to sort out her past, she forgot about good common sense and fair play. Nothing seemed as important as this, certainly not the consequences of some of her recent stunts. She had, in the last few days, been compelled by events to admit she might have taken a more prudent path. Some of the things she'd done could be ready to come back and bite her on the ass. But she'd been driven, and now she was here and committed and that was that, however it played out.

Evelyn Edwards looked around at her reflection in the old mirror she had nailed up on the office wall so she could put on makeup. Beautiful? Maybe. Skin the color of coffee with real cream in it. Long hair made longer with extensions. She had three good suits and lots of accessories. Surely he would be proud when he saw her. She looked away from her image, disgusted with herself for such a thought, such a weakness.

Evelyn pulled the telephone toward her. She had some damage control to do if she was going to survive this latest crisis. And survive she must, so she could be here in the middle of things for the dedication. Right in the middle of the action, where he would be as well.

As she fiddled with her electronic address book, looking for a number, the door opened behind her. When she organized her office, she'd debated over whether to be able to see the door or to look outside. Outside won. She continued to dial, not looking around. "Well, big sister, I hope you brought me some of that cornbread you're so famous for."

Mona Kirk stepped up next to the desk. "I don't know who you're expecting, but I haven't brought you anything but a warning." Mona's eyes were blazing with anger.

"Mona, I'm busy here. What's your problem?"

Mona snorted. "You're the one with a problem, miss. You

have been dishonest and now you're caught. And I, for one, am steamed about it. You're jeopardizing a project that is near and dear to my heart."

She tried to get up but Mona had her wedged in her chair. "Get off me, woman," Evelyn protested. "I don't know what you're talking about."

Mona pointed her finger at Evelyn and leaned toward her. Evelyn was surprised at the old girl. She'd taken Mona for a widow with too much time on her hands, not a crusader.

"You," Mona declared, "have been demanding kickbacks from the vendors who are helping us with the gala dedication. And that's not right. That's stealing from the people of Kansas City."

"I really don't have time for this, Mona. I don't know who's been lying about me, but I'm sure there's not a speck of proof that I've asked anyone for money to be a part of your little ol' dedication."

Mona straightened up with a look of triumph in her eyes. "That's where you're wrong, young lady. You better start packing up your stuff, because after tonight, I'm betting you'll be gone from Eighteenth and Vine. You have been found out!"

Evelyn twisted her way out of the chair and stood up to face her accuser. "I don't think so. Now, beat it. I'll see you at the meeting this evening, and you better not be making these silly accusations then. We still have a lot of work to do before next week. You certainly don't have time to fire me and hire another event planner, so if I were you I'd just shut up and mind my own business, which is finding volunteers, as I recall."

"I won't let you take advantage of this town and this committee. We can dedicate this district without you," Mona snapped. "I intend to make sure of that."

"Get out."

"I'm going," Mona said as she swept out and slammed the door.

Evelyn sat back down and fiddled with the pages of her desk calendar. She was so close. It was that florist. She knew she'd made him mad when she asked for ten percent of the gross. But Evelyn didn't intend to stay in Kansas City, so she couldn't very well ask him to landscape her yard or something like that. Besides, she needed the cash.

The door opened again, and Evelyn turned angrily. But it wasn't Mona Kirk, back for a second round. It was a beautiful black woman dressed in vintage clothing. Her hair was marcelled; her platform shoes and gloves and hat all matched her burgundy-colored 1940s gabardine suit. "I didn't know when to expect you," Evelyn said.

"Surprise is always a good weapon, don't you think, sister? And now is as good a time as any for you to explain why you think we are sisters."

"Half sisters," Evelyn amended, still mesmerized by the physical presence of this other woman. She filled the room with her energy. Evelyn thought she saw one of the Eighteenth and Vine ghosts dart into the room and out again. Even the dead were attracted.

Evelyn slipped two photos out of the desk drawer and held them up. The other woman took them in her hand and stared at the images intently. "There the bastard is. One with you and your momma, one with me and my momma," Evelyn said.

"Where'd you get these?"

"Just last year, when Momma passed, I found them in a box, along with some other things that belonged to our long, lost father. He must have left them behind and forgot about them, like he forgot about me and my mother," Evelyn said, the pain of remembering all there in her voice.

"But what brought you to me? That could be any little black girl."

"Don't give me that shit. That's you, and you know it. And I've done my homework. I didn't just call you up out of the blue," Evelyn said with more confidence in her voice than she felt.

"Were there any letters?"

"Wouldn't you like to know?"

"Calm down, Mona," Heaven said. "Haven't I been working on this celebration for months now? I'm not going to leave you in the lurch, not when we're this close to the finish line."

Mona Kirk tugged at her glasses—cat eyes, of course—and sat down beside Heaven Lee. They were at Sal's Barber Shop, across Thirty-ninth Street from Mona's cat gift shop and Cafe Heaven. Mona had put a Be Back in Five Minutes sign on the door and gone across the street when she saw Heaven heading for Sal's. "You have worked like a Trojan, H, but I just want you to be prepared for the meeting tonight. It's getting close to the big gala weekend and everything is all in an uproar, believe you me. The mayor's office is mad at the Ruby Theater people. The Ruby Theater people are mad at the Negro Leagues Baseball Museum people, and everybody is mad at the Parks and Recreation people, who are supposed to have had the parking lot paved but it isn't. And don't get me started on Evelyn Edwards."

"What's she done now?" Heaven asked.

Mona pinched her lips together. "You'll find out tonight, and I'm hoping it will be the last act for that little crook. I just can't abide what she's done. After so many people have worked for years to get Eighteenth and Vine renovated, we can't let some party planner ruin it."

Sal d'Giovanni looked up from the sink. Sal kept tabs on his whole shop through the mirrors that covered the walls. He rarely turned toward the person he was talking to. Now he chewed on his unlit cigar and grinned at the same time. "That's what happens when you volunteer for stuff, Mona, you have to contend with the fact that most people are incompetent. Heaven, what's your part of this wingding? Are you catering?"

Heaven rolled her eyes and shook her head, looking embarrassed and proud at the same time. "Of course not, nothing that would actually produce income. I am the volunteer chairman of the food committee for the dedication of the Eighteenth and Vine Historic District."

Mona looked around for something to eat. It was the middle of the afternoon, so there was no thought of drinking Sal's coffee, which was frightening even in the morning. She spotted a bagel in a see-through plastic bag, gave it a poke. It was impervious to her touch, so she put it back on the counter. "Now, Heaven, remember we asked you to cater the fancy party Friday night, the opening gala. And, Sal, she said that the black community should do the catering because this was celebrating the history of the black community. She was right, of course."

Sal started scrubbing his combs and brushes. "So she works just as hard for free. Smart move, H." Sal knew Heaven had been so busy at the restaurant she barely had time to go home and change her clothes. Folks in Kansas City came out of the woodwork in the spring, going out to eat, listening to music, enjoying the good weather that would end when summer and the humidity hit. Now she'd taken on a big volunteer job. Sal would have to ask Murray to keep an eye on her. Heaven never knew when to say no.

"Who's Evelyn Edwards?" Sal asked.

"A smarty-pants party planner who has been hired to coordinate the entire gala weekend," Mona said tartly.

"And?" Sal said. "Don't give me a one-sentence description, especially when I can hear from the tone of your voice that there's more to the story."

"Mona doesn't like Evelyn, Mona doesn't like Evelyn," Heaven chanted in a singsong voice.

Mona got up and looked over at her shop. There was a small gray kitty sitting in front of the door. "Sal, it isn't that I don't like Evelyn. I just don't trust her, and it turns out I'm right. Something's not kosher, and as the chairman of volunteers for the entire weekend, I'm not about to put up with it. Oh, look, a new kitty. I better go feed it."

Sal glanced across the street via the mirror and shook his head. "So you think you can get out of telling us about this Evelyn gal by changing the subject to a stray, do ya? Every cat in Kansas City that no one wants ends up here on Thirty-ninth Street. There must be a sign somewhere: 'Leave all unwanted cats on Thirty-ninth Street, because Mona is a soft touch.' "

Heaven got up and patted Sal on his bald head. "You must be bored today. You're trying to start trouble."

"I don't see a cat blocking the entrance to your place of business, Mr. d'Giovanni," Mona sniped.

Heaven put her arm around her friend and headed toward the door. "We'd better get back to work so we can go to the meeting. Do you want to ride downtown together? The meeting is at six, so I'll have to come back to the restaurant anyway. You can leave your car behind the shop."

Mona smiled. "I'd like that, but you're always late and we have to leave on time, have to, have to. We have lots of ground to cover tonight. I'll come over and get you. Be ready at five-forty." The two women waved to Sal in the mirror and went across the street.

Sal surprised them both by sticking his head out the door of the barbershop. "Heaven," he called across the street. She turned toward him with a question in her look. "It wouldn't hurt you to take a night off, you know. You work too much."

Heaven rolled her eyes. "Coming from you, that's a compliment," she said, and blew him a kiss.

The truth was, Heaven didn't want a night off. Hank was in Houston for two months and Heaven was lonely.

She hadn't planned it this way, but most of her life had been spent in tandem with a man. It certainly hadn't been traditional, one man for life. But when one relationship had gone wrong, another had rapidly taken its place. Years ago she'd walked out on her first husband and childhood sweetheart, Sandy Martin, after a miscarriage left her anxious and skittish. She married her second husband, rock musician

Dennis McGuinne, before she realized how impossible it would be to live that lifestyle. In a year she was divorced and back in Kansas City with a baby daughter, Iris. Iris was going to college in England now, spending time with her father. She was the light of Heaven's life always.

But Heaven hadn't stopped needing a man in her life just because she had a daughter. Ian Wolff, the painter, had been the next husband. When he broke Heaven's heart, she found a wonderful man, Sol Steinberg, a uniform manufacturer, to replace him. When Sol died suddenly of a heart attack soon after they were married, designer Jason Kelly came knocking at her door. Then Heaven opened Cafe Heaven, and Jason quickly tired of her late hours and her preoccupation with business. Heaven and Jason divorced, and because of her hours, she was sure that—barring falling in love with the man who serviced the dishwasher and was around far too often—she was through with men.

She was going to concentrate on making money for a change.

But this guy from her neighborhood—he was just a kid, really—wouldn't stop coming around. He was a young doctor in his last year of residency, and he was handsome and funny and wise beyond his years. Huy Wing was his real name, even though most of his American friends called him Hank. His father had been killed execution-style during the fall of Saigon because he worked for the United States. Hank and his mother and sister had been on one of the last planes to leave for the United States and had been sponsored by a Catholic church in Kansas City. Hank had been four when they arrived at their new home. In Heaven's mind, Hank deserved a storybook family that would somehow make up for the heartbreak of his childhood, not a love affair with an older woman.

Heaven told herself this kid would get over his crush. In the meantime he spent more nights at her house than at his own. Hank was very comfortable with their relationship, even though Heaven was always telling him how he would grow up and move on. Hank said that losing his father and his country had given him an understanding of how the world really worked. He lived in the moment better than anyone Heaven had ever known. She was always letting her fear of the future get in the way of their time together; he was always bringing her back to the present.

But this current separation, only ten days old, was giving Heaven time to stew about how she had allowed this guy, who she was positive should be dating someone his own age, to become so important to her. She was glad the Eighteenth and Vine event needed her attention right now. She could certainly use the distraction.

Heaven headed down the alley to the back door of her cafe and opened the kitchen door just in time to put out a spectacular oven fire.

The filling from Pauline's plum tarts had run over, and the sugar and fruit syrup had found some grease that had spilled the night before from the lamb shanks. The result was a mini bonfire that was fed by the oxygen that rushed in when Pauline opened the oven door. She yelped and looked around for the baking soda, which was across the room. Heaven was closest to the baking station. She grabbed the box of baking soda and emptied the contents on the bottom of the oven.

"Thanks, boss," Pauline muttered as she pulled out her tarts. They were fine, golden brown, the bottom of the pan the only thing blackened from the flames. Heaven thought she recognized a plum in the mess below. "This is such a drag," Pauline whined. "Now I have to let the oven cool down so I can clean it out, then heat it up again. I have flan and bread pudding yet to do, and I know Brian will need the ovens for something."

Both Brian Hoffman, the day chef, and Robbie Lunstrum were suddenly very busy on the other side of the kitchen. They were fighting back smiles. It wasn't that they wished

Pauline ill, it was just the usual competition of any professional kitchen. When someone was really in the weeds, they usually got help, but not until they'd been teased about it.

"Guess you filled those tart pans too full, eh, Pauline?" Brian quipped. Heaven cleared her throat loudly to warn him he better shut up. The look on Pauline's face was somewhere between despair and rage.

Robbie Lunstrum saved the day, something he was famous for. Robbie was a sixty-something elf, a recovering alcoholic who relished every day of his sober life. He was the day dish washer, shrimp peeler, and handyman. Cafe Heaven couldn't open the doors without him. "Let me handle the cleanup, Pauline. I have asbestos hands. I'll be able to wipe that mess out in ten minutes or so. You do something else," Robbie said.

Pauline smiled. "Thanks, Robbie, I'll fill the flan pans. Heaven, will you please call the produce guy? He wants to know what you need for tomorrow."

Heaven called the organic produce supplier, Max Mossman. Then she made salad dressing, cleaned a crate of spinach, caramelized twenty pounds of onions, and prepped fifteen chickens and stuck them in the oven. Suddenly Mona was at the pass-through window, sticking her head all the way into the kitchen. "Heaven, I knew you wouldn't be ready," Mona fussed, her finger wagging. "Put that down right now and wash your hands. We *cannot* be late to this meeting."

The whole kitchen staff grinned involuntarily. It was rare to hear someone boss the boss around.

To everyone's surprise, Heaven obeyed without argument. "I'll be right there, Mona." Heaven washed her hands and stepped into the kitchen bathroom. When she emerged she had taken off her baseball cap, fluffed her short red hair into some semblance of order, and applied lipstick, hot pink. She hung her chef's jacket on a peg and slipped on a black linen jacket in its place. "Let's go. The van is out here."

"Heaven, you always have to drive. I'm driving tonight."

Heaven nodded distractedly. "Whatever you say."

When the two women got into Mona's car, Mona dangled the keys in front of Heaven's nose, then threw them out the open car window on the passenger's side.

"What are you doing?" Heaven asked, getting out of the car and picking up Mona's keys. "You've gone mad. I thought you said we had to be on time, then you pitch the keys out the window," she snapped as she got back into the car.

Mona calmly took the keys from Heaven and started the car, pulling out of her parking space behind the cat shop. "You've been so obedient and docile I thought the real you was gone and you'd been replaced by the pod people. I was just checking."

Heaven grinned. "I'm just getting ready for the meeting, putting myself in a Zen trance."

Mona nodded. "That would help. You're generally the calm one at these meetings. I tell you, I'm certainly not going to be calm tonight."

"When are you going to tell me what Evelyn is up to?"

"When we come face-to-face with her and the rest of the committee," Mona said determinedly as they pulled out of the alley and headed downtown.

Escargot with Pernod

4 T. butter
36–40 canned snails
3 cloves garlic, sliced
1 cup tomato concentrate, recipe below
Pernod

Melt the butter in a heavy sauté pan. Add the garlic. Rinse the snails and sauté for 5 minutes. Add the tomatoes and sauté another 5 minutes. Remove from heat and sprinkle with Pernod, between 1 T. and ¼ cup, depending on how you like the licorice taste. Serve with toast or good French bread.

Tomato Concentrate

4 lbs. peeled, seeded, and chopped tomatoes, or a 28 oz.
  can of good-quality canned tomatoes
2 bay leaves
8–10 stalks fresh herbs—thyme, oregano, tarragon,
  marjoram, any or all
1 T. sugar
1 T. kosher salt

Combine all these ingredients in a baking dish and bake in a slow oven, about 300 degrees, for at least 30 minutes and up to 2 hours, until the moisture is completely gone. Remove aromatics, cool, and store. This is a very good way to add tomato flavor to sauces and recipes that call for sun-dried tomatoes.

Two

Jim Dittmar sat outside on a bus stop bench looking over at the Ruby Theater. Spring was his favorite season in Kansas City. Of course, spring hadn't been too shabby in Paris, either. But all in all, Jim was glad to be back home. Two years of bouncing around Europe was a long time.

What a time to be a jazz player in his hometown, what with this Eighteenth and Vine renovation. Maybe now players wouldn't have to leave Kansas City to make a living. Leave town or live off their wives and girlfriends. Of course, that can't last forever. In his case, Teresa had a good job at Hallmark, but she got sick of carrying the load after seven years. Jim always said he got kicked out. Teresa always said that she'd asked Jim to get a real career, something he thought he already had.

Tomorrow, first thing, he had to call Teresa. He'd been home three days now, staying at his parents'. Last night he'd played at a jam session and lots of friends who knew both him and his ex-wife had seen him. If he didn't call her tomorrow he would be in more trouble than he already was. Even before he came home, Teresa was pissed at him. His folks had confirmed that. He had missed a few months of his child support payments. His parents finally kicked in five hundred dollars, just to keep Teresa from calling in Family Services.

Jim needed to see Josh as soon as possible. He was sure Josh was pissed, too. He did pretty well for the first year, calling Josh every week, coming home three times for special occasions like Josh's birthday. The second year he lapsed. But now, now he better take Josh to a Royals game and make plans for them to take a trip this summer, just the two of them.

He would pay everyone this week. He would repay his folks the five hundred and Teresa the four months he owed her. She could have the extra five hundred for the aggravation. When he rented an apartment and bought a secondhand car, he would be lucky to have a few thousand left. But that's what money was for, wasn't it, to spend?

He'd had some good gigs just as he was leaving Paris. He'd decided to have a great meal at Restaurant Alain Ducasse and come home. He would miss the food in Paris, especially those snails with the Pernod they made at that little bistro around the corner from his apartment in the Marais. And the cheeses. And the pâtés. You just couldn't get that stuff in the States, at least not that tasted so good. But they didn't have good fried chicken in Paris, either. Everything in life was a trade-off of some kind.

Jim watched the workmen on the scaffolding and saw trucks bringing deliveries of boxes and crates to the museum building. Maybe this was really going to change things for jazz in Kansas City. The jam last night down in the River Market had been crowded and it was only the beginning of the week. Maybe this Eighteenth and Vine redo made people want to hear music again. A couple of the players last night had promised to check out some possible gigs for him. He'd follow up with some phone calls. If things went right, he could be playing by next weekend.

A cool breeze ran down the street, stirring up the trash in the gutter as it traveled east. A spring rainstorm during the night had brought the temperature down into the low sixties.

The air was full of ozone and promise and danger.

Jim stuck his hand into his jeans pocket and pulled out a loose diamond, a big one, eight carats at least. His lucky diamond. He loved the thrill of having a loose stone worth thousands just stuck in his jeans. He tossed it up and caught it with one hand, stuck it back in his pocket. Then he checked his watch. He'd just sit here and watch another ten minutes, then maybe mosey over to the Ruby.

He wanted to see what they'd done to the old place. And he did have some work to do.

"I think's it's interesting we don't have one musician on the committee for this big weekend. The city of Kansas City is dedicating a whole district to the memory of its long lost fame in the music world, and we don't have a single musician on the planning committee," Heaven said.

"I agree one hundred percent, Heaven. But before you came on board Evelyn Edwards had already chased off the one musician on the committee. She said she would be the one to interface with the music community."

Heaven wrinkled her nose. "Interface?"

"Some techno biz term for 'work with,' " Mona said. "I understand the need for event planners in principle, just like I understand the need for interior decorators. But a bad one can ruin your life. Dealing with the musicians herself is just another one of Evelyn's scams, I bet."

"What got you sucked into the project, Mona?"

Mona turned the car east on Eighteenth Street, toward the new historic district. "Samantha Scott," she said.

Heaven was surprised. "The jazz singer? What about her?"

"We were best friends all through high school in Saint Joseph, Missouri," Mona said with regret in her voice.

"You're kidding. Are you the one who got her to come for the opening?"

"No, we don't speak."

Heaven turned and looked at her friend. "Let me get this straight. You and Samantha . . . Did you call her Sam, like they do now?"

"Yes, she's always been Sam."

"You and Sam Scott were friends and then you had a falling-out and then you found out she was coming to the dedication and you decided to volunteer?"

"I only knew that her husband, Lefty Stuart, was one of the first baseball players they asked to be a part of the dedication of the Negro Leagues Baseball Museum. I hoped she'd come along, what with the jazz connection and all," Mona said.

"Why?"

"I did something terrible and I've been too embarrassed to try to fix it and all this time has gone by and I hope I can apologize now."

Mona sure seemed full of secrets tonight. Heaven was dying to ask what the fight with Sam Scott was about, but she was sure Mona wouldn't tell her, not yet. She seemed torn up about it, whatever it was. Heaven would have to ease her into telling her everything by acting uninterested. She'd start that play in a minute. "Have you seen her in the last twenty-five years, I mean except for on television?"

Mona shook her head. "I last saw her the summer after we graduated from high school. I went off to college and Sam was already singing with a big band. She never came to visit her folks at the same time I was home visiting my folks. I got married, moved here to Kansas City, and my folks mostly came down here to visit Carl and me because my mom always wanted to go shopping, rest her soul. All of a sudden it's twenty-five years later." Mona pulled into a parking space in front of the Ruby Theater. The crew was still clambering on the scaffolding even though it was evening.

The two women got out and walked toward the main entrance. "This is so exciting. This time it's you instead of me having a run-in with the past. A real-life personal drama to accompany all the historical fanfare," Heaven said.

Mona tried to smile but she looked worried. "I'll be glad when the whole kit and kaboodle is over. I hope Sam will . . ." Mona's voice trailed off, and Heaven let her have her private thoughts for a minute.

But there was only a minute for reflection.

The fighting had already begun. They could hear it as they approached the conference room. The door opened violently, almost knocking Heaven down. "Whoa," both women said at once.

Nolan Wilkins, the mayor's top aide, was making a rapid exit. Nolan, a handsome black man, was almost beet red. "So sorry, Heaven. Something's come up. I'll be back," he muttered as he strode down the hall.

Inside, everyone was talking at once. Mona looked triumphant. "I guess Nolan already told them."

"Slow down a minute and catch me up," Heaven demanded, holding on to her friend's arm so she couldn't escape.

Mona looked like she was considering making a break, but she knew Heaven wouldn't stop bugging her.

"Evelyn Edwards came into the shop and said she needed a new florist for the Eighteenth and Vine gala," Mona said.

"Into the City Cat? Boy, was she in the wrong place," Heaven said, knowing that wasn't what Mona meant.

"No, into that nice young man down on Westport Road's flower shop. When I came in about twenty minutes later I heard him on the phone to another florist. They both had the same tale to tell."

"About?"

"Kickbacks," Mona said impatiently. She wanted to hear what Nolan had told the rest of the committee. "Evelyn wanted him to give her ten percent of the gross sales total in cash when she delivered the check from this committee. Then I asked the florists if they would put in writing what she'd said and done and they did and I gave it to Nolan and told him he'd better fire her," Mona said loudly. She was pleased to see other committee members nodding as if to confirm her story. At least Nolan hadn't tried to take credit for catching Evelyn Edwards all by himself. "The florists all said they didn't mind taking someone out to dinner or giving them a bouquet for a big job but this gala was for the city, not some big corporation, and it seemed like she was stealing from everyone," Mona explained.

"I don't get it," Heaven said. "Why did she, instead of an established Kansas City event planner, get this job?"

Mona turned to her friend with eyebrows arched. "Why, indeed. There are plenty of mysteries about this whole thing. We've all tried to keep our noses out of them and just take care of our own little areas of responsibility. Now, it seems we were wrong."

A voice boomed from the direction of the door. "You got that right, honey. Wrong is what that piece of Tulsa trailer trash is, if she thinks she's gonna get a cent out of Miss Ella!"

Heaven had never laid eyes on Miss Ella Jackson before, although they had recently talked on the phone. Miss Ella's Soul Food was a Harlem fixture, famous for its catfish and cornbread. Two years ago, Ella had branched out and opened cafes in Atlanta; Washington, D.C.; and Chicago. Kansas City was going to be home to the fifth Miss Ella's, and the location was the new historic Eighteenth and Vine district. The grand opening was to coincide with the dedication.

Miss Ella was big, black, and beautiful. She had on a vintage dress from the forties. Heaven recognized it as what *People* magazine called her trademark fashion statement. What's more, she had on vintage accessories, long black gloves, a sassy hat with feathers, platform heels. Her hair was marcelled. She was a knockout, and it was only a Tuesday. Heaven wondered what happened when she wanted to really strut her stuff on a Saturday night.

Right now, Miss Ella was angry. "Which one of you is Heaven Lee?" she asked. Smoke was practically coming out of her ears.

Heaven got up and held out her hand. "Well, this wasn't exactly the face-to-face meeting I'd planned, but I'm brave. I'm Heaven Lee."

"Why'd you sic that crazy woman on me, sugar? Surely you didn't think Ella was a fool, now, did you?" Ella grabbed Heaven's hand and pulled her close. The rest of the room tensed. The gesture had something erotic about it, and an element of danger, too. Was she going to slap Heaven or kiss her?

Mona walked toward the door, using hand signals to tell Heaven she was going to use the phone. What a chicken Mona was, Heaven thought.

Heaven used her free hand to pull a chair back from the conference table. She deftly guided Ella to the chair, and when she sat down, Heaven sat beside her. "Let me guess. Evelyn Edwards wanted a kickback from your catering?"

"And made no bones about it, girl," Ella said. "Aren't you in charge of how the food goes down for this weekend?"

Heaven nodded. "Ella, we just found out that Evelyn is hitting up some of the other vendors for money. Believe me, this is not how we do business in Kansas City. Don't let this leave a sour taste in your mouth, please. As chairman of the food committee, I guess I'd better call the rest of the caterers and see if they've heard from Ms. Edwards."

"And I'll call the tent company," someone chimed in. Suddenly the room was a buzz, with everyone talking about how they knew something was rotten in Denmark but hadn't wanted to be the first one to mention it. Hindsight was, as usual, making geniuses out of everyone. No one defended Evelyn Edwards or even suggested they get her side of the story.

Heaven looked around the room. "How come she isn't here?"

"She breezed in before the meeting started and said she had to check with the tech director, something about lighting cues for the big concert," a city planner chimed in.

Heaven stood up. "I know we need to give our committee reports tonight. But our chairman and fearless leader left in a snit as I came in. I'm assuming that was about the Evelyn Edwards situation?" She looked around for an answer.

Mona, who had slipped back into the room, looked like she'd seen one of the Eighteenth and Vine ghosts. Her mouth was pinched into a thin line. Heaven held her hands upward, looking at Mona as if to say, What's going on?

Mona hemmed and hawed. "Nolan was . . . ah . . . hopping mad on the phone to someone and . . . said 'she' should be arrested. I hope it was the mayor he was talking to and Evelyn Edwards he was talking about."

Heaven stood up. "Well, we aren't going to get anything else done tonight. I suggest we reschedule the nuts-and-bolts meeting for tomorrow and then ask Evelyn Edwards to come in here and have a little talk. She turned to Ella. Are you in Kansas City until your restaurant opening?"

Ella got up slowly, as if trying to decide if she would allow herself to be dismissed or stay around for the fireworks. "Yes, I am, sugar. I have to put those finishing touches on the place that only Miss Ella can do. You and I will talk tomorrow, Heaven. I expect you to take care of this little problem very soon."

Heaven looked at her watch for effect. "It won't be a problem much longer, I guarantee it."

The rest of the committee members mumbled soothing words to Miss Ella.

Suddenly, the lights went dim. Two flickers, then darkness.

"What the hell?" Miss Ella's booming voice demanded.

Heaven was closest to the door. She opened it and let the fading sunlight from the windows in the hallway shed some light on the darkened room. She looked down the hall. "The electricity is out everywhere." She could hear workers yelling outside. "Come on, it's brighter out here. Maybe the workers cut a cable or something."

All the committee members, plus Miss Ella, trooped out into the hall. Through the window, they saw Nolan Wilkins running down the sidewalk. "Do you think Nolan has a generator in his car?" Heaven joked.

As they passed the open door of the concert hall, the lights flashed back on. The stage was bathed in fuchsia, purple, and midnight blue light. "They must have been looking for the perfect lighting colors for Tony Bennett," Mona said.

"Wait a minute, honey," Miss Ella barked, holding her arms out to block the hall path. "That sure don't look like old Tony up there on the stage," she said as she pointed stage right.

Next to the lighting board a figure lay crumpled on the floor. Everyone ran down the aisle. Mona, the most nimble of the group, leapt onto the stage. She stopped short when she saw a stream of water ending in a puddle near the body. "Oh, Jesus, Joseph, and Mary," she said softly. "It's Evelyn Edwards."

The smell of singed hair was not a good sign.

Plum Tart

Enough pastry dough to cover a one-crust tart pan, or a
   frozen pie crust
4 oz. marzipan (almond paste)
4–6 plums, halved and pitted
½ cup cream
½ cup sugar
4 eggs
1 T. vanilla flavoring
½ cup slivered almonds

Combine the eggs, sugar, and cream and beat until frothy.
Add the vanilla and the nuts.

   Spread the marzipan over the crust. Place the pitted
plums facedown on the marzipan. Fill the shell with the
custard mixture. Depending on the size of the tart pan, you
may have custard left over. I just put it in a little glass custard
cup and bake it along with the pie.

   Bake at 350 degrees for about 40–50 minutes, until the
custard in the middle of the tart is set. This is more beautiful
baked in a tart pan as you can fit in more plum halves.

Three

Detective Bonnie Weber slipped off her high heels. "I tell you, it's a hell of a thing when a friend requests your presence at a homicide investigation like she was asking for her favorite waiter at a restaurant."

"Hush," Heaven said as she set out a platter of cold soy-and-peanut noodles, half a plum tart, and some dessert plates and forks. "Just because I've been involved in enough murders to have a favorite homicide investigator, you think that's bad? And I needed you to be there, especially since you finally got rid of your nasty partner. What do you want from the bar?"

Bonnie looked over at the bottles of booze lined up, and reflected a second time in the mirror behind the bar. "Harry went to Vice; I didn't get rid of him on purpose. Beer, no, wine. You're going to have wine, aren't you?"

"Wine for the table?" Heaven asked.

Mona Kirk and Ella Jackson nodded. "Red," Ella said.

"White, please," Mona said glumly, not looking up or noticing she hadn't gone along with the crowd. Mona wasn't used to finding dead bodies. It had taken the starch right out of her.

Heaven went over to the bar. The cafe was closed. By the time the women were released from the crime scene, it was almost eleven, the time Cafe Heaven stopped serving food during the week. Only one waiter and a busboy were working, resetting the last tables. Usually, the bar stayed open until midnight, one-thirty on the weekends. Tonight, Heaven had told the bartender to start his checkout early. Now he was down on his knees, restocking the bottled beer cooler. She grabbed a wine list and looked at it for a minute. "Tony, while you're down there, can you reach into the white wine cooler and pull out a bottle of Newton unfiltered Chardonnay?"

Tony glanced up at his boss and scooted over to the next cooler on his knees. "What are you celebrating? We don't get much of this stuff."

"I know we don't, but I don't care. We've had a rough night. And the answer to your question, what are we celebrating, is a death. Now, don't ask any more questions. I think for red we'll have that Ridge Monte Bello Cabernet."

"Wow. The '94?"

Heaven nodded. "The vintage of the decade, that's what they said last year at least. The decade's not over yet. I know, Tony, don't fuss at me. I know I'm spending the week's profits that we haven't made yet. Like I said, I don't care."

Heaven took glasses over to the table.

"And then this one here says 'She won't be a problem much longer, I guarantee it' and looks at her watch," Ella Jackson said, pointing at Heaven. "You sure got that right, baby. What did you have, a timer."

Bonnie shook her head and moaned. She had her trademark legal pads in front of her, the ones marked "Motive," "Means," and "Opportunity." "Great, Heaven. You forecasted the victim's demise just moments before she turns up fried on the stage of the Ruby. Just great."

Tony brought the wine to the table and uncorked the bottles. "Tony, when you're done with whatever you're doing back there, take off. We'll be fine." Heaven turned to the women. "And I didn't say anything about her being fried. I was referring to her larcenous ways' being nipped in the bud."

Bonnie Weber lifted her glass for a toast. "I hope this is the last time you three show up in this investigation. I would hate to have to pin Evelyn Edwards's murder on any of my drinking buddies. To Eighteenth and Vine, long may the joint jump."

Mona blanched. "Please, Detective, don't use the word *jump* after what happened to Evelyn. I have a feeling the electricity made her . . . , you know."

"Sorry, sorry," Bonnie said soothingly. "Mona, I didn't know you were such a wimp. You should see gunshot victims."

Mona's chin jutted forward. "I didn't choose a career in blood and guts, thank you very much. And as much as I disliked the woman, I'm sorry she touched the wrong knob, or whatever happened. I still hope it was a tragic accident. This is a good tart, by the way."

The other three women looked at Mona as if she were speaking an alien tongue. They had all decided that Evelyn Edwards had been murdered.

"Yeah, Mona, someone just happened to stop up the stage sink and leave the water running so it would run over and reach Evelyn's size-ten feet while she was tinkering with the light board," Heaven said. Mona was gazing out the window and just moaned. Heaven was immediately sorry she'd mentioned Evelyn's feet; they were charred on the bottoms, not a pretty sight.

Bonnie pointed to her legal pads. "Motives for killing this broad are available by the dozens. Mona, you didn't get along with Evelyn, and you just happened to leave the room to use the telephone minutes before she was found dead. Ella, you came to the meeting late and were gunning for Evelyn. You could have stopped up that sink before you came into the meeting."

"If I were gonna kill someone, I sure wouldn't leave

everything to chance. No sir, too many ways the whole thing could have fallen apart before the old girl kicked. Besides, if she weren't such a bitch, this would smell more like an accident than a murder," Ella said coldly.

"I don't know, Ella. Maybe this had nothing to do with Evelyn Edwards," Heaven said.

"What do you mean?" Mona said, jolted back to the conversation.

"Well, it could be part of a bigger plot, or someone could be after the tech director, or maybe Tony Bennett..." Heaven murmured.

"What did the tech director say?" Mona asked with worry in her voice.

"He'd gone to the lighting supply shop. Evelyn had asked for some gels he didn't have. She told him she'd work on the lighting cues while he was gone, as if she could do cues without knowing the running order for Tony's set. He said he thought she was just wasting time. Then he said he personally hadn't touched the sink for hours, claimed everything was fine when he left, everything except her attitude, of course," Bonnie answered. "Although he might have had the means, I doubt he had the motive. He hadn't known her long enough. That's more than I can say for Nolan Wilkins. If he was talking on the phone about having her arrested, he might have decided to stop her himself. I wonder where the guy went."

"Have you tried to call him?" Mona asked.

"Someone at the station has him on redial even as we speak. I hope he has a good reason for running away," Bonnie said. "I have to go pee," she added as she got up and headed to the women's room.

Heaven looked up and saw Tony motioning to her. "I'll be right back."

"So, sugar, when are you going to tell the cop you were yelling at Evelyn Edwards in her office just this afternoon?" Ella asked pleasantly.

Mona Kirk let the wine slop out of her glass as she set it

down with a jerky movement. Her already pale face turned paler. "What are you talking about?" she asked, a little tremor in her voice.

"Don't you think Detective Bonnie would want to know you two had a big old-time blowout just hours before she ends up dead? I think she would."

Mona tried to mount a defense but her face collapsed back into a worried frown. "I don't know anything about lighting and electricity. My family was in air-conditioning. And I guess it wouldn't do any good to ask where you were while I was having what I thought was a private conversation?"

Ella looked at Bonnie Weber, coming back to the table. "Doesn't air-conditioning involve electricity here in the sticks, Mona? Or do y'all still have houseboys with big old feather fans?"

"What'd I miss?" Bonnie asked as she slid into her chair, kicking her shoes out of the way.

Ella slapped Mona on the back, and Mona shrank even smaller. "I was just getting acquainted with Mona here."

Heaven had been watching Mona and Ella in the mirror behind the bar. What had transpired that had upset Mona even more? Heaven sat down again and put two glasses in front of her, one of white wine, the other of red. Finishing off the white, she started on the red.

Ella Jackson burst out in a big hearty laugh. "I like your style, Heaven. And who ever said Kansas City was a dull little cow town? I've been here ten hours and I'm around for a murder and got me some new friends. I love Kansas City. And I'd like to buy whoever killed Evelyn Edwards a drink. Good riddance, as far as I can see." She laughed that big laugh again. The other women couldn't help but laugh along with her. Everyone but Mona Kirk.

Nolan Wilkins was pacing. He couldn't put it off much longer. He had to return all the calls that the police had left on his answering machine or have a good explanation for why he hadn't. The messages hadn't mentioned Evelyn, of course, but he knew that was what they were calling about.

Nolan had no idea why he had panicked. It wasn't like him. People in politics couldn't afford to panic. He had been so angry at the stupid bitch, he could feel the pulse in his temples throbbing even now. He had longed to wring her neck.

Giving Evelyn Edwards the contract to manage this gala, some might have called it bad judgment from the first. But wasn't everything in life based on give-and-take? Doing favors for friends, using people you knew to do jobs, hiring people who might be able to help you later or had helped you in the past, that was how business worked. The private sector thrived on it. Why did government have to be different? Nolan paced, sickened by his own pitiful whining. Government was not the private sector, and that was that.

If the press discovered all the facts, they would yell blackmail or extortion—Nolan couldn't remember the exact legal definitions of the two. To an observer, it might seem that Evelyn had exerted some illegal pressure on Nolan. Who was he trying to kid—it had sure as hell felt like that to him. But it wasn't like he put a pipe welder in charge of brain surgery. She was an event planner, had been for years. He just didn't know she was a crooked one. Of course, if she was blackmailing him, why did he think he would be the only one? Now that she was dead Nolan hoped he wouldn't get caught in the undertow. He hadn't counted on Evelyn Edwards's business dealings being examined under a microscope.

To make a bad thing worse, he had run away from the theater in view of several dozen construction workers and who knows how many people inside the building. It was obvious why the police were calling every fifteen minutes.

He had weighed the options. He could call the mayor, tell him everything. But why put the burden on his shoulders? There were those who would never believe that he wasn't working on orders from the mayor in the first place. He would have to resign, would probably end up a murder suspect, if he wasn't already. It would certainly give him a motive. No one had seen him in the auditorium. If he came up with a convincing reason why he left the meeting in such a hurry, he might get yelled at by Detective Bonnie Weber but he wouldn't crash and burn.

Nolan's wife came into the bedroom. "I could lose my medical license for this, you know," she said tensely.

Nolan smiled at her, knowing that to her he must look like a miserable excuse for a man. This was going to cost him in their relationship, big time. "No one will know, trust me."

She tapped the syringe and pointed to his arm. "Let me see your vein. You better hope I know what I'm doing."

Nolan rolled up his shirtsleeve and made a fist. "I believe in you, baby. Let me have it."

Four

Boots Turner was tired. It was two in the afternoon and he had just eaten breakfast. He and the band had played another college concert last night, so it hadn't been the late hours of a club date. Still, by the time they'd gone out for something to eat, it had been almost three in the morning when Boots hit the sack. The habits of musicians don't die easily, Boots had noticed. Even on the nights he didn't gig, sleep never came until well after midnight. And God knows, it took longer to get up and running than it used to.

He was old—seventy-five, he thought—although he had guesstimated for Social Security. He'd been born at home in Clarksville, Tennessee, and the year of his birth seemed a little murky even to his own mother. She bore a baby a year for ten years. Only two of them survived to old age. Boots's brother Jesse had been the musical director of the Boots Turner Big Band for more than fifty years; he did all the arrangements and produced their recordings.

Now Jesse had cancer. He had been determined to go to the dedication in Kansas City, but Boots was worried about him making the airplane trip. Come to think of it, Boots was worried about his own ticker. Last night his heart had pounded so hard during the encore he thought it was going to burst.

Then there were these damn letters and phone calls. A young woman's voice that he didn't recognize on the answering machine, computer-generated letters with different postmarks, the latest one from Kansas City. Boots didn't know what to make of them. Was someone laying a trick bag on him, or was there a chance that it was the real thing? Everything was possible, life had taught him that. He couldn't do anything about it until he got to Kansas City. Then, according to the phone calls, he would get a big surprise.

Most of all, Boots was worried about seeing Sam Scott and that son of a bitch she had married. It was hard to admit he had carried a torch for one woman for thirty years. Through four marriages. For years he imagined that Lefty Stuart would die and he and Sam would pick right up where they left off. Then for years he was mad at Sam; anger choking him every time they ran into each other. Now he found, when they were thrown together, the anger was gone, replaced by the kind of melancholy and longing Boots had never felt for anyone.

He had every recording she'd produced. Absentmindedly, he went over to the CD cabinet and picked out a disc. Soon the room was full of Sam's voice, from the Gershwin songbook, singing "Bidin' My Time."

"I've been bidin' my time; now my time is almost up," Boots Turner said to his image in the mirror. "You better make hay while the sun shines, my man." With that he pulled his suitcase out from under the bed and opened it. The first item he packed was a .357 magnum.

Samantha Scott picked up the phone and quickly put it down again, for the tenth time, or maybe the twentieth. She couldn't shake the feeling she shouldn't go to Kansas City.

Once again she started to call and cancel, tell them she was ill or her voice was gone. Anything. Then she thought about Lefty going without her. That wouldn't work at all, and she knew Lefty was looking forward to the whole weekend. He had worked hard raising money for the Negro Leagues Baseball Museum. It would be selfish of her to ruin his plans when she didn't even know what she was afraid of.

At the time she had agreed to perform in Kansas City for the dedication, she was thinking of the early days of her career. Some of her first gigs had been there with Boots' band, when she was still in high school in Saint Jo. And Kansas City was where she met Lefty.

She could remember it like it was yesterday. She and the horn section had gone to the baseball game in the afternoon to see the Kansas City Athletics. Lefty had thrown out the first ball and the trumpet player had explained that Lefty was one of the first black men to play on a white major league team. That night he was at the club where they were playing. He was treated like royalty. You would have thought he was Joe DiMaggio. Between sets she went over to Lefty's table with Boots to say hello. The first time Lefty Stuart smiled at her, her heart melted.

A touch brought Sam back to the present. "A penny for your thoughts," Lefty Stuart said as he slipped an arm around her waist. He smiled and her heart melted again, just like it had that first time. She turned and kissed him, not a peck on the cheek but a big juicy one, right on the mouth. "Oh, Lord, you'll give this old man a heart attack, acting like that," he said.

"I was thinking about the day I met you, you handsome devil."

"Little did you know I was gonna steal you away from that piano player," he teased, rumpling her short gray hair.

Her eyes filled with apprehension. "Boots Turner is probably waiting for us in Kansas City, ready to chase us out of town with one of your old baseball bats."

Lefty held her out at arms' length, studying her face. "You're not kidding, you're worried about this, aren't ya, baby?"

"You know as well as I do he hasn't spoken to me for almost thirty years. Last year at Lincoln Center, he almost softened. It was after that concert of Duke Ellington music. Everybody was high on the evening, it had gone so well. They had a reception for all the performers, and someone tried to introduce us, one of the kids who didn't know the story, it could have been one of the Marsalis boys. Boots smiled this sad smile and said, 'We've met,' and just walked off."

Lefty hugged her close. "He's a fool. If I couldn't have you for my wife, I'd have taken anything I could get. If I were Boots, I would have never made you stop singing with my band. He could have been part of that wonderful talent, played along with that angel voice of yours, this whole time. That's something I can never do. You and Boots made fine music together. Plus, I'm an old man. I was retired from playing ball when we met. If he'd played his cards right, he might have had a second chance when I pass."

Sam shook her husband gently, shaking her head at him. "He's almost as old as you. And I'm no spring chicken, sugar. Don't you be talking like that. Which one of us makes it to those golden gates first is in the Lord's hands. I'm bettin' you'll outlive us all."

"Not if I don't take my walk. I hear Central Park is nice this time of year. How about going with me?"

Sam smiled. "I go with you when it's freezing and covered with snow, baby. I'm sure going on this beautiful May evening. That's why we live in this damned expensive apartment, honey, so we're across from the park. I'm gonna take advantage of it till I can't walk anymore."

The two went out of the apartment, arm in arm.

* * *

"So we all agree that a musician should be asked to be on this committee during these crucial last ten days. And because of my big mouth in suggesting it, I'm going to have to try to fill that slot. I'll make some calls tomorrow. Why don't we take a ten-minute break?" Heaven Lee said. "We only have two reports left, Mona's and mine. Everyone has been great, staying focused when I know we all really want to be talking about Evelyn Edwards. Let's get a soft drink and stretch our legs. I brought a cream cheese spread and some lavoosh; it's on the counter by the Coke machine in the lunchroom."

When the rest of the committee had left, Heaven got up and swung her arms around in circles. "Mona, how am I doing?"

Mona had slipped out of one of her shoes and was rubbing the bottom of her foot. "You run a good meeting, Heaven. Were you the president of something in college?"

"Law school. I was the president of something in law school. How's Nolan?"

"Well, I guess he had a heart attack," Mona said. "Or had pre–heart attack symptoms. His wife is a doctor, you know. He got so worked up about Evelyn and the florists and the kickbacks that he started having chest pains. When the lights went out, he panicked. I guess that's when we saw him hightailing it down the street. He went home and his wife the doc checked him out and then took him to the emergency room. He's in the hospital. Or at least he was last night, when we were getting drunk at your place. Boy, did I have a headache this morning."

"Buck up, Mona. You're playing with the big girls now. I commend you for your information gathering. Between your headache and this interminable meeting, when did you have time to get the word on Nolan? And what's the diagnosis? Does he have to have valves replaced or anything, like bypass surgery?"

Mona smiled at the praise. "The headlines come from

Sal, of course. I told him it was an emergency, that he had to get info fast. That little piece on the front page of the Metro section didn't say squat, just that the mayor's aide was admitted to Saint Luke's last night. But, as of noon, word was Nolan would be released today or tomorrow, so I guess no surgery."

"Poor Nolan. Working for the mayor must be tough, lots of pressure."

"Nolan has really shepherded this whole Eighteenth and Vine revival from start to finish. It's the mayor's favorite project of his reign," Mona said.

"Mona, only kings have reigns. Mayors have terms," Heaven said with a grin.

"You know what I mean. Now, let's get this show on the road," Mona said as their cohorts began returning.

With them came Pam Whiteside, the public relations aide for the mayor's office. She chirped, as she was paid to do. "Guess who's here and wants to talk to the committee? This is so exciting."

Heaven didn't think she or anyone on the committee needed 'exciting' at this point, but there didn't seem to be an option. "Gosh, Pam, we don't have a clue. Are you taking over for Nolan?" Heaven asked.

"Just for a few days," Pam said. "I talked to Nolan, and he gets to go home tomorrow morning. He promised his wife he would stay home for two days. He really wants to see this project through to the dedication. He didn't need angioplasty or anything. They think it was just an anxiety attack. But I didn't come here to talk about poor Nolan. Bob Daultman, the famous documentary filmmaker, has come to Kansas City. And the big news is, he wants to bring his crew to the dedication weekend. But I'll let Bob tell you all about it," she effused while avoiding eye contact. She knew the committee didn't need the strain of a filmmaker hanging around after what had happened yesterday. Giving a little gesture toward the hall, she exited, coming back with the famous man in tow.

Heaven had seen pictures of Bob Daultman, but she couldn't believe he really wore a black turtleneck and beret when he wasn't at a photo shoot. It was so hokey. But there he was in the flesh, being led in by the mayor's P.R. person, turtleneck and beret in place and not a camera in sight.

"*Bonjour*, Kansas City," he said solemnly, as if he were addressing a new alien nation.

Heaven said little during the next twenty minutes as the rest of the committee members fell all over themselves to impress the filmmaker. If he had asked them to have the official dedication at midnight, instead of noon, they probably would have agreed. Even Mona batted her eyelashes at the guy.

"So I see, here in your quaint city, a chance to show my fans, especially those in Europe, the essence of the Kansas City jazz style as it is in the present day and as the old-timers who will be here for the dedication represent it," Daultman intoned, waving his arms expressively. "And there is the famous Charlie Parker. I hear you will put the plastic sax in the new museum, the one that Parker bought when he was short on money. That will be amusing."

Heaven couldn't help but grin. Amusing, indeed. When the city paid a fortune for that saxophone at auction, the taxpayers went wild. They weren't sure they wanted to spend their money on some junior high band instrument that once belonged to a junkie musician, famous or no. Now this documentary filmmaker was going to show the world what Kansas Citians spent their money on. She looked at her watch and realized she better take control of the meeting or they would be there all night. "I hate to interrupt, Mr. Daultman, but we have to move along here. If I read my fellow committee members correctly, I'd say we are sold on having you on board."

Everyone murmured yeses and grinned like fools. "How long are you going to be in Kansas City?" Heaven asked.

The filmmaker did a 360 degree turn, complete with

hand gestures. "Just another day, to get the feel. Then we will come back next week."

"Please let us know, through the mayor's office, if you will have special needs," Heaven said. "I'm very happy this is a documentary shooting. That's certainly easier to integrate with a live audience. Of course, the sooner you can let us know what you need, the better."

Bob Daultman smiled vaguely. "We have simple needs. Remember my coal mining film? We crowded down in a narrow shaft, down, down, down, into the earth, along with the miners. Then there was the piece about the Kabuki theater in Kyoto. The hours and hours of listening to that droning music. Why, one of my crew members went bonkers, brought a boom box into the theater one night and played a Nine Inch Nails CD at full volume. He had to be sent to Bali for R&R. Now usually my crew can handle adversity. Do any of you remember one of my early films, it was in 1963, or was it '64, in the meat packing plants of Chicago, the one with the Carl Sandburg poem and the Frank Sinatra song, all over the shots of the cattle being . . ."

Heaven realized these reminiscences could go on forever. There's nothing an artist likes better than talking about his projects. "We hardly think of this coming celebration as adverse conditions, Mr. Daultman," she said tartly, cutting him off before he started describing the cattle slaughter. "Thank you for your interest in Kansas City and our jazz heritage." She stood and held out her hand. He bent over it and took it grandly, placing a kiss on her knuckles.

The P.R. aide swooped in to whisk him away amidst a chorus of thank-yous from the committee members.

Heaven didn't even give them time to discuss this new turn of events. "Mona, what about the volunteers?"

Mona stood up, beaming. "I have such good news. The old-time social clubs of Kansas City have all agreed to provide volunteers for the weekend."

"What social clubs?" a businessman representing Kansas City Southern Railroad asked.

Mona's voice slipped into a lecture tone. "There were black social clubs created in the 1940s and 50s when black people in Kansas City couldn't go to white people's places. So they organized these clubs to have dinners and dances and do volunteer work together. And then they started picketing for equal rights for black people in front of department stores and such. Lots of these groups still exist in Kansas City, even though their members are getting up in years. They are a real part of Kansas City history. It will be wonderful to have them participate in this celebration."

"Mona, aren't these people too old to be of any help?" Heaven asked.

Mona sniffed at Heaven's lack of tact. "Every social club member will have a younger club or family member with him or her. Even though the original purpose of the clubs isn't necessary anymore, I guess younger people have joined, you know, since the 1950s. I'm meeting with someone from each club next week. I've asked them to bring photos of their club activities in the old days. I thought we could put them up someplace."

Heaven smiled at her friend. "Good thinking. Mona, I'm assigning you the job of figuring out where. Sounds like the social clubs should definitely be a part of the celebration."

Heaven passed out copies of a calendar of the dedication weekend that she had printed out on the computer at the restaurant, complete with the food plans for each day. "As you can see, the first event, the Friday night concert and gala, is being handled by Miss Ella's Soul Food, from New York, and ten of the local soul food restaurants."

"How is that working out? I thought all the local soul food restaurant owners hated Miss Ella for bringing her restaurant into the new historic district?" Mona asked.

"They do, but Miss Ella has only been here since yesterday, so I haven't seen any face-to-face confrontations yet. I'm sure the tasting on Sunday will be very interesting. All the restaurants are bringing their dishes to my restaurant and we're sampling the menu. You're welcome to come; it starts at six. As you know, the Friday night event will be an outdoor buffet on Eighteenth Street with tables set up in front of the Ruby Theater, where the concert will be that night. We'll have two food lines set up in the blocked-off portion of the street. Then there will also be two dessert stations, at opposite ends of the street. On Saturday, the governor and congressmen and all will dedicate the Eighteenth and Vine district. Barbecue will be available from seven different barbecue restaurants at a food court across the street from the stage when the musicians will be performing. People can eat and enjoy the music at the same time. And before you ask, these barbecue folks aren't crazy about each other, either. At least they aren't as vicious as the barbecue competition people are, trying to RUB each other out." She looked around for laughter, expecting them to have heard about the murders surrounding a barbecue competition she'd been involved in.

When committee members started glancing at their watches. Heaven realized she had digressed. "Guess that dry rub joke was one of those you-had-to-be-there things. Moving right along to Sunday, when the Negro Leagues Baseball Museum is dedicated, we will have a gospel brunch featuring Cajun and Creole cooking. There are three restaurants catering that event, and they seem to get along."

"This sure has made me hungry," someone quipped.

Heaven nodded. "The food should be excellent the whole weekend if everyone behaves. Meeting adjourned and we'll meet back here at our regular time next Tuesday. Be prepared for a long meeting. It will be our last full get-together before all hell breaks loose. I hope Nolan is back to preside by then."

There was a stampede for the door as it was well past dinnertime for most of the businesspeople on the committee who had been at offices all day. Heaven imagined families all over Kansas City being very glad when this whole gala was over.

"Come on, H, let's get back to midtown. I suppose you

have to go back to work," Mona said. It was almost eight at night, but there were dozens of workers still installing the seats in the auditorium. Mona paused and stared at the stage as they passed by an open door. "Have you heard anything from Detective Weber today?" she asked anxiously.

Heaven shook her head. "I didn't hear a word. Poor Bonnie, she sure has her work cut out for her. It will be hard to prove Evelyn's death was a homicide, I would think. It's not like there was a smoking gun lying beside her or a knife stuck in her chest."

Mona grimaced.

"Well, you know what I mean. We think it's murder, but I suppose the sink could have overflowed by accident. When someone is shot or stabbed, it's easier to make a call. They either committed suicide or they were murdered."

"Sure, I'd stab myself if I wanted to commit suicide. And what about when someone accidentally shoots someone else?" Mona cracked.

"You know what I mean, smarty-pants. You're certainly getting to be an expert at this homicide stuff," Heaven shot back.

Mona didn't look proud at the compliment. She walked on silently.

Suddenly, Heaven remembered the conversation between Ella and Mona the night before. What was going on with her friend? "I'm tired of thinking about ol' dead Evelyn. I'm changing the subject. Mona, that was a real coup getting the social clubs to cooperate. How did you find out about them?"

Mona pulled her car away from the curb with a big smile on her face. Maybe she was reading too much into Mona's moods, Heaven decided. It would upset anyone to find a body in the way they'd found Evelyn's. Everyone was upset, except Ella Jackson, who hadn't seemed to be fazed.

"There was a story about them in the newspaper," Mona explained, "about how all these years later, even after Kansas City was integrated and the original purpose for the

clubs was gone, they still met, that their friendships continued. I guess the piece struck a chord with me because I
don't have any forty-year friendships, so I clipped the article
out. When I got involved with this gala, I fished around in
my file cabinet and found the article. I called up the reporter, he was real nice and gave me some leads, as they
call it."

Heaven saw a chance to get the scoop on Mona and her
feud. "Were you thinking of Sam Scott when you said you
didn't have any forty-year friendships?"

"More than you know," Mona said, and clammed up.

Heaven let her be silent until they got to 31st Street.
Then she went in for the kill. "Come on, Mona. I'm going
to find out sooner or later. What was your fight with Samantha Scott about?"

Mona fidgeted as her eyes filled with tears.

"Wow, I'm usually the one crying, not you. It must have
been a doozy," Heaven said.

"I'm ashamed to admit it. But remember, I was raised in
northern Missouri. It's not the heart of Dixie, but it was a
Confederate state."

"What in the world are you talking about?"

"The thing that came between Sam Scott and me. It was
prejudice. Mine," Mona said sadly. Heaven didn't open her
mouth so Mona went on. "Sam had this great voice and she
started singing professionally when she was in junior high.
At first she just performed around Saint Jo. But by the time
we were between our junior and senior years of high school,
she was touring with Boots Turner and his big band. When
she came back at the end of the summer for our senior
year, she was in love with him."

"Boots Turner?"

"Yes. And I just could not accept it, a white girl with a
black man. And I told her so. I hurt her. She couldn't believe I was like that," Mona said. They were in front of Cafe
Heaven, and she stopped the car but didn't turn off the
engine.

"Come on in and have a drink, Mona. I'm so sorry. I know you were wrong, you know you were wrong, but it was the late fifties and there weren't many interracial marriages in your neighborhood, I bet. You probably didn't want Sam to be hurt. After all, she grew up in Saint Joseph, too."

"No, Heaven, it was worse than that. I was thinking about myself. I didn't want my folks to find out. I remember like it was yesterday. I knew they wouldn't want me to see her anymore, for us to pal around. Not that it was a problem for long. After I opened my big mouth to Sam, she told me that being my friend had been a mistake. That I was just an ignorant white trash girl who didn't know right from wrong. She said Boots Turner would make her rich and famous and he was good to her, and a fantastic piano player, to boot. She was right about it all, of course," Mona said quietly.

"Park the car, Mona. I don't want you to go home alone feeling this way. God knows, I've had too many of those nights myself. They aren't fun."

"Thanks, Heaven, but I can't. Let me go on. I'll be fine tomorrow."

Heaven got out of the car. Mona waved and took off. Heaven walked slowly into the cafe, using the front door for a change.

There was a line of men waiting to talk to her.

Murray Steinblatz got to her first. He had been running the room tonight at Cafe Heaven, like he did three or four nights a week. "Hey, boss. You look down. Did someone else get fried on the stage of the Ruby Theater? By the way, I'm going to write about the dedication for my column. People that read about the midwest in the *New York Times* will get a kick out of all this."

"No one else got fried, as you so beautifully put it. And I would hope you'd tell this story to your faithful readers in New York City. They only know two things about Kansas City, barbecue and jazz. How's the restaurant going, Murray?" Heaven looked around the room. Only two tables were vacant.

"We're having a good night, H. But you didn't tell me why you look so down," Murray said. Murray could be very persistent, that was why he had been such a good journalist.

"Oh, it's nothing that you—or I, for that matter—can do anything about. Life is hard to figure out, Murray."

"And that's the truth. There's a guy here, sandy hair, beard, tie-dye tee-shirt. He said you called him and asked him to come over. A theater lighting guy, I think."

Heaven looked around. "Hart Kenton. Where is he?"

"Went to the john. And there's this other guy. A musician. I remember his face but I don't remember his name. He said he's been out of town, just came by to say hi."

Heaven looked over at the end of the bar. She felt her face flush. "Jim Dittmar. He plays keyboards."

"Heaven, are you blushing?" Murray couldn't believe it.

"Can it, Murray," she said without taking her eyes off the man at the bar. She walked over. "Bartender, buy this man a drink," she said.

Jim Dittmar looked over and smiled. "Hey, Counselor."

"You haven't been gone that long, Jim. I haven't been a lawyer for years."

"You got me a good deal on my first record contract. You'll always be 'Counselor' to me."

"Your music career certainly went better than my law career. Will you do me a favor?"

"Name it."

"Stay here for a few minutes. I asked this lighting guy to come by. I need some information. It won't take long."

Jim grinned. "That's an easy one. You're buying me a drink, I think I can wait."

Heaven was glad her heart had stopped pounding so fast. She turned right into the arms of Hart Kenton.

"Whoa, Heaven. What's up?" he said as he untangled them.

"Hart, thanks for coming. By the way, the lighting at the production at the Unicorn is terrific—electrifying, you might say."

"A little lighting designer's joke, eh, Heaven?"

"Can I buy you a drink?" Heaven asked, leading Hart to the other end of the bar.

"Yes you can. I would love a cognac, if you've got it. You said you needed to pick my brain. What about?"

"Tony, will you give my friend here a big ol' snifter of cognac, the oldest we've got."

Tony raised an eyebrow. "You've certainly been generous this week. Expensive wine last night, free drinks for an army tonight."

Heaven raised an eyebrow back. "Hardly an army. It's been an unusual week. But don't let me get in the habit of this or we'll go broke." She turned to Hart. "Did you read the paper today about the woman found electrocuted on the stage of the Ruby Theater?"

"Of course. I'm supposed to go over there tomorrow. I'm doing lights for Sam Scott this weekend."

Heaven perked up. "Well, then I'm glad we talked before. Hart, I think the woman, Evelyn Edwards, was murdered. And my question is, how would you kill someone on that stage with that equipment?"

Hart swirled his glass of cognac, sniffed deeply, and drank. "Is this just your idea or the police's?"

"The police's too," Heaven said.

"Then I assume they have experts working on this question."

"Yes, but I want to understand it myself. The police aren't necessarily going to confide in me. Will you check it out and let me know what you think?"

"I feel like Mickey Spillane. Yes, I'll get in touch after I go to the Ruby for a walk-through. I'll be working with the tech director, so I should be able to get some answers," Hart said. "I do know that the Ruby is a road show theater, a venue that was built for traveling one-night shows. That makes a difference in how the lights and sound are wired. If your venue is just for one type of entertainment, you have a lot more of your electricals wired in permanently."

"That makes sense," Heaven said thoughtfully. "A road show venue. The set-ups are temporary to accommodate various electrical needs. Thanks, Hart. You don't know how much this means to me."

Hart grinned and held his cognac up in a mock toast. "I've heard all about your crime-solving exploits. Now I'm part of the junior G-men team."

Heaven kissed him on the cheek. "Isn't it fun? Now I'm going on to my next victim." With that she walked to the other end of the bar, where Jim Dittmar was watching her with amusement.

"Still have the boys lining up for kisses, don't you, Heaven?" he said as he patted the seat beside him.

Heaven sat down. "Tony, may I have a glass of the Sancerre, please, the Ladoucette?" Only after she got her glass of wine and had the first sip did she look Jim in the eyes. He waited through the ritual without a word.

"So, where have you been? And how long have you been gone? And why?" Heaven asked rather breathlessly. She was embarrassed at the tone of her voice, flirty, but it was too late now.

"Europe, two years and some months. Teresa threw me out," Jim said as he played with his glass.

Heaven laughed. "This is going to be the shortest catch-up conversation on record. Teresa comes in to eat once in a while. I did know you were divorced."

"Who does she come in with, anyone special?" Jim asked.

Heaven rolled her eyes. "Such a guy question. She's usually with people from work, if it's any of your business. Or with your son. Josh, isn't it?"

"Yeah, Josh. Isn't he something? We went to dinner tonight. I think he might forgive his old man for going away."

"What happened with your family, Jim?"

"The same old thing. You've been married to a musician. Yours was rich and famous and still you didn't stick around. Just imagine living with a struggling jazz player and footing all the bills. She finally got sick of it, lost respect for me. No matter what you say in the beginning, it does matter who makes the bread.''

Heaven put her hand over his for a minute, then used it to wave down the bartender. "Tony, I think this calls for two shots of our best aged one hundred percent Agave tequila. Enough said about love.''

"I don't know, Heaven. Enough said about Teresa's and my marriage. Love is a different matter.''

Heaven felt another blush coming on. "Don't go there,'' she said.

"Why not? As I remember it was quite spectacular.''

"Yes it was,'' Heaven admitted. "But it wasn't love. Now, let's move on. Tell me about your life on the Continent.''

The tequila had arrived. They clicked shot glasses and drank silently. Whoa, Heaven thought to herself, I sure didn't expect this luscious little piece of my past to be sitting at the bar tonight. Watch yourself, girl.

"I played in Paris and the Riviera, Berlin, Barcelona. There are lots of jazz clubs. People go to them willingly, without being begged, unlike here. And I dabbled in a few other things, learned to lose money with style at the roulette tables in Monte Carlo, sailed a boat around the Greek islands.''

"Recordings?'' Heaven asked.

"That's the good news. My stock is up. I got a little cash up front—an advance, they call it—and I have a new CD coming out in a month or so. A live recording. *Jim Dittmar Does Europe*, that kind of thing.''

Heaven was genuinely happy for him. She knew how hard it was to make it in music; jazz was doubly hard. "Well, then, I'd better ask you for a couple of favors this month, before you become rich and famous.''

Jim moaned. "I should have seen that coming. Okay, lay it on me, baby. What can I do for you?''

"I'm on the committee that's planning all the celebrations around the Eighteenth and Vine dedication. It goes down the weekend after next, and the event planner who was in charge of the whole affair was killed yesterday. She refused to have a musician on the committee. Now we know it was because she was ripping everyone off for a piece of the action, you know, a little cash from the tent company, the flowers, the caterer. I'm the food committee. I honestly don't know a thing about the music. I know a concert of jazz greats who played in Kansas City in the old days is planned for Friday. Saturday, all the local guys are supposed to be playing. But we, the committee, decided we need a musician on the planning committee and now I'm asking you."

"Oh, man, Heaven. Don't do this to me," Jim said, shaking his head.

"You've got to. I don't know who Evelyn Edwards asked to play, if she screwed them out of money, if she even asked the good old guys who aren't famous but should be a part of this weekend. The big corporations, like Hallmark and Kansas City Southern, have thrown money in for this weekend, so it isn't like asking your friends to do a gig for free. You've got to organize this, for the cause."

Jim looked around the room, pretended to be thinking about what Heaven had asked. This would give him a chance to make some phone calls to other players, let everyone know he was back in town, plus it would put him in the position of knowing exactly what was going on next weekend. It couldn't have been better if he'd planned it himself. And it had the added bonus of putting Heaven in the position of thinking he was doing her a favor. He looked earnestly into her eyes. "Well, when you put it that way, when do I start?"

Heaven beamed and put her arm around Jim's shoulders and squeezed, then quickly let go, as if the contact were burning her. "Go by the Ruby Theater tomorrow after ten in the morning. That'll give me time to let them know you're on board."

"It goes without saying that if it's me it would be after

ten in the morning," Jim said. "It's been too long since you've been involved with a musician, Heaven."

"Hush, now. I'll call and let them know you're coming. You're going to help us avoid a disaster, Jim, I can just feel it. Call me afterwards."

Jim gave Heaven a mock salute. "Aye, aye, Counselor. I can't wait to hear what the second favor is. The first was a beaut."

"It's an easy one. We have this open mike night on Mondays. And we have an upright piano. I know it's not much, but we do get it tuned twice a month. Would you come play this Monday? Just one song, it would be your triumphant return from the honky-tonks of Europe, blah, blah, blah."

"Get the piano tuned this Monday and you've got a deal."

Heaven held out her hand and they shook on it. She got up.

"You're still that way?" said Jim. "Use me and abuse me. Get me to agree to everything and then leave me alone with an empty glass at the bar."

"Tony, get this man another whatever. I've got to go check out the kitchen. I told them I'd be back to help hours ago."

"Now, wait a minute," Jim said, grabbing Heaven's arm. "Come with me down to the Phoenix. I hear Gerald and the guys are playing." Jim pulled Heaven close and nuzzled her hair. She slipped out of his grasp.

"Call me tomorrow, and thanks," Heaven said as she walked toward the kitchen and never looked back. Her palms were sweaty.

So were his.

Nolan Wilkins gazed out the hospital window. He couldn't wait for tomorrow morning so this part of the charade could come to an end. Having to persuade his wife to shoot him up with enough digitalis to almost give him a heart attack was bad enough. Next he had been compelled to stay in the hospital for two nights, wasting space that a sick person should be taking up. What a tangled web we weave, as his grandmother used to say.

Of course, this little stay was costing him money. His insurance had a $1,000 deductible, so he was in for a thousand at least. And he knew there were always other costs, radiologists, emergency room doctors. Nolan sighed. He was a fool. And now he was a fool two days behind in his work. When he got home he could work the phones, but it would look suspicious if he went in to the office first thing in the morning. He would have to wait until Friday or Saturday for that.

Who knew if this expensive little ruse had even helped? He could still be a suspect. Bonnie Weber was a sharp cop. She could have seen through the whole thing. She could get his medical records and find out he had no record of heart trouble. She could pressure his wife, threaten her career. And surely she was looking into Evelyn Edwards's background. What would she find in Tulsa? Why had someone who had moved to Kansas City only six months ago gotten a choice contract to pull together the biggest celebration of the decade?

Fear was nibbling away at Nolan's stomach. He hadn't even been able to keep down the mashed potatoes and Jell-O on the dinner tray. He didn't have time for fear. Pam had called him from the office and told him about the new player on the field, the filmmaker. More details, more personalities, more problems, even if everything went like clockwork.

Nolan knew he had to buck up. He'd started down this path, now he had to finish what he'd started.

The door of his private room opened and he turned, expecting a nurse coming to take his blood pressure. His wife had made it clear she wouldn't be back to visit. She was still furious with him.

"Well, well. So you almost had a heart attack, Nolan sweetie," Miss Ella Jackson said. She laughed that big laugh of hers and slammed the door behind her. "In a pig's eye."

Hoppin' John

1 lb. dried black-eyed peas
2 ham hocks
1 stick cinnamon
2 bay leaves
1 inch fresh ginger
1 jalapeño
kosher salt
½ tsp. each ground coriander, ground white pepper,
    cayenne
1 lb. Polish sausage
1 lb. spicy sausage such as Italian
1 lb. pkg. frozen greens, collard or mustard
1–2 cups chicken stock
1½ cups rice, Carolina if you can find it, but a good long-
    grain rice such as Basmati will do
1 onion, peeled and diced

Hoppin' John is one of the original American dishes created through the tragedy of slavery. The Carolinas were good rice-growing country, and this dish was a taste memory of Africa for the slaves who ended up in the Carolinas. The first written records of it indicate it was just beans and rice cooked together in the pilau manner, as opposed to cooking beans and rice separately. As the dish moved up to the Big House (the white landowner's plantation) and became a staple of southern cooking, salt pork, bacon, or ham hocks were added. I kept the original spices mentioned in early recipes that set it closer to Africa, like the stick cinnamon and coriander, but added two kinds of sausage and the greens. This Hoppin' John makes a great one-dish party meal, as does its Louisiana counterpart, jambalaya.

Cover with water to 4 inches over the dried peas and soak for at least 2 hours. Add the stick cinnamon, the ham hocks, 2 bay leaves, ginger, and jalapeño to the dried beans. Bring to a boil, then reduce to a simmer. Cook until tender, from 1–3 hours. Start checking the beans for tenderness at about 40 minutes. At that time prick the Polish sausage and throw into the pot. Make sure to add water as needed.

While the beans are cooking, prick the Italian sausage and roast on a baking sheet for 15–20 minutes at 400 degrees.

When the beans are tender, remove from heat and take out all the aromatics, the ham hocks, and the sausage. Let sausages cool and cut in chunks. Remove ham from the bones. Sauté a diced onion and add to the beans at this time, along with the chicken stock, the rice, the sausages, the remaining spices, the ham, and the greens. Bring to a simmer and cook uncovered until the rice is tender, about 30–40 minutes. Start tasting the rice at 20 minutes. Salt. As it is written here, Hoppin' John has a medium heat. If you like less heat, omit the jalapeño from the cooking process, reduce the cayenne, or use a sweet Italian sausage instead of a spicy one.

Five

"Bonnie, really, we don't need you," Heaven said in a tone that could have been construed as unkind.

Bonnie Weber didn't take offense. She calmly continued her assigned chore, which was polishing wineglasses. "Heaven, I could have put in for overtime to be here today. Even in a police department that loathes overtime, I would have had no argument from the brass, what with your record of entertaining on Sunday nights. I'm not even going to hark back to two or three years ago. Why, just last September the whole bread bakers club got all whacked out on bad rye bread, and I had to drive busloads of bakers to the medical center myself."

Heaven shrugged. "That was out of my control, if you recall. This is just a little food tasting for the big party next week. Ten restaurant owners and caterers are bringing dishes, and I'm going to try to make them happy and get a good menu for the gala." Heaven suddenly remembered what had happened to Evelyn. "Now that I think about it, maybe you should stick around."

Bonnie was in the dining room, polishing wineglasses. Heaven was in the kitchen, making Hoppin' John. They were yelling across the pass-through window, only occasionally actually looking at each other. Right now Bonnie Weber was watching Heaven pulling the meat off a ham bone. "I thought you didn't have to cook for this, just supervise."

Heaven smiled. "I know, but you can't invite cooks over to your restaurant without offering them something. It wouldn't be right. Now, this Hoppin' John is really interesting. It comes from . . . well, historically it comes from Africa, but in American food history it comes from the Low Country, the Carolinas, where they grew rice. It was beans and rice before beans and rice were cool." Heaven dumped the ham into the pot with the black-eyed peas. She had been itching to ask Bonnie about the Evelyn investigation. They were alone now. She wiped off her cutting board with bleach water and wiped her hands dry. "I'm coming out for coffee," she announced.

As Heaven pushed through the doors to the dining room Bonnie Weber was already making espressos.

"Well, la-de-da. When did you learn to be a *barista*, little miss?" Heaven said as she poured herself a glass of water from behind the bar.

"I don't know anything about being a *barista*, but I got a home version of an espresso machine for Christmas this year. We love it. Speaking of home, how's Hank?"

Heaven didn't want to waste this moment on discussing her personal life. She wanted to talk about Evelyn, but she had to be civilized. "Hank is fine. He's in Texas for two months going to ER school. Iris is fine, too. Now, what about Evelyn? It's been five days. Didn't you tell me once that if you don't find a good suspect in the first week of an investigation, you're in trouble?"

Bonnie nodded. "Yes, that's true, but then most of my victims don't die under such cloudy circumstances. You find the gun that killed the victim in the boyfriend's dresser drawer. The boyfriend was the only other person in the house when the victim died. The boyfriend doesn't have a clue; he was passed out drunk at the time. The boyfriend guesses a burglar came in while he was asleep and killed his girlfriend, then put the gun in the boyfriend's dresser.''

"Then you question the boyfriend and he spills his guts in a fit of remorse?'' Heaven asked cheerfully.

"You took criminal evidence in the same class I did,'' Bonnie reminded her friend. "Most crimes are committed by our loved ones.''

"Or, now in the nineties, by a stranger who gets pissed off at the world and goes postal. I don't think Evelyn's death easily falls into either of those categories.''

Bonnie nodded in agreement. "From what I've learned about Evelyn, she doesn't have any close family. She had an event planning business in Tulsa for five years. Before that she worked at a hotel in Fort Worth, in the catering department. Her mother is dead. Father unknown.''

"What about Tulsa? Did you go down and find out if she ripped people off when she was doing parties down there?'' Heaven asked, eager for dirt.

"Now, you know good and well I didn't go to Tulsa. If the king of Sweden was killed in Kansas City, the budget to investigate would still be about five dollars. But I did go to Evelyn's office and riffle through her stuff enough to see the names she used for references when she made proposals,'' Bonnie said.

"And?''

"Nolan Wilkins was on the reference list. And I did have the budget to call Tulsa and talk to another reference, the Convention and Tourist Bureau. They said she did a great job for them on several big events, then they started getting complaints. And the complaints were about the same scam she was trying to pull here: you can do the flowers if you pay me ten percent. They were surprised she used them as a reference.''

Heaven shook her head. "You know how many times people don't check those, especially the out-of-town ones. Still, I can see a kickback scheme getting you dead if it were government contracts worth millions and you'd been skimming for years. But this stuff is kinda penny-ante. How much money do you think Evelyn relieved folks of over the years?"

Bonnie got up and headed toward the espresso machine. "Want another?"

Heaven paused for a minute, then said, "Yeah. I'll need all the energy I can drink for when the soul food folks get here."

Bonnie looked troubled while she tapped out the old coffee grounds and refilled with freshly ground coffee. "This case is a mess. The paint rag just happened to get stuck in the sink. The water just happened to be left on. Evelyn's feet just happened to be touching a big fat plug box with big fat cables plugged in. But Heaven, you're making the same mistake you always make. You're looking for the logical connections. One thousand dollars isn't enough to kill for, but two thousand is? If that were true, then the poor homeless guy who got stabbed last night over a blanket and a refrigerator box would still be alive."

Heaven went over to where the espresso machine was gurgling away. She sat down and waited for her next cup of the inky brew. "I know I'm always looking for those logical answers. That's why I became a lawyer and you became a cop. Is it moral? Is it civilized? Those weren't questions either of us could deal with. You went for solving the puzzle and I went for interpreting someone else's version of what was right, the legal code."

Bonnie interrupted with the coffee and a smile. "Or we would have both studied to be rabbis."

Heaven giggled. "Now, that's a frightening thought. Is the homeless guy another new case of yours?"

"Yes, and I've already got a confession and the perp in jail. It was his friend, another homeless guy. They'd lived near each other for a year. Last night the cheap wine took them both over the edge."

"Even though Evelyn Edwards and her death are still a mystery, the homeless wino case probably provides you with a clue," Heaven said thoughtfully. "Something Evelyn did pushed someone over the edge."

Bonnie shrugged. "If Evelyn were murdered, it wasn't an impulsive act like the two wino buddies. Someone had to lure her to danger on that stage, then cause the flood without her noticing until it was too late, and then arrange for Evelyn's feet to be there at the same time. It was premeditated."

"Oh, I knew I'd miss something. What was premeditated?" It was Mona Kirk, rushing in from the back door. Mona was resplendent in a cat sweatshirt with glitter sparkling on the cat's whiskers worn over leopard pedal pushers.

Heaven started back to the kitchen. "Bonnie was just saying that if Evelyn was murdered as opposed to just unlucky, then someone planned it, it wasn't an act of passion."

"Bonnie, don't tell me you can't figure out if the woman was murdered yet," Mona said.

"In this case, the act doesn't reveal the intent, Mona. If "x" amount of volts go through you, you die. It wasn't as though we found her in the bathtub full of water with the hair dryer bobbing like a rubber duck in the water, like on television."

Mona was not going to be deterred. "Someone rigged it and you know it, Bonnie Weber. I think she must have a musician boyfriend and she broke his heart; maybe she told him he couldn't play at the dedication. Or maybe it was the florists and rental companies and caterers, they all plotted it together, like that murder on the train."

"Well, I will admit I don't think it was an accident. But about the only chance I have of finding out who did it is if killing Evelyn Edwards was only the beginning," Bonnie said.

Both Heaven and Mona pondered that for all of two seconds. "What else do you think is going to happen?" Mona asked.

"The beginning of what?" Heaven asked.

"What if someone wants to sabotage the whole Eighteenth and Vine project, or at least the dedication weekend?" Bonnie asked.

"I have to go stir my beans. Don't you dare say another word until I get back," Heaven said as she scurried into the kitchen.

Mona pursed her lips. "Why would anyone want to do such a thing, Bonnie? This will be a great tourist attraction for Kansas City."

"It also will cost a great deal of money, and knowing taxpayers the way I do, I'm sure at least half of them think it's a waste."

Heaven yelled from the kitchen. "Maybe it's someone who hates jazz."

Mona looked like she had remembered something. Her eyes clouded over. "Or someone who hates black people. Eighteenth and Vine is in a part of town where mostly African Americans live, and suppose the event gives the area a big boost."

Bonnie nodded. "And it celebrates the achievements of African Americans. It could be that Evelyn was only chosen for effect."

Heaven stuck her head through the kitchen pass-through window. "So, the killer is a disgruntled racist taxpayer who hates jazz. Bonnie, go get 'im."

Bonnie Weber leaned over toward Mona Kirk, talking quietly so Heaven wouldn't hear in the other room. "Why didn't you tell me you went to Evelyn Edwards's office the day she died?"

Mona blanched. "I don't know what . . . How did you know?"

Bonnie shook her head. "You were going to lie to me, weren't you, Mona old buddy? You actually started to try to tell me you hadn't gone over to Evelyn's and had a scene with her. Why are you so nervous, Mona? What have you got to hide?"

"Nothing! I was just so angry about what she was doing,

how she was trying to make money illegally off this celebration. I went over there and told her . . ." Mona's voice trailed off.

Bonnie Weber leaned in even closer. Bonnie was at least six inches taller than Mona, but Mona stuck out her chin in a brave gesture of defiance, looked up at her interrogator, and spilled her guts. "I told her she wouldn't get away with it, that after the meeting that night she'd be gone from the project."

Bonnie turned back toward the espresso machine. "And you were right, Mona old buddy, you were right."

"You're talking without me," Heaven yelled from the kitchen.

Bonnie stared silently at Mona from across the cafe.

In an hour, Evelyn Edwards, if not forgotten, was no longer the topic of conversation.

Except for Miss Ella, who had called and said she would be a little late, all the participants for the soul food extravaganza were gathered. Waiters Chris Snyder and Joe Long had arranged the dining tables into one long row and placed pitchers of ice water, and bottles of Salice Salentino, an Italian red wine from Apulia, on the table. On the bar sat a copper tub filled with ice and assorted bottled beers and some Tuscan white wine from Villa Antinori. A few members of the dedication committee had showed up, but it was the presence of Detective Bonnie Weber that had everyone buzzing.

"We gonna have some po-lice watching us cook, like it was the president or something?" Ruby Singer asked.

"Oh, now, don't be braggin', girlfriend," Maxine Frey said. "Just because you *have* cooked for the president." The room erupted in laughter.

Heaven lifted her glass of wine in the air. "Welcome to you all. We'll wait just a few more minutes for Ella to arrive . . ."

"As far as I'm concerned, we can go ahead on without her. Didn't need her in the first place," a voice called out from over by the bar.

Bonnie Weber looked in that direction. "Now, don't be talking like that," Heaven said. "Detective Weber here would call that a motive."

Another round of laughter. "Motive for what? Miss Ella ain't dead."

"Yet," someone else piped in. This time even Bonnie had to laugh.

Heaven moved on. This was the only day of the week the cafe was closed, and she knew Joe and Chris wanted to get home as soon as possible. "I asked you all to bring your dishes in disposable aluminum pans so we can do a blind tasting," she explained.

"Kind of like how Ernest cooks," a smart aleck cracked. Ernest was a busy caterer who had just recently had cataract surgery. Before the operation there had been several mishaps in the kitchen like the one in which Ernest mistook cayenne pepper for paprika. Now Ernest turned toward the wise guy and pointed a finger. "I can see just fine now, and I'm takin' names." The others all howled.

"Now, you all know this is not a contest. Every one of you could do this whole dinner and do it fine," Heaven said. "The reason we decided to have a blind tasting, if you remember, was because no one could decide what they wanted to contribute."

There was a rumbling through the crowd that told Heaven they still were far from a consensus. She hurried on. "Everyone thought they had the best yams, the best greens."

"And I know I have the best cornbread," someone shouted.

Heaven smiled. She loved cooks who knew what they were good at. "So we'll all decide together. I made up a ballot on the computer. Joe and Chris, who have no idea who brought what, will put numbers on each item." Joe Long, looking nervous after hearing how serious this was to these chefs, pointed to the numbers on several pans like Vanna White showing letters on *Wheel of Fortune.*

"All you have to do is eat your way around the table," Heaven said, "and mark the number of the dish you like best in each category. For example, number six in sweet potatoes, number twenty in corn pudding. Does everybody understand?"

"What if there's a tie?" Mona asked.

"We'll have a taste-off. If it's still tied, we'll flip a coin."

Detective Bonnie Weber grabbed a plate. "Do we have to wait any longer for Ella, Heaven? I'm a nonvoting eater, but I'm starved."

Again a rumble of discontent went through the crowd. Heaven gave her friend a glare that said, Thanks so much. "We'll start soon. Have another glass of wine," she said, and went to help herself to another.

"Well, one thing about this white girl's restaurant," Ernest said loudly. "I like the drinks better than the lemonade and the sweet ice tea over at mine." That brought back the friendly camaraderie that was evident when they weren't talking about Miss Ella Jackson. They attacked the beer and wine supply with gusto.

Suddenly there was a commotion at the front door. In walked six young men who could have qualified for a Calvin Klein ad or an all-star basketball team. Tall and dark and handsome, they each carried boxes filled with disposable pans full of food. Bringing up the rear, Miss Ella sashayed up to the bar. She had on a 1940s navy crepe dress with a peplum that played over her hips. She wore a red hat with navy trim, short red gloves, and big red lips. She glanced around at the rest of the Kansas City restaurant crowd with a look that said, Is this my competition?

"Heaven, honey. I do apologize for being tardy. But a good entrance is so important. Let the games begin," Ella proclaimed with a flourish of her hands.

Chris and Joe made a beeline for Heaven. "Boy, is she beautiful," Chris said.

"Boy, does she have balls," Joe added. "Doesn't she know these people hate her?"

Heaven looked around. Ella was working the crowd like a politician. She moved fast, while they were all still stunned from her grand entrance, shaking hands and barely listening to the names they stammered out before moving on to the next restaurateur. Everything about her attitude proclaimed, Stand back, Miss Ella is in town.

Heaven decided she better move fast herself. "Let's eat," she yelled. "Joe, will you explain to Ella how we're doing this?" she said in a voice that said he had no choice.

Bonnie Weber sidled up to Heaven. Bonnie was 5'10" and was a big woman, not fat at all, but big. She could wrestle a drunk male suspect to submission. "I'm filling my plate before the food fight begins. This is going to get ugly, and I hate to see good food wasted," she chuckled.

As hard as Chris Snyder had worked to arrange the food pans and disguise the ones Miss Ella had just brought, Heaven was sure everyone recognized her numbers right away. She saw them sniff and pass over certain offerings. They wouldn't even take the chance it might taste good.

Heaven herself tried to obey the rules. The table was a bounty of goodies. Beans of every kind, including her own Hoppin' John, which wasn't an official candidate, cornbread dressing, macaroni and cheese, sweet potatoes with all kinds of toppings from marshmallows to pecan strudel, rice, grits, mashed potatoes, corn pudding, squash casserole, turnips, turnip greens, green beans, smothered cabbage, fried green tomatoes, okra prepared in several ways, collard greens, mustard greens, pickled beets, Brunswick stew, and fried apples were all represented. Then there were the main dishes: fried chicken, chicken and dumplings, chicken pot pie, baked chicken, salmon croquettes, catfish, meat loaf, oxtail stew, smothered pork chops, neck bones and rice, braised turkey legs, Swiss steak, and fried chicken livers and gizzards. The only thing Heaven asked them not to bring was barbecue, because that was for Saturday, or gumbo and jambalaya, because that would he served on Sunday.

She started marking her own ballot: Best chicken dish, #24, the chicken and dumplings. Heaven had never been able to make a dumpling that didn't weigh a ton. These practically floated off the plate; the sauce was full of chicken flavor and speckled with parsley and black pepper. Heaven also knew they could never make fried chicken for the crowd that was due to show up on Friday night. Chicken and dumplings would be easier. Best greens, #3. Heaven decided it must be a mix of all three, collard, mustard, and turnip, plus diced apples with some hot sauce and vinegar. She was interrupted in her analysis by the beginning of the end.

"Don't you talk about my squash soufflé that way!" a voice cried from a table in the corner.

"Is that your mess? I guess you cooked it a little too long, honey. I call that slimy squash," was the retort.

Heaven turned to see Ruby backing Miss Ella across the room with her pointy finger. "Nobody wants you in this town, sister. Why don't you take your pitiful excuse for cornbread and get, now!" she said with surprising vigor for a seventy-year old.

"Those aren't my greens. They gritty. I never served a sandy pot of greens in my life," someone else replied defensively.

"I've eaten those tired, old smothered chops at your place. You can't fool me. You think Nancy Wilson wants some nasty, ol' chops that're so thin you can hardly taste the meat?" a male voice snarled.

Suddenly everyone turned to Heaven.

"Heaven, I won't have my greens served in the same meal with these neck bones."

"You can always tell when Ernest makes ham hocks and white beans. You can smell the raw garlic from over here."

"Heaven, now you better count these ballots up and tell

me her nasty macaroni and cheese didn't win, *if* it ever saw any real cheese."

To say the crowd was getting ugly wouldn't quite capture the intensity of the mood. Cafe owners who had been friends for years were turning on each other over black-eyed peas. Joe and Chris retreated behind the bar. Bonnie Weber continued to eat. Mona Kirk tried to reason with each and every cook, none of whom wanted to hear her. Finally, Heaven yelled—"Hold it a minute"—at the top of her lungs.

"No, you hold it," Miss Ella said as she crammed her ballot into Heaven's hands. "I won't have my food on the same buffet with this trash. If you want me to, I'll do the whole party. Otherwise, I'll be over in my new restaurant, drinking champagne, celebratin' 'cause it's gonna be so easy to steal all y'all's business. Come on, boys," she ordered. And they left.

After that, it was a stampede for the door. Ballots were torn in half and stomped on. Pans were snatched. Dressing and gravy and greens were spilled on the floor. The spirit of cooperation to honor Eighteenth and Vine was a distant memory. Not one cook and restaurant owner would allow his precious and delectable sweet potatoes or cheese grits or cabbage or baked chicken to share a table with the inferior dishes made by his former friends. It was no longer even about Miss Ella.

When the room was empty, save for Heaven, Joe, Chris, Mona, and Bonnie, the detective got up from her perch at the bar, surprisingly chipper. "What do you know? No one died. What's for dessert?"

The candidates for Dessert had been put in the kitchen for lack of room on the table. Heaven and the rest of the survivors went out and started lifting tinfoil. "Oh, boy, I was hoping there would be banana pudding, just like this, with vanilla wafers," Heaven said as she found spoons and bowls and set them on the counter.

"Look at this cobbler," Joe said appreciatively.

"When's the last time you saw a German chocolate cake made from scratch?" Bonnie murmured as she cut a big hunk.

Mona was horrified. "How can you be so cavalier, Heaven? You're in charge of the food for the whole weekend, and you just lost an entire meal."

Heaven shrugged. "I guess I was asking too much. I was trying so hard to be fair, I forgot the fact that everyone likes their food to take the spotlight. It's the same the world over. It's the same for fancy French chefs and grandmothers from Kansas. 'I made this lemon pie and I'm proud of it.' "

"Where's the lemon pie?" Joe asked with his mouth full of chocolate cake.

"I was just giving an example. We don't have lemon pie."

"I'm assuming by the lack of panic on your part, you already have a plan B," Bonnie Weber said. "But don't count on me for the sweet potatoes or anything else. You know what a terrible cook I am."

Heaven looked at Mona. "I do have a plan B, but it might not work. What do you think about asking your social clubs to help? Each one could make one dish for five hundred people and give the money we would have spent on the catering to their charities."

Mona frowned. "Cooking for five hundred is a lot, Heaven. Most of these ladies are older. I don't know if they could handle it."

Heaven wasn't ready to concede defeat. "I can help them. Most of them have a church kitchen they can use, I bet. They can make a social event out of it. Do part one day, part the next. And we can use all the photographs that you asked them to dig out to decorate the tables. These women are part of Kansas City history. People will be thrilled to meet them."

Mona could tell she'd better give up. Heaven had a good idea, and just because she, Mona, had panicked at losing the professional cooks and Heaven hadn't, that was no reason to shoot a good idea down. "I guess you know it's really a better idea than having all the soul food restaurants cater. Why didn't you think of this before?''

Heaven pushed her finger on some chocolate cake crumbs and then put the finger in her mouth. "Because I was an ignorant white girl and didn't even know about the social clubs until you told me. Will you set up a meet?''

"I'll call first thing in the morning," Mona replied.

"Heaven, now you sound like a cop on undercover assignment, with your 'set up a meet' talk," Bonnie Weber said. She looked at her watch. "It's eight o'clock and all is well. I'm going home. This is the best Sunday night I've ever had here at Cafe Heaven.''

When Jim Dittmar walked in through the swinging kitchen doors, everyone jumped. "Shit, you scared us. I guess we forgot to lock the front door," Heaven said.

"I'm very quiet," Jim said. "I could have stolen all the good booze while you all were back here eating. Is that German chocolate cake?''

Heaven realized she was blushing again, and so did her friends.

Bonnie and Mona got up. "We're out of here," Mona said, and they went out toward the dining room.

Joe and Chris looked at Heaven for instructions, Joe impatiently checking his watch. The dining room was a disaster.

"Guys, please do a twenty-minute job on the front. I'm afraid the mess will be set in stone by tomorrow. Just put away the beer and wine and bus all the plates in here. Robbie can put the tables back in the morning and work on the carpet." The two were gone like a streak of lightning, knowing they could get everything done in fifteen minutes if they concentrated.

"Wait," Heaven said, embarrassed all over again. "Do you remember Jim Dittmar? He's from Kansas City . . .''

"And a famous jazz piano player," Chris said, trying to be polite. "Great to have you back. We're looking forward to you playing Monday.''

"And we're getting the piano tuned, like Heaven said," Joe piped in as they headed for the dirty dishes in the dining room.

"They run open mike night," she explained. "I'm sorry Mona and Detective Weber got away so fast and I didn't introduce you. I don't know what happened to my manners," Heaven muttered as she put a scoop of each dessert on a plate for Jim.

"What are you trying to do, Heaven, kill me with sweetness?"

"Don't start," Heaven said with a little grin. "You don't have to eat it all. Just taste what you want." All of a sudden she was very busy putting clear plastic film over all the desserts.

" 'Just taste what you want.' Why, that's the best offer I've had since I've been home," he said, knowing he had her flustered.

She tilted her head and tried to look mean. They both laughed. "Jim, I didn't tell you the other night, but I have a perfectly good relationship going. Don't rock the boat."

Jim nodded. "I heard all about it. A doctor, a tall Vietnamese, beautiful eyes. The women say he's a hunk with a ponytail," he said as he ran his hand over the top of his head, where not too much was growing. "A young hunk. Is he working tonight?"

Heaven couldn't help herself. She could have lied and saved them both the temptation. But she didn't. "He's in Texas for some special training. He's thinking of becoming an emergency room specialist."

Jim put a dollop of banana pudding on his spoon and made a spectacle of himself licking it off. "Getting them before they decide what they want to be when they grow up, eh, Heaven? Pretty steamy stuff."

Heaven bristled. "This is where I say if you only knew the half of it, isn't it?"

Joe and Chris wheeled in a cart loaded with dirty plates and glasses. "Do we have to do the dishes?" they whined.

"No," Heaven said. "But you do have to scrape and rinse

them so Robbie doesn't lose it totally. Getting out the food on the carpet will be bad enough," she said, and winked at the guys. "Thanks for helping. And yes, you have my permission to turn the soul food contest into a performance piece for open mike night." She jerked her head toward the dining room, and Jim put down his plate of desserts and followed.

Joe and Chris were dying to go into the dining room and watch them. They could feel the sexual tension. But as much as they wanted to spy on their boss, they wanted to get out of there more. They started on the dishes.

"When I came in, this room looked like a disaster. Was there a fight? Is that what brought the cops?" Jim asked.

Heaven looked puzzled for a minute. "You mean, because Bonnie Weber was here? No, she came because we've had some weird food disasters on Sunday evenings. She was practicing preventative crime fighting. We didn't need her this time, thank God."

"What kind of cop is she?"

Heaven looked puzzled again. She was looking through the assortment of tequilas but Jim could see her face in the mirror. "A good one. Oh, like what assignment? She's a homicide detective. She just took the Sergeant's test."

Jim looked relieved. "So you were afraid someone was going to kill someone tonight?"

"It's a long story. Actually, it's several stories. But you didn't come by here to hear about my recent run-ins with the law. You know we're not really open on Sunday nights."

"I saw the lights on and took a chance."

Heaven brought out a bottle of aged Herradura and poured two shots. "Is this about your new position as unpaid music coordinator for the Eighteenth and Vine dedication weekend?"

They clicked glasses and drank. "Wowie, Counselor, you didn't tell me I had a title," Jim said. "Yes, as a matter of fact, I do have a task at hand. I want to use your computer. I've booked people and written myself a few notes." He pulled cocktail napkins and other assorted scraps of paper out of his pockets.

Heaven had to admit Jim looked cute. He dressed only in black, and tonight he was wearing faded jeans and a jean jacket over a black Gap pocket tee-shirt. He wasn't tall, probably about 5'10", but he had long limbs that made him kind of gangly, and of course the graceful long fingers pianists need.

"So Evelyn Edwards hadn't filled Saturday up with players?"

"I could bore you with more stories of how Evelyn Edwards was fixin' to mess up your dedication, but to sum up, she was trying to get most of the players to give her back fifty bucks of the hundred and fifty she was offering. She didn't have the nerve to call it a kickback. She must have known that wouldn't go down quietly. She said it was for the Musicians' Union Building, that the city felt all the players should throw in for the repairs. I'll have to say she chose the one thing that most of us would want to contribute to, so she didn't get much shit. Stealing a third of these poor players' money. What a loser."

Heaven nodded. "And she lost. Let me turn on the computer for you." She walked into the office and turned everything on while Jim watched her from the door.

Joe stuck his head in from the dining room, glancing back at the musician quickly with an appraising eye. "We're done, boss. Are you coming?"

Heaven walked over and gave Joe a kiss on the cheek. "Thanks for hanging in there. It got pretty hairy, didn't it?"

"It was the best fight I've seen in years. Are you coming? Can we put on the alarm?"

"Lock up the back and I'll lock you out the front. Jim needs to use the computer. He's trying to book the music for next Saturday for me, I mean, for the committee," Heaven explained, blushing again.

"Another Evelyn Edwards screw-up?" Joe asked.

"I'm afraid so," Heaven said. "I'll see you two tomorrow."

Joe came close to glaring at Jim. "Don't keep her up too late," he sniffed.

"I promise not to keep her up a moment more than I have to," Jim said. Heaven gave him a hush-up look and walked to the door with Joe and Chris.

"Heaven, are you going to be all right? We don't know this guy," Chris said. "I have the feeling the position he has in mind for you instead of up is down, as in bed."

"He's just an old friend. Don't be so dramatic," Heaven said, pushing them gently toward the door.

"Is he an old boyfriend?" the two young men asked more or less at the same time, and louder than Heaven thought they should.

"Shhhh. He's an old something. Something like a boy-friend. Now go, please."

"You're not going to *do* it, are you?" Chris asked, shocked at the idea. He thought of Heaven and Hank as a couple.

"No, I'm not going to *do* it. How come, all of a sudden, I can't be left alone with an attractive man?"

Suddenly, Chris smiled wickedly. "We're leaving, but you are blind and dumb if you don't know the heat you two are generating."

"Sparks are flying," Joe said as he disappeared out the door. Heaven slipped the top lock in place.

She turned around to see Jim Dittmar standing at the door to the office, grinning. "Sparks, did I hear the word *sparks?*"

"Get back in there. I want to go home," Heaven snapped.

"I'll go with you. I can do this in the morning."

"How about another shot of tequila instead?"

"How about in addition to?" Jim said.

"Jim, forget it. You are not coming home with me. But I will entertain you while you work with a rousing rendition of how I lost an entire evening's worth of chefs and caterers tonight," Heaven said.

"Come talk to me, then," Jim said.

And she did. It was second choice for both of them, but neither was ready to force the issue.

Heaven pulled into the garage of her house on Fifth Street, in the old Columbus Park area of the city. It wasn't really a house. It was a building that had been a bakery, and the man who owned it had lived upstairs. Heaven and her daughter, Iris, had lived next door. To everyone's surprise, when Angelo Broncato died, he left the building to Heaven. He had no relatives in the United States. He and his wife had never had children, and his wife had been dead for many years.

Heaven always thought Angelo knew she and Iris needed a home. And that's what it had always been, even in the times they had lived elsewhere, like when Heaven had been married to Sol and moved to his house in Mission Hills. Fifth Street was always home base. It was also a professional kitchen that Heaven had catered out of before she opened the restaurant. The first floor was one big kitchen and entertainment area. The upstairs had big bedrooms/sitting rooms for Iris and Heaven, rooms that had been created by knocking down the walls of lots of small rooms. Upstairs and down there was a jumble of collections: antique glass, quilts, Mexican carved animals, the paintings of Heaven's third exhusband, the famous Ian Wolff.

Tonight Heaven went upstairs without even turning on the lights on the lower floor. Then she stopped near the top of the stairs and ran back down to the kitchen, returning with a glass of amber liquor in her hand. "Port and tequila, always a good combination," she muttered.

Quickly, she stripped off her clothes and jumped into a huge tee-shirt with a Paris Metro map printed on it. She sipped her port, and hopped into bed, dragging the phone toward her. She dialed and broke into a huge smile when her daughter answered. "I know it's Monday morning there in England, but I didn't want to miss our Sunday call. Hi, honey. How was your week?"

"Hi, Mom. I'm so glad you called early. I have to leave soon."

"I miss Hank," Heaven said rather shamefully, as if she had just confessed to a crime.

"That was an abrupt transition. Of course you miss Hank. But he's already been gone a couple of weeks. He'll be home in no time," Iris said cheerfully. "Why is this a big deal, Mom?"

"Well, I'm always trying to get Hank to think about the rest of his life, when he's done with his residency and ready to move out into the world. Now that he's gone away, even for just two months, I really miss him."

"I hardly call going to a special education seminar for two months moving out. You can be so dramatic," Iris said sharply.

"You're right. I'm doing what your grandmother used to call borrowing trouble. Speaking of trouble, you remember that I'm working on that big dedication of the Eighteenth and Vine district?"

"Yeah. I told Dad and he wanted to come over for it. He loves Charlie Parker."

"Your Dad owes me a visit, but it's too late, the event is next weekend. I'm in charge of the food—that is, coordinating, not catering."

"How's it going?"

"Just fine except for a couple of minor problems. Tonight all the caterers for the gala on Friday night quit."

"Mom, why are you so calm? That's a major problem. What's the other one?"

"The event coordinator was electrocuted the other night, and I was there," Heaven said.

"Not again. Did you see this person get fried? God, how awful."

"What do you mean, not again?" Heaven said with a little

80

laugh. "I've never been party to an electrocution before. And I didn't really see the actual, you know . . . I was in a meeting in another room."

"And you know very well what I mean by not again. You're involved in another mysterious death. Will you promise me you'll be careful?"

"Haven't I survived so far? The caterers are more of a threat than some mad killer who wants to sabotage the new Eighteenth and Vine district."

"Is that what the police think is happening?"

"Of course not. I'm just kidding. When we talk next Sunday the whole thing will be over and done with." She paused. "Honey would you ask your father something for me?"

"Of course."

"Ask him if he's heard anything about a jazz player from Kansas City who's been playing around Europe for the last couple of years. His name is Jim Dittmar."

"Why? What's he done?"

"No big why. He's back in Kansas City and he's helping me with the musical end of this."

"As if you needed help with musicians, Mom."

"I need help this week, sweetie. I can't deal with all these temperamental cooks and temperamental musicians at the same time."

"So what do you want to know about this Jim Dittmar?"

"Anything your dad can find out. And if Dennis knows anything, would you call me back before next weekend?"

"Wow, sounds like I have an assignment."

"I guess you could call it that. I'm beat, honey. Say goodnight to your mom."

"Night, Mom. Have a good week. I'll call if I find out anything."

"You too. Thanks." Heaven put down the phone and turned out the light. Her hand knocked over a rag doll that sat on the bedside table, a memento of her mother's antique business. It lay there, flopped on its side. Heaven patted it and started to set it up again. Instead, she pulled it over into bed with her, putting it under the covers with its head on the pillow where Hank's head used to be.

Greens with Leeks and Apples

3 bunches greens, usually about 1 lb. a bunch, either
  collard or mustard or a combination of the two
4–6 leeks
2 Granny Smith apples, cubed, unpeeled
2 T. each olive oil/butter
apple cider, or in a pinch, apple juice
kosher salt, freshly ground black pepper

Slice the leeks just up into the green, discarding the green
tops or saving them for your stockpot. Soak sliced leeks in
water 20 minutes, changing the water twice and rinsing out
the pan to eliminate the sand and grit. Do the same thing
with the greens, trimming the bottoms and discarding bad
leaves as you go. The idea is to separate the vegetables from
the dirt and sand that collects in them, so don't drain the
water off of them as this just coats them with what you just
separated out in the water. Lift the greens and leeks out of
the water, put them in a colander, then replace the water
and put them back in for another soak. Rinse at the end of
this process to remove any extra grit, but just rinsing will
not get the job done. Coarsely chop the greens.

Heat a large heavy pan with 2 T. each of butter and oil.
Sauté the leeks slowly until they start to get tender, about
20 minutes. Add the coarsely chopped greens and increase
the heat to medium. After the greens have initially wilted,

reducing their bulk by half, add enough apple cider to cover and then add the cubed, unpeeled apples. Cook for 40 minutes or more, until the greens are tender, adding more cider or water as needed to not burn the greens. Season with salt and pepper.

Six

I can tell you right now, the Twin Citians Club will not fight you to make the greens. None of us has ever bragged about our greens," a tall, patrician woman standing by the window declared. Her fellow club members backed her up with a chorus of "That's right" and "uh-huh."

Heaven Lee smiled from ear to ear. "You don't know how glad I am to hear you say that. How are your sweet potatoes?"

"Now, sweet potatoes we can throw down," the same woman said. The Twin Citians echoed their agreement. Heaven had asked Pauline to whip up a couple of coffee cakes and Heaven had served coffee, tea, and juices. The women all knew each other so it had not taken long for the meeting to slip into a comfortable, friendly rhythm.

"Well, then, we've almost got it done, ladies. Would it help if I threatened you by saying I'll be glad to make the greens here at Cafe Heaven?"

Moans followed. "It's not that we don't trust you, but if your greens got more compliments than our catfish, you'd have to go, leave Kansas City for good. You don't want to have to do that, do you?" a sprightly seventy-year-old cracked from the front row. "The problem is the room it would take to soak that many greens. Not even the church kitchen has a big-enough sink for all that mess."

"What if some of you come over here to the cafe on Thursday," Heaven offered. "I'll order twelve cases of greens and you can soak them and get them ready. Then on Friday you can come back and finish the job."

"Now, who's going to come over here to work on the white side of Thirty-ninth Street when all her friends are back on the other side of town? That's just asking to get talked about, child," the president of the Mo-Kans club proclaimed. The crowd chuckled.

"Very good point, Julia," Heaven said. "How about this. I'll buy the greens and clean them Thursday night. Then a couple of you can come pick them up. We'll load them in a trash bag and you can cook them along with whatever else you're cooking."

"Agreed," the patrician woman with the short gray natural haircut said. "You gonna do the hard part for us, Heaven?"

"You all have saved my butt and saved the big party for Eighteenth and Vine. You came here on just a few hours' notice, you buckled down, and together I think we solved the problem. The least I can do is clean some greens for you," Heaven said humbly.

"Would you go through the list one more time. My memory isn't like it used to be and I want to write everything down," a cute little lady called out. She was joined by a chorus of testimonies about the loss of memory, not being able to find glasses, missing appointments, even forgetting grandchildren's birthdays.

Heaven held up a pack of brightly colored Post-it notepads. "These are my memory. I'll get you all some. Here we go," she said, then paused as Mona Kirk entered. "Ladies, I know some of you have already met Mona Kirk when she asked your clubs to volunteer for the weekend. She's the one to blame for making you chefs for the big party.

Mona, take a bow while you still can. By Thursday or Friday they'll probably be cursing your name."

Mona smiled bravely and waved. The ladies clapped, and one of them wagged her finger in Mona's direction. "You should have asked us to cook in the first place. Then you wouldn't have got in this fix."

Heaven quickly stepped in to take the blame. "That was my own stupid mistake. It's through Mona that I found out about the social clubs and when the sh . . . sorry, ladies, when it became apparent last night the restaurant owners were not going to be able to work together . . ."

"Go ahead, honey, when the shit hit the fan. You can say it," the wisecracking seventy-year-old piped up. "When the shit hits the fan, that's when we work best. That's when we started these clubs, that's when we picketed together. This is what we do, honey."

"And Kansas City is better for it, that much I now know. Okay, we better stop before I get sappy and sentimental," Heaven said, embarrassed by how emotional she felt about these women and what they'd done. "Here's the duty roster: Twin Citians, all the fried foods, catfish, chicken livers, and hush puppies, plus the sweet potatoes. I'll rent propane burners and stockpots, and we'll set up in the alley behind the Ruby. We'll get some of the high school groups that have volunteered to run the food and platters back and forth. Mo-Kans, the vegetable side dishes, except the greens. Socialites, the smothered pork chops and neck bones and rice. Inter-City Dames, the chicken and dumplings. Twentieth Century Girls, the cookies and cakes. Geace Club, the cobblers. And the other groups that aren't here, you all are going to take them their assignments: rolls, cornbread, pickles, coleslaw, jellies, and all the other cold sides. Two of you will share the greens with me. Are we in agreement?"

Heads nodded all over the dining room.

"Just for the record and so there are no surprises," Heaven continued, "each of the principal clubs will be repaid for the price of the food. You will need to turn in your receipts, so be careful and save them. You will also get a check for five hundred dollars for your favorite charity. The clubs who make the smaller dishes will get their expense money plus three hundred dollars for charity."

"Did the mayor sign off on this?" someone asked.

"I made his office fax me an authorization this morning," Heaven replied, waving a piece of paper. "I didn't want any surprises later when it came time to pay for this party, and I know you wouldn't want any, either. I'll copy this so everyone can have one for their files."

"Do we meet again?" Mona asked anxiously.

Heaven shook her head. "There isn't time. But please, call me here if you have any questions. If I can't come to the phone, I'll call you back as soon as I can. I usually work on the line from six to ten at night. I can't talk then." She went to the front of the restaurant and got business cards for everyone and passed them out. As the women left, Heaven felt a great surge of relief. She turned to Mona, threw her arms around her, and lifted her in the air.

"Heaven, put me down. You'll throw your back out," Mona shrieked.

Heaven smiled as she returned Mona to the ground. "I think these good women can pull this off. How can I thank you? I know the cafe folks are expecting me to call them today and grovel. Now I won't have to."

Mona shrugged. "I feel sorry for them. Now they won't be a part of the celebration. Oh, double darn! I forgot to remind everyone to bring their photos."

Heaven patted her friend's arm. "You already told them that last week, didn't you?"

Mona was headed out the door. "Yes, but now I think I need them sooner than Friday. Those photos are more important than ever now that the social clubs are cooking. I better call everyone," she said under her breath.

* * *

Heaven circled the City Hall office one more time. It was a cheap trick, but effective. Watching someone bouncing around a room like a pinball tended to make people who weren't bouncing come unglued.

"Heaven, won't you have a chair?" Nolan Wilkins pleaded, pressing on the sides of his forehead.

The cheap trick was working. Heaven smiled pleasantly and sat down. "When are you going to cut the crap and tell me the truth?"

Nolan put on his best injured civil servant look. "I almost died six days ago and you're accusing me of lying? Isn't there a term in the criminal justice system, something about the confession of a dying man being above reproach because the dying have nothing to lose?"

"Are you dying?" Heaven asked mildly.

"No, but only thanks to my wife. If I hadn't gone to the emergency room when I did, who knows what could have happened."

"That's what your nurse said, too. She thinks you're a swell guy, by the way."

"Heaven! Don't tell me you went to the hospital and nosed around?" Nolan whined. "I just hope you didn't do anything to hurt my wife's reputation. She's on staff there, you know."

Heaven's eyebrows shot up. "Now, why would I do a thing like that, Nolan? I was just visiting a friend there, that was all I was doing. I just kind of forgot that you were released last week. Why would that reflect on your wife's reputation?"

"You haven't forgotten anything in all the years I've known you. Now you just happen to forget I've been out of the hospital for three days. What's going on?" Nolan asked.

"First, let's get the niceties out of the way. How do you feel?"

"Fine, thanks, but as you know, I'm way behind in my

work, so maybe you could get to the point. Do you want to fill me in on that message you left for me? The one about the dinner Friday night?"

"Soul food restaurants out, their choice. Social clubs in. I'll spare you the details since you're so behind."

Nolan grinned. "I'm not going to be able to avoid whatever you want to discuss, am I?" He leaned back in his plush desk chair and shrugged, indicating surrender.

Heaven warmed to her task. "Here's the thing. Little Miss Evelyn Edwards was sitting at the sound and light boards, stage right. Someone jammed a rag into the drain of the backstage bathroom sink and turned on the water. The bathroom was on the same side of the stage that Evelyn was on. It was a small sink, Nolan. Pretty soon the water had overflowed and started running out onto the stage. But Evelyn was looking up at the lights didn't notice this little puddle coming toward her. It was noisy in the Ruby, what with all the workmen, so she didn't hear the water running, either, I guess. There was a floor pocket down by her feet. Do you know what a floor pocket is, Nolan?"

Nolan gulped and slid his finger under the collar of his shirt, pulling it out slightly to get more air. He was having trouble breathing. Maybe he really was having heart palpitations. "A fancy term for a plug?"

Heaven nodded affirmatively. "And there were lots of big, thick cables plugged into those floor plugs and by chance, or on purpose, one of those cables had exposed wires right near where it entered the plug. When the water reached the floor pocket, it also reached Evelyn Edwards's feet. Now what do you think, Nolan? Was that homicide?"

"Maybe the rag got stuck in the sink by accident?"

"I thought about that," Heaven said. "It was a paint rag, and there were lots of painters around. But I checked with a foreman, and he said that the workers didn't use that backstage bathroom. The outdoor workers use the Porta Pottis. The indoor workers use the lobby john."

Nolan drummed his fingers on his desk. "Yes, but if you

were a painter who had gone to the wrong john and dropped a paint rag when you washed your hands and forgot to turn off the water, then someone is electrocuted because of the rag and the water, you probably would not mention it, would you?"

"No, if I were that painter, my lips would be sealed, you're right about that." Heaven couldn't wait any longer. "What did Evelyn Edwards have on you?"

"Why would she have something on me? Why are you so suspicious?"

"Because you recommended her for a job that plenty of locals could have done. She moved here and suddenly seemed to be on the fast track, introduced to the right people, all that jazz, pardon the pun," Heaven explained. "Sooner or later someone would have noticed she had some mighty nice connections."

"I slept with her at a convention."

Heaven perked up; she never thought she'd get a confession so easily. "You've been in public life for twenty years. You wouldn't do anything that stupid. Come up with a better lie."

Nolan looked sheepish. "Clinton had been in public life a long time, too, remember. He thought with his dick: so did I that trip. It was a Convention and Tourism meeting in Dallas. She was, well, she was nice-looking and I must have got hammered on margaritas. I swear I don't do, didn't do, that kind of thing when I went out of town." Nolan hung his head. "This is so trite. Evelyn called me the next week and said she had decided to move to Kansas City, that there seemed to be unlimited possibilities up here. I tried to talk her out of it but she wasn't hearing it. She was blunt. Unless I helped her get established, she visits my wife and chats about certain things I whispered in her ear."

"How sleazy," Heaven said with a little grin. "Are you a screamer, Nolan?"

Nolan fidgeted. "She was playing the odds that certain things I did would be familiar to someone else who had shared intimate moments with me. I didn't want to take the chance. I told myself she was certainly qualified, she ran her own event-planning business in Tulsa. What would be the harm?"

Heaven felt sad. "First a gig, next some cash. Where would it all end? Is that what you wondered, Nolan? And so you decided to put an end to Evelyn before she further damaged your life."

"Heaven, I swear to you I did not electrocute Evelyn Edwards." Nolan got to his feet.

"Why did you tell me about the sex part?"

"I trust you. After all, you've been through some, some . . ."

"Scandals? Yes, Nolan, I do know about finding yourself in embarrassing situations. But what makes you think I won't be a sister and tell your wife?"

"I promise you I'll tell her myself. Just give me until we get the dedication weekend over."

"Does Bonnie Weber know?"

"I don't know. Does she?"

"If she doesn't know today, she will soon. Heads up, Nolan. She's good at what she does."

"Lots of people didn't like Evelyn Edwards. Just before she died, I saw her arguing with your buddy Mona Kirk. Mona was steaming."

Heaven stopped at the door to Nolan's office. She turned back. "So were you, as I recall. Mona was plenty mad because we were being ripped off. I'm sure she'll be just as mad when she learns you're the one who created the situation. Good luck, Nolan."

Heaven continued down the hall to the elevator, trying to look cooler than she felt. She was going to kill her friend. Why hadn't Mona mentioned she'd talked to Evelyn that night?

Why?

* * *

Heaven had meant to go back to the cafe, she really had. But instead she found herself on Eighteenth and Vine, looking up at the windows of what had been Evelyn Edwards's office. Heaven looked around guiltily. Bonnie Weber would be furious with her if she found out Heaven was conducting her own little investigation.

Heaven walked up to the street-level door as if she belonged there, hoping it wasn't locked. It wasn't. She climbed the stairs quickly and passed a young black man in a suit. He looked back at her. "Are you looking for the accountant?"

Startled, Heaven said, "No, why?" loudly.

He cocked his head. "Oh, well, I'm the accountant who has an office up here. I just thought . . ."

The building wasn't that big. It could be that Evelyn and the accountant were the only two offices on the second floor. How was she going to explain her presence? Heaven caught sight of a sign on a door out of the corner of her eye. "I'm going to see about some hair extensions," she said, and turned away. A white chick with short red hair going to see about hair extensions. Yeah, sure. She hoped he didn't think about it too hard.

There were only four offices: the accountant, the hair place, a door that read "J. J. Maloney, ESQ.," and one with yellow crime scene tape still stretched across it. Surely Bonnie was done with the place. Probably no one from the city had time to clean out a dead woman's office when there were so many other things to be done before the weekend. For the first time Heaven wondered about Evelyn's body. Was it still in the morgue waiting for an auntie or a distant cousin to be found? Did anyone who jumped rope with her when she was a little girl know she was gone? Was there an ex-husband, a lover, perhaps a child?

Heaven turned the handle on the office door, and to her surprise, it opened. For a minute, she thought the police had tossed the place the way they do in the movies. But she remembered Bonnie saying she had gone through Evelyn's office herself. No way would she leave it like this. A guy maybe, but Bonnie was precise. Heaven walked over to the desk. The drawers were pulled out, the papers scattered. A file cabinet was pushed over on its side and files had fallen everywhere. A mirror had been pulled off the wall and lay cracked on the floor.

"Seven years bad luck for someone," she murmured out loud. She reached down to pick up the mirror. The mirror back, a thin sheet of wood, fell off, and several shards of glass fell to the floor.

Two photographs fluttered out as well. Heaven sat down in Evelyn's chair and leaned over to pick up the snapshots. The same man was in both of them, a big, joyous-looking guy. A little girl and a woman were standing beside the man, different ones in each shot. Everyone looked vaguely familiar. Were these hidden photos what someone had torn up the office looking for? Or was there something else, something that had already been found and removed?

Heaven stared out the window for a long time, clutching the photos. Suddenly she was watching Eighteenth and Vine in 1940. It was easy to imagine the street in early afternoon filling up with the players in this musical scene, bar owners opening the front doors to let in fresh air, musicians coming around, looking for advances on money they hadn't made yet, drug dealers in double-breasted suits and fedoras reading the newspaper and grabbing some barbecue for breakfast. Perhaps this major renovation effort had stirred up all kinds of powerful memories, little moments stuck away in the corners of these streets, convection waves of riffs, heartaches, all-night jams.

Heaven looked longingly over at the file cabinet. Maybe she had time for a quick peek. She glanced at her watch and shook her head, telling herself to resist the temptation. She slipped the photos into her jacket pocket and left.

You could tell they were from Eastern Europe. Nowhere else on the planet did they manufacture such ill-fitting menswear. The man and the boy were probably father and son. They had the same nose, the same ears set apart from their heads just a shade too much. They paused at the door of Cafe Heaven, then walked in.

Heaven heard a soft "Allo?" coming from the dining room.

"Are you the piano tuner?" she yelled through the pass-through window. The man and his son looked at each other, unsure. "I'm sorry, I was expecting a piano tuner," she said. Suddenly, Heaven appeared in the flesh, not a disembodied voice, before the strangers in the dining room. She wanted to figure out what the two wanted before they had a chance to make their pitch. It wasn't an easy one to guess. Maybe they were truck farmers, new in the area, with some baby lettuce or early vegetables. But those clothes. Truck farmers would not be wearing bad polyester suits that looked straight out of the seventies. "I'm Heaven Lee," she said, and extended her hand.

"And I am very glad to meet you. I am Sergei Vangirov and this is my son, Louis Armstrong Vangirov," the older man said as he took Heaven's hand and pumped it up and down.

"Great name, kid," Heaven said with a grin. Louis smiled back. Now that the introductions were over, silence and smiling ensued. I guess I'm going to have to pry it out of them, Heaven thought. She turned toward the father. "What can I help you with? If you have a green card, you could start bussing tables tonight. Monday nights are busy here, and we can always use another busser."

"No, we have come for the open performance program," Mr. Vangirov said firmly. "Louis is a great jazz piano player. He will play for you now." With that announcement, Louis went over to the piano and sat down, a serious look on his face.

Heaven knew when she was whipped. Louis would play now. She would listen now. "Okay, Louis, let 'er rip," she said as she sank onto a dining room chair near the small stage. She could use a break anyway. The elder Vangirov stood at attention by the side of the piano, discussing what Louis should play with his son in a tongue that Heaven guessed was Russian or at least somewhere in that Slavic vicinity.

The next twenty minutes were amazing. First, Louis played perfect stride piano in the style of Eubie Blake. Then a Count Basie tune, "One O'Clock Jump." Then he went right into a Jay McShann classic, "Jumpin' the Blues." As his father was announcing a Thelonious Monk piece, Heaven stood up and waved her arms. "I give. Save it for tonight. I would be honored if Louis would play here tonight, but you understand I don't pay anyone. This is an open mike night, a chance for talent to play or sing or perform in front of an audience. Your son is a prodigy, Mr. Vangirov. He should have a recording contract. How old is he?"

Louis swiveled around on the piano bench and beamed at Heaven.

"Eleven years. Yes, yes, he is gifted," Mr. Vangirov agreed. "I know no money, but a chance for Kansas City to hear Louis."

"Louis, do you speak any English?"

Louis ducked his head and spoke rapidly to his father in their native tongue, whatever that was. "He only knows some jazz slang that he has picked up from recordings," the father explained apologetically.

"Give the drummer some. Give the bass a taste," Louis said woodenly to Heaven with a hopeful expression. She gave him five, and he slapped her hand joyfully.

"Mr. Vangirov, how did your son learn to play like that? And what are you doing here—in Kansas City, I mean?"

"From recordings mostly. We live in Belorussia, in Minsk. I loved the jazz always. I found few recordings and in the fifties and sixties, many jazz musicians come on goodwill tours. I once met Louis Armstrong," he stated proudly.

"From the very beginning, Louis could play perfect after hearing something once." Mr. Vangirov remembered the second question. "I saved so we could come to Kansas City, New York City, Chicago. We found out when we get to New York about the Eighteenth and Vine celebration. We will hope that Louis can play next weekend when they open the museum. Louis wants to be a part."

"Boy, have you come to the right place," Heaven said. "I'll introduce you to the person who can make that happen, another piano player, he'll be here tonight. Now I have to get back to work. Come early, about six-thirty, and I'll feed you. The show starts at nine, and we'll get you on early so Louis can get to bed. I forget, how old are you, kid?"

Louis knew that one. "Eleven years."

Mr. Vangirov grabbed her hand and pumped again. "Thank you, thank you. We are so proud."

Heaven walked them to the front door, finally retrieving her hand. "And so am I to break Louis in Kansas City. See you later."

As the pair walked across the street, they paused in front of Sal's Barber Shop. "How'd I do, Pop?" the boy asked in decidedly broken English, but English nonetheless.

"The tempo was off a little on the McShann piece. I think you were rushing—"

The young man broke into his father's critique. He knew he'd rushed the first part of the McShann. "No, I mean, how'd I do? Do you think she bought it?"

The father slapped his son on the back and pulled him into a hug. "Of course. Louis, you're a pro."

Heaven went back into the kitchen but her mind wasn't on her prep work. She took off her apron and yelled "I'll be right back" to no one in particular as she went out the back door. As she walked down the alley, she tried to second guess the motives of Mona Kirk. She stomped into The City

Cat and demanded, "So, what in the hell is this? You just conveniently forgot to tell me where you were just before Evelyn got fried?"

Mona Kirk looked up guiltily and scowled at Heaven. A mother and her young daughter were buying matching cat tee-shirts. They looked over at Heaven with trepidation. Heaven smiled sweetly and started paging through a cat journal while they paid. The minute they left Mona sniffed, "Go ahead, scare my customers off."

"Answer the question, little missy," Heaven persisted.

"I couldn't stand it. I wanted to drag that smarty-pants into that meeting by her ear and make her take her medicine. I'd warned her earlier in the day that we had the goods on her," Mona stormed.

"Oh, really," Heaven said. "Earlier in the day, you say? And when was that, if I'm not being to nosy, and obviously I haven't been nosy enough."

Mona remained defiant. "I went over to her office in the morning and told her she should just resign because we knew she was a thief."

"And?"

"She denied it, of course."

"Mona, what in the world is wrong with you? The woman is murdered ten minutes after you yell at her—for the second time that day. You're the one who jumped up on the stage and looked for a pulse. Wouldn't that have been a good time to mention that you'd just been in the theater and she'd been alive?"

"I hadn't been in there, not really. She was talking on her phone, and I just walked down the aisle halfway to the stage. I didn't see the water, not that I would have known what water meant. She didn't even see me until I yelled."

"What did you yell?" Heaven asked.

"Evelyn Edwards, don't think you can hide on this stage, you thief. You come in the conference room right now!" Mona said with authority.

"Well, aren't you the little schoolteacher," Heaven said.

"Mona, you sat and drank with the homicide officer in charge of Evelyn's case that very night. You told about neither your huffing and puffing at the Ruby nor your trip to her office earlier in the same day. You must be nuts trying to hide anything from Bonnie Weber."

"I've noticed over the years that you don't always tell Bonnie everything you know," Mona parried.

Just then four ladies-who-lunch types came into the store, faces flushed from a couple of glasses of Chardonnay. They started ohhing and ahhing over the latest shipment of cat-inspired jewelry. Mona glared at Heaven, daring her to continue the conversation.

"Only when it won't make me a suspect," Heaven snipped as she walked out.

Eggplant Roll-ups

2 eggplants, sliced the long way about ¼" thick
1 lb. ricotta cheese
2 eggs, beaten
½ cup Parmesan cheese
½ cup shredded Mozzarella cheese
¼ cup chopped basil or parsley
¼ cup toasted hazelnuts, chopped
½ cup caramelized onions
kosher salt and ground black pepper
marinara sauce, or 1 large jar commercial marinara sauce

Soften the eggplant slices by placing on a baking sheet and roasting for 4–5 minutes in a 350 degree oven. Cool while you make the filling.

Combine all the ingredients but the red sauce and a small amount of Parmesan. Roll the eggplant slices up with about 2 T. cheese filling in each. Place the roll-ups in a greased baking dish with the sides touching. Cover with marinara sauce, top with the Parmesan. Bake for about 30 minutes at 350 degrees, until the cheese is browned and the sauce is bubbling.

Caramelized Onions

4 large, sweet yellow onions
2 T. each butter and olive oil
1 T. kosher salt
1 T. sugar

In a large, heavy sauté pan, heat the butter and olive oil. Peel, split, and slice the onions. Sauté over low heat until the onions start to turn translucent. Add the salt and sugar, and continue to cook over a slow heat for about 1 hour, stirring every 5 minutes or so. The onions should turn the color of caramel sauce.

Marinara Sauce

½ cup each peeled and diced onion and carrot, and diced celery
6 cloves garlic, minced
2 T. olive oil
2 28 oz. cans Italian-style tomatoes, one crushed tomatoes and one whole tomatoes that you crush with your hands
1 small can tomato paste
1 cup chicken stock
1 cup red wine
¼ cup chopped basil
1 tsp. dried oregano
2 bay leaves
1 T. sugar
kosher salt, freshly ground black pepper

Heat the oil in your heaviest sauté pan and sauté the mirepoix (onions, celery, carrots). When the carrots are soft, add the garlic. Sauté until the garlic just starts getting brown, then add all the other ingredients except the black pepper. Simmer for at least 1 hour, preferably 2, stirring every 5 minutes or so to prevent sticking as the sauce has a high sugar content from the tomatoes. Add a little more stock or wine as needed. Cool and chill. I like my sauce chunky, but you can use one of those long mixers that you just stick right in the sauce to smooth it out if you prefer. This sauce can be frozen in plastic bags for future use.

Seven

Heaven peeked out the pass-through window from the kitchen. She could see Jim Dittmar at the table with the Vangirov duo. They were deep in conversation, probably about some obscure piano riff, Heaven figured. She had called Jim and asked him to come and have dinner with the father and son. She had also asked him to fit Louis into the program next week. If he agreed of course, after hearing him play, that the kid was a genius at the keyboard.

Murray Steinblatz was standing in the kitchen, getting in the way. "Murray, don't you have something to do? We're busy back here. That must mean the dining room is full. Go greet someone, for God's sake, and get out of the way," Heaven grumbled.

Murray chomped on a red pepper strip. He appeared to be in no hurry to go anywhere. "So, you'll do it?" he asked.

"You know I hate going out to the stage when I've been on the line cooking. I'm hot and sweaty and messy. Why won't you?"

"Come on, H, this kid is your discovery."

"Big discovery. All I had to do was go into the dining

room. He came to me. It's not exactly like John Hammond scouring the South for guitar pickers."

"And Jim is your friend, and famous at that. You should welcome him back to town yourself."

Heaven pushed past Murray with two orders of eggplant stuffed with ricotta cheese, caramelized onions, and toasted hazelnuts, and topped with marinara sauce, one of the most popular meatless dishes on the menu. "Okay, you've made your point. Give me a ten-minute warning, though, so I can at least put on some lipstick."

"Now, will you please stop bothering the boss?" It was Sara Baxter, the grill queen at night, talking. Sara and Murray teased each other constantly and mercilessly. "If you don't leave the kitchen now you won't be in any shape to introduce anyone," Sara muttered to Murray as she plated two orders of salmon and one duck breast.

"Promises, promises," Murray said, but Heaven noticed he left the kitchen rapidly.

The next hour was a blur of orders, plates going out, pasta being sauced, shrimp being seared. The noise level from the dining room told Heaven it must be approaching nine o'clock. Suddenly a familiar face peeked into the kitchen from the pass-through, and it didn't belong to a waiter looking for salads. "Guess what, Heaven? This is so exciting!" It was Pam Whiteside from the mayor's office. She must have decided from the look on Heaven's face that it wasn't the time for a guessing game. "Bob Daultman is back in town, and somehow he heard about your open mike night and he wanted to be here. He brought one cameraman, too. You don't mind, do you?"

The next two faces Heaven saw were those of Chris Snyder and Joe Long, who produced these open mike nights. They had obviously been shocked by the sight of a camera crew, however small, and were trying to get Heaven's attention by jumping up and down behind Pam Whiteside. They were making gestures suggesting that they could kill Heaven for not filling them in.

"Surprise, surprise," Heaven said over the top of Pam's head. "Joe and Chris, this is Pam Whiteside, who works in the mayor's office." She didn't give them a chance to get a word in. "Pam has brought the *famous* filmmaker Bob Daultman, who is going to be filming here in town through the Eighteenth and Vine district dedication. Say hello to Pam."

Pam turned and threw the young men a smile. Heaven hurried on. "I'm sure Mr. Daultman would like a drink. Why don't you get him set up, gentlemen? Pam, I'm so sorry there isn't a table for you all. They're usually all filled up by eight. But do you see Jim Dittmar out there? He's sitting with an older man and a young boy, who is an exceptional pianist. I bet we could crowd you and Bob at that table, couldn't we, guys?"

Chris and Joe had been ready to tell Heaven there was a Bob Daultman look-alike in the dining room with a bogus cameraman. Now they were smiling and nodding yes to Heaven, with the kind of expressions people in the theater get on their faces when a famous director pops up, even one who makes documentary films and so can't cast them in his next production. "I'll go downstairs and get some extra chairs," Joe said.

"And I'll take you over and introduce you to everyone at the table," Chris said grandly. "You won't believe this kid when he starts to play his Duke Ellington medley," he proclaimed, even though he had no idea if the boy knew any Duke Ellington. It sounded right.

In just a minute, so it seemed to Heaven, Murray was poking his head through the pass-through. "It's time," he said firmly.

"Sara, give this risotto another minute. It goes with the quail you're working on," Heaven said as she threw a handful of Parmesan on the rice and whipped off her apron. She stepped into the kitchen bathroom and came out a minute later with eyes and lips, something accomplished with the first aid makeup kit she kept in there. On the hooks where the kitchen staff hung their jackets and aprons there was a man's sport jacket from the sixties, one of those sharkskin, iridescent, skinny-lapel numbers. It was the emergency, I-have-to-look-like-a-hip-businesswoman jacket. She had dressed up the jacket with several bug pins from the fifties: a dragonfly with rhinestones, an enamel ladybug, and a great spider with multicolored glass legs. Heaven removed her chef's jacket and put the sports coat on over her James Beard Foundation tee-shirt and black leggings. It worked. "I'll be right back," she promised, and went out into the dining room.

Heaven scanned the darkened room. Her eyes met Joe's. She gestured to indicate he should come to her. He made his way through the crowd. "What's up, boss?"

"The beatnik film guy . . ."

Joe nodded. "Who knew he actually wore the beret in real life?"

"Usually," Heaven reminded him, "I don't interfere in your staging of the show, but let me just give you a tip. I heard this guy talk about himself at the committee meeting the other day, and he will put a serious cramp on the timing of your evening. Not that it isn't interesting stuff, it just isn't the kind of thing that keeps folks on the edge of their seats. Let me ask him to come up to the stage and tell the crowd about the jazz project that he's in town for, then we'll follow it up with the real thing, jazz from the kid, then Jim Dittmar. I know that the kid will blow the house down, and Jim is a homeboy who made good."

Joe nodded. "Then Murray can pick right up with the list of performers I gave him earlier. Sounds like a plan."

Murray was already up on the small stage at the back of Cafe Heaven, warming up the crowd. "This show tonight is so big, I knew you wouldn't believe me when I announced all the talent. So I asked our fearless leader to come out and tell you about it herself. And here she is in person, our angel of mercy, Heaven Lee."

Heaven couldn't help but blush when the guests started

stomping and yelling "Hea-ven, Hea-ven" like she was a bad talk show host.

"Cut it out or I'll start watering down the margaritas," she threatened. "Tonight, in addition to our usual swell combination of hipsters, players, and candlestick makers, we have three very special people here. Bob Daultman is world renowned for his documentary films. He's in town to film the dedication of the historic Eighteenth and Vine jazz district next weekend."

Bob Daultman stood up and tossed a few kisses into the air. The crowd applauded enthusiastically.

Heaven continued. "Today, a great talent walked into Cafe Heaven. He's only eleven years old, and already he's a jazz pianist extraordinaire. He's come even farther than Bob Daultman to be in Kansas City for the event. He's from Belorussia, which was a part of the Soviet Union."

The crowd murmured, looking at the only child in the room.

"He's going to play for us tonight, and believe me, you're in for a real treat. Stand up and take your first bow in Kansas City, Louis Armstrong Vangirov," Heaven said as she pointed at Louis and smiled. He rose and bowed solemnly. The crowd went wild. With the name, the bad polyester suit, and the ears that were just a little too big for the head, Louis was already a star.

"And that's not all," Heaven yelled. The crowd calmed down a little. "One of Kansas City's own has returned home from two years in Europe. Jim Dittmar has agreed to be the music coordinator for the Eighteenth and Vine dedication. He also has a new CD coming out soon, *Jim Dittmar Live in Paris*, and tonight he's live at Cafe Heaven."

Jim had always had a good following in Kansas City. Most of the crowd hadn't heard he was back in town yet so there was much clapping and stomping again. Heaven let it go on for a while, then she whistled, not exactly a ballpark whistle, but loud enough. "So, now you know how special tonight is. I want you to tip your waiter well. I want you to drink and eat and enjoy yourselves like there is no tomorrow. I also want you to welcome Bob Daultman to the stage for a minute. Bob, will you tell the Cafe Heaven crew about your jazz documentary?"

Heaven pointed at the celebrity table again, and the film-maker, making sure his cameraman was catching it all, stood up with a modest expression on his face, as if he were really honored to be asked to talk. Daultman smiled graciously at her as he stepped up onstage. Heaven hoped Joe had briefed Murray and they had come up with a way to keep this guy's speech down to ten minutes. She took a last look around the room for trouble spots. Everyone looked happy, so she went back to the kitchen.

The night had been a big success. Heaven had listened and watched as much as she could. People had taken her advice and continued to order food, so she hadn't been able to leave the kitchen.

Bob Daultman had been charming and brief, spending only five minutes onstage.

Louis had wowed them, of course, playing the same tunes he'd auditioned with in the afternoon. Then Jim Dittmar had played and sung *"My Little Red Top,"* a King Pleasure tune that he dedicated to Heaven. The crowd loved it. After that he called Louis Armstrong Vangirov to the stage and together they played *"Moten's Swing,"* a tune from Kansas City bandleader Bennie Moten, whose hey day had been the 1920s and 30s. The duet, four hands on the keyboard, brought the house down.

Two hours and a dozen acts later, the show was over and the guests were slowly clearing out. Heaven had turned her sauté station over to the night staff to break down. She was working the room. Louis and his father were heading for the door slowly, because everyone wanted to shake the hand of the kid. She wanted to, too.

"Well, what a Kansas City debut," Heaven said as she approached them. "Thank you for making it at my cafe, Louis. By the way, how come you took your jazz tour of America in May? Aren't you supposed to be in school in Belorussia?"

Louis's father smiled and shrugged. "His mother and I, we thought this was more important—for his future. We brought all the books and lessons with us. Every morning, Louis and I study."

Louis was excited, eyes bright with the thrill of a good crowd. "Thank you, Heaven," he said, and gave her a little bow, then he looked to his father for approval on his English.

Heaven bowed back. "Thank you, Louis." She looked at his dad. "Is Jim getting you fixed up to play at the dedication?"

"Next Saturday," Mr. Vangirov said proudly. "And the two will do another number together. We will see you there?"

"I'm setting up all the food, so I'll be there for the duration. Now, go home and get into bed, or I'll get in trouble for endangering the welfare of a minor." Both of the Russians looked blankly at Heaven. She hugged them and then turned toward the bar. She hoped there was a glass of wine with her name on it. Her eyes searched the room. If Jim Dittmar was still around she'd buy him a drink, just to thank him for being so nice to the kid. He was nowhere to be seen. Heaven felt a little let down. Of course, she had been discouraging him, hadn't she? He probably left with some cute thing from the Art Institute. It was just as well.

"Tony, may I have a glass of that Viognier from Calara?" she asked with disappointment in her voice.

Jim Dittmar paced up and down the alley behind the cafe, afraid Heaven would come out the back door any minute and ask him what he was doing there. So far, only the dish washer had come out to make a trip to the Dumpster.

Jim checked his watch for the fourth time in five minutes. He hated this part. This slinking around in alleys, it made him feel so guilty.

"Jim, darling, what an amusing group. I couldn't get people to stop talking to me, asking for my autograph. They love me here in the heartland." Bob Daultman came up the alley with a cheerful gait, his beret at the perfect tilt.

"Let's get this over with. I hate these clandestine meetings."

"Fine," Daultman snapped. "Do it Thursday and the kid is your mule. I don't recall you being so offended by our meetings in Europe. We drank some good wine had some fun while we planned our little jaunts."

"Yes, and I came back home because I didn't want to make those little jaunts anymore. But the next thing I know, you're on the phone, giving me an ultimatum."

Daultman patted Jim's cheek. "What did you think, that the buyer wouldn't miss a five-carat perfect diamond? You were so naughty, Jim. And this celebration is too good to pass up. Besides, I love seeing your roots. I hope I get to meet your son while I'm here."

"Don't even think about it, Bobby," Jim said quietly. "We're not thugs. Don't even hint at threatening my family. I'm in, like I told you."

"Good, because I hated losing the cash we would have got for that stone. But now you're going to make it up to me, like a good boy. And that was innocent curiosity about your son. After all, we were like a family in Europe, now, weren't we?" Daultman turned without another word and disappeared down the alley.

Jim Dittmar paced for another minute. He wanted to go back into the restaurant, have a drink, flirt with Heaven. But he felt disgusted with himself. He knew he'd get over it, but right now he didn't have the stomach to look at his own reflection in the mirror behind the bar. He headed for his mom's car, parked down the street, his footsteps ringing hollow in the empty alley.

Eight

art. Over here." Heaven was leading a scraggly group of
men and women down the middle of Eighteenth Street. She
had spotted Hart Kenton when they had walked through
the Ruby Theater earlier. Now he was leaving the building,
and Heaven wanted a word with him before he took off.

Hart waved at Heaven and headed her way. "What's up?"

Heaven indicated the group behind her. "The barbecue
titans of Kansas City are arguing about the placement of
their food stands. I thought this would be easier than the
soul food folks. They are selling their product, not being
hired to cater, so I don't see what difference it makes what
order the stands are in."

Hart glanced over his shoulder. Everyone seemed to be
pointing in another direction. "It seems to make a difference to them." He paused. "Can you talk about the Evelyn
Edwards situation for a sec?"

Heaven nodded. "The cookers can fight it out on their
own. Did you find out anything interesting?"

"Pretty much what you already know. Because the Ruby's
a road show venue, it has big power capabilities in those
floor pockets, as opposed to a venue that has all the lighting

and sound permanently wired. It was set up to meet requirements for lots of different kinds of stage shows.

"I asked the stage manager about that day. He said he'd gone to get more gels because the chick, ah, the party planner, had come in out of nowhere, real interested in how the lights were going down for the first number and the grand finale of the concert. He was frustrated, he said, because she was a real bitch."

"And that brings up another point. Whoever did it would have to know that Evelyn was going to work on the lights that afternoon," Heaven mused.

"Well, Heaven, that's true only if the accident was specifically meant for Evelyn. What if it was supposed to postpone the opening of the Ruby? Then it wouldn't make any difference who got it, or when."

"Is that what the stage manager thinks?"

"He thinks it could have been him lying dead on the stage, no matter who the accident was meant for," said Hart solemnly.

"Good point," Heaven said reluctantly as her precious theories about motive went down the drain. "It's kind of like the Unabomber. He didn't know for sure who would open his nasty little packages. He just sent them to those who represented the enemy in his mind. If you really have a specific target, one person, you don't booby-trap a whole city, or even a building."

"Unless your target is the whole city."

"Hart, you are a great junior G-man. Anything else?"

"Yeah. The stage manager said that Evelyn was talking on a cell phone when he left the stage to get the gels. And she was upset, seemed to be having a big argument. He also said he got the impression she had an eye on the doors to the lobby, like she was watching for someone or expecting someone."

Heaven's face lit up. "Hart, now, that's a clue!" She hugged him. "I better get back to the barbecue boys. Thank you so much," she said, turning toward the knot of angry-sounding people down the street.

"Okay," she shouted as she waved the paper that showed the layout of the street for the next Saturday. "The bands will be at the far west end of the blocked-off portion of the street. The food booths will be at the far east part. The middle will be filled up with tables and chairs. Who doesn't like where their booth is placed?"

Everyone but the person from Arthur Bryant's held up a hand.

It was going to be a long afternoon.

Sam Scott closed the suitcase. She was ready. She'd packed Lefty's suitcase, too, everything but the toiletries she would throw in at the last minute Thursday morning. Distracted, Sam sat down in the old-fashioned window seat and pulled her legs up to her chin, staring out at Central Park. What would this weekend bring? Her mind kept going back to the note she had received via her agent.

Did she want to mend fences with Mona Kirk? She reached over to her desk and picked up the note.

> *Dear Sam,*
> *Greetings from a part of your past. You probably want to leave me back there, but I thought I should warn you that I'm an active member of the committee putting together the Eighteenth and Vine dedication in Kansas City. I'd like a chance to talk to you alone sometime over the weekend. I owe you an apology.*
>
> *The Best,*
> *Mona Kirk*

It surprised Sam how hurt she still felt when she read the words. It was as if she were eighteen all over again and her best friend had turned out to be . . . not who she seemed.

Even now, as she read the note for the fourth or fifth time, her eyes filled with tears. The first disappointments of a young life never go away, never even seem to diminish in their ability to hurt. But now Mona wanted to make amends, even if they both knew that wasn't possible. So the weekend threatened a confrontation with her old friend, whether Sam agreed to meet with her or not.

Not only that, she was very nervous about both Boots Turner and her husband being in the same city at the same time. Lefty's health was, well, frail. He would deny it, of course. But she knew his arthritis made walking and using his hands painful. She also knew that Boots had undergone heart surgery last year. Would the two men act their age? Neither one of them should be taking a swing at the other, yet she could see it happening. If anything life threatening—or even an emotional scene—occurred, she would feel responsible. After all, she *was* responsible for the decision that had changed all their lives. Sam Scott got up and walked through the spacious apartment, looking around each room in turn. "Honey, where are you?" she called.

Lefty Stuart was in the book-filled room he called his office. He loved to kiss Sam good-bye at the breakfast table and say with a wink he was going to the office. There he made his calls, read the newspapers, worked on the book he was writing about his days in Negro League baseball. Now, when Sam poked her head in the door, he looked up from a pile of newspaper clippings. "Come in, sugar. Boy, a lot of these guys are feeding the tulips," Lefty said sadly.

"You must be looking at photos of the bands I used to sing with. Half of 'em are dead," Sam said. She glided into the room, perched on the arm of Lefty's roomy leather chair, and put her arm around his shoulder.

"No, I'm lookin' at the men I used to play ball with. Look, here we are the year the Kansas City Monarchs won the championship. That was 1941," Lefty said.

Sam studied the photo and pointed at Lefty's image. "There you are. You were just a teenager."

"It was my first year." He pointed at the player standing next to him in the photograph. "There's Rainey Bibbs. He was my roommate that year. Snored louder than a church choir can sing. We had a time."

Sam snorted. "Yeah, when you could find a place that would let colored baseball players stay. It sounds like you spent most nights sleeping on the bus."

Lefty nodded. "In the heyday of the Negro Leagues, before the Depression, that sure was true. I came aboard when the whole thing was almost over."

"The Depression really hurt black baseball, didn't it?"

"The old-timers told how they would have twenty, thirty thousand fans at the games," Lefty said with a glimmer in his eye. "The Baltimore Black Sox, the New York Black Yankees, the Chicago American Giants, they drew big crowds. The Depression comes along, that twenty-five-cent admission was grocery money."

"Next thing that happens, integrating the majors finishes off the black leagues. Even though we've talked about it a million times, it still seems a little too ironic," Sam said as she sorted through the clippings on her husband's lap.

"The crowds really never came back after the war. Then when Jackie Robinson made it to the big leagues . . ."

"Followed by you," Sam interjected.

"Followed by me, Satchel Paige, and the rest. The black families went with us to the majors. It was like the players left in the Negro League, and there were plenty of good ones, were the second string. No one wanted to see the second string."

"So fewer black baseball players had jobs," Sam said sadly.

Lefty Stuart looked up at his wife. "Now, what's the use of crying over milk spilt that long ago? Are you feelin' all right, Sam?"

Sam got up and kissed the top of Lefty's head. "I'm just a sentimental fool today, honey. Our past is waiting for us in Kansas City. It's just got me thinking. And the thinking has got me hungry. I'll make lunch." And she slipped out of the room before Lefty could question her further.

Sam went back into the guest bedroom, where two suitcases lay on the bed, packed and ready. She opened the closet and rummaged around on the linen shelf. When her hand emerged, it was holding a small .22-caliber pistol. She opened her own suitcase and slipped the weapon in between the carefully folded clothes. "Just in case," she murmured, and headed for the kitchen.

Heaven hurried to the kitchen. It was four, almost time for dinner service, and she had promised to be back by three. If this gala wasn't over soon she would have a kitchen rebellion on her hands. "Sorry," she muttered breathlessly as she slipped on her chef's coat. "What can I do?"

Sara Baxter was tossing a pan full of pecans as she fried them in olive oil. "Stop feeling guilty, that's what you can do. It's Tuesday, the slowest night of the week. If we can't get ready for Tuesday night without you, then you need a new kitchen crew."

"I know, but I wanted to make the stuffed cabbage. I know how irritating it is to fiddle with those leaves. You have to keep dipping them in the boiling water to soften them, then try to peel them off without tearing them . . ."

Sara whistled. "Hold it right there. Didn't I cook for a Hungarian count back in 1972? You think a little stuffed cabbage is going to set me back?"

"How foolish of me," Heaven said with a grin as she opened the hotel pan filled with cabbage rolls simmering in a sweet-and-sour tomato sauce. She took a big sniff. "This smells like heaven right here on earth, if you'll pardon the pun."

"Hank has called twice and said he'd call back," Sara said as the kitchen phone buzzed.

Heaven had mixed feelings about even having a phone in the kitchen. It was a terrible temptation for the crew.

When the night was slow they were supposed to take a quadrant of the kitchen and clean, not talk on the phone. But the fact that Heaven worked in the kitchen made it imperative to have a phone. She'd never get anything done if she had to go to the bar every time she got a call. It also meant she had no privacy.

Heaven hunched toward the wall as she talked. "I was hoping it was you. Oh, just fine. No, they don't know any more about the victim. Well, I don't at least. Of course, my friend Hart Kenton, the lighting designer, said . . . You know, I should call you back. I'm late and it's almost time for service. The most wonderful kid came in last night. Russian, eleven years old, and he can play jazz piano like nobody's business. I'll tell you all about him later. Hank, I miss you. Me, too."

Everyone in the kitchen acted busy.

"I just have one more call," Heaven said apologetically. She dialed quickly. "Bonnie, did you find a cell phone with the . . . with Evelyn's stuff? Well, if I were you, I'd go to the evidence room and see if there's a cell phone and if it has redial. Why? Because the stage manager told a friend . . . Just check, please? I don't know, maybe he just remembered. He said Evelyn was arguing with someone on her cell phone. Maybe we'll catch a break. Call me later—or tomorrow," Heaven said, and hung up. The crew didn't even try to act like they weren't listening this time.

"So, who do you think the dead broad was talking to?" Sara asked.

The kitchen phone buzzed again. Chris Snyder poked his head in the kitchen window. "Heaven, you've got to take that call. It's one of the social club ladies. I told her you couldn't talk now, but she said it was really important."

Heaven wheeled around toward the phone and picked it up. "Yes? Hello, Julia. What's up? Oh, that can't be. Did you call everyone on that list I gave you? Well, there has to be some explanation. I'll call Pisciotta's and the other wholesalers in the morning. We'll figure out something. Now, calm down and tell everyone not to worry." She hung up the phone slowly.

"Well, what now?" Sara asked.

Heaven shrugged her shoulders and walked toward the sauté station. "Someone has bought up all the vital ingredients for the Friday gala buffet. There's not a black-eyed pea left in town."

Mona Kirk turned the sign on the shop door over, from OPEN to CLOSED. Then she checked her watch for the tenth time in the last five minutes. "What could be taking her so long?" she muttered.

Suddenly, Detective Bonnie Weber appeared at the door. "What's up, Mona?" she asked as the door opened. "You sounded upset."

"Well, I am. I've been upset ever since this horrible Evelyn Edwards thing began. So, now, I'm ready to confess. There's something I haven't told you."

Bonnie Weber looked surprised, something she rarely did. She leaned against the counter and crossed her arms. "Let me have it, Mona. I hope this isn't going to ruin our friendship."

It was well past midnight. Jim Dittmar parked the van he had purchased earlier in the day two blocks away. He had the temporary license plate taped on the back window, but he could take it down quickly if necessary.

Jim had spent several days looking for the perfect situation.

It had to be a familiar house, one where he had played a party or been inside as a guest. The homeowners had to be older and preferably have a cat. Older people with cats often didn't turn on the interior component of their alarm system, fearing they or their cat might set off the motion sensors. But it couldn't be an older woman alone. They always turned on the alarm, even if it meant putting the cat out for the night. And the house most certainly had to be on the Missouri side, not in Mission Hills in Kansas, where the biggest mansions were. The Mission Hills, Kansas, police were to be avoided. They kept watch for stray cars, especially vans, and strangers walking when or where they shouldn't be. They were there to prevent crimes against property, something their residents feared more than a gunfight in the front yard, which was rare over there.

Jim felt good about this mark. It was a couple in their late sixties, a retired insurance executive and his wife. They were actually acquaintances of Jim's parents. He had been in their house several times. It was situated right off Ward Parkway, where the mansions on the Missouri side were located. Thanks to a good memory for details, he knew where he was going. Even if the alarm started ringing the minute he slipped the lock, he was confident the couple wouldn't leave their bedroom. They would stay there and let the police handle it. They wouldn't try to be heroes. If he was lucky and the alarm wasn't set, they wouldn't even know until they got up in the morning that someone had stolen their Jasper Johns painting, leaving them only an empty frame.

Jim Dittmar slipped on his black stocking cap, his surgical-quality latex gloves. He had a smile on his face. Despite his promises to himself to reform, he would miss the excitement, the adrenaline rush. And with what he was facing in the near future, he needed the practice.

Chicken with Green Dumplings

2 whole chickens, or 10 lbs. of bone-in chicken breasts if
  you can't stand dark meat
2 onions
4 carrots
1 stalk celery
2 flat cans sliced water chestnuts, or one 10 oz can.
1¼ cup flour
½ cup yellow cornmeal
2 eggs
1 tsp. each baking powder and kosher salt
⅓ cup milk
2 T. melted butter
1 10 oz pkg. frozen chopped spinach that has been
  defrosted by running warm water over it in a colander,
  then squeezed to remove most of the moisture
kosher salt, white pepper
Option: 1 cup heavy cream

Stock

To make stock, you really need two large stockpots so you
can transfer the broth back and forth as you do these steps.
In your largest stockpot, place the 2 chickens, the end and
leaves of the celery, 1 carrot, washed but unpeeled, and an
onion, quartered, with the onion skins. Cover with cold

water, bring to a boil, then reduce the heat to keep the pot simmering until the chicken is falling off the bones. Remove from heat, drain the chicken and vegetables out of the stock. You can separate the chicken and the broth by using long kitchen tongs and fishing it all out piece by piece, or by putting a colander or china cap (a cone-shaped strainer) over pot number two as you pour the contents of pot number one into pot number two, thus saving the chicken parts and the aromatics in the colander. This sounds much harder than it is. I'm just mentioning it so you will be prepared with the equipment you need. Let the chickens cool, then separate the meat and coarsely chop. Strain the stock and let cool, then remove the fat that has gathered on the top. This step can be done anytime and the stock frozen in plastic bags. You want about a gallon of finished stock.

Dumplings

Combine the dry ingredients (flour, cornmeal, salt, and baking powder) in a mixing bowl, beat eggs and add to the dry ingredients along with the milk, the butter, and the drained spinach. Combine and let set while you make the sauce.

Sauce

In a large sauté pan, sauté 1 cup each diced and peeled onion, celery, and carrot in 4 T. butter or a combination of butter and canola oil. When the onions are turning translucent, cover the vegetables in stock and simmer until the carrots are tender. Add the water chestnuts and remove from heat.

To finish the dish, heat remaining stock to simmer in a large pot. Drop tablespoons of the dumpling dough into the stock, making sure each dumpling gets submerged. Let simmer about 5 minutes, then add the chopped chicken and the vegetables, salt and pepper. If you want the rich version, add the cream now and simmer another ten minutes. Serve in bowls. This dish freezes well.

Nine

Sal's Barber Shop was packed. Joe, Chris, Mona, Murray, and Heaven were drinking coffee that Heaven had brought to Sal's, along with glazed donuts from Lamar's Donuts. This meeting was too important to drink Sal's coffee. Mona was scanning the morning *Kansas City Star*. "Someone broke into a house out on Ward Parkway and stole a painting worth . . ."she said to no one in particular.

Heaven snatched the paper away from Mona. "We don't have time for the news," she declared. "Has everyone made their calls?"

Everyone started talking at once. "Okay, okay, one at a time. Chris?"

"Well, not even the most devious villain can make all the chicken in Kansas City disappear. There's still chicken in town. But, now, ham hocks are another matter. I called Fritz's and the other big smokehouse, over in Kansas City, Kansas, and someone had come in and bought all the ham hocks at both places," Chris said. "And the pork chops."

"Did you ask—" Heaven started.

"For a description?" Chris finished. "Two good-looking black guys. Body builders."

"Like the guys who were with Ella the other night, maybe," Heaven said.

"I was in charge of produce," Joe piped up. "And the collard green situation is bad. And there's a real sweet potato shortage, too. Turnips? Someone bought cases of them. And it looks like you might have to go with canned green beans."

"Never!" Heaven snapped. "Mona, how's the catfish inventory?"

Mona shook her head. "Someone called in early this morning and asked the wholesale fish guy to hold all the catfish he had for them, that they would be in later to pick it all up. And they also said they would take all the catfish that comes in on Friday. Said they would pay cash."

Murray stood up as if he were reciting in class. "I checked out the grocery stores, like you asked me to, H. The black-eyed peas have taken a hit, there are some wilted mustard greens at a few places, and no one can buy up all the cornmeal. So, chicken and cornbread are still on the menu."

Did you talk to the grocery store managers? Could they tell you who bought up all the greens and peas?" Heaven asked with fire in her eyes. She was past the point of panic and had moved on to anger.

Sal stopped his neck trim. The old gent in the barber chair was hard of hearing and thought they were talking about a picnic. "Fried chicken would be nice," he said, trying to get into the spirit of the conversation. Sal twirled him around. "What haven't you told us, Murray?" Sal demanded.

"Some of the stores remembered the boys. And then some remembered a woman in, ah, vintage clothes," Murray said.

"That witch! She thinks we'll have to come begging her to do the gala. She's cornering the market, as if she were Bill Gates and Microsoft." Heaven said.

Mona blinked a couple of times, trying to figure out the Gates allusion, then got up and put her arm around Heaven. "I thought you'd outsmarted them when you came up with the idea of having the social clubs cook, H. But it sounds like Miss Ella had a trick or two up her sleeve as well. How can she afford to do this just out of spite?"

"She'll probably freeze the stuff she can't use right away. And dried beans don't go bad, the evil snake," Heaven huffed. "I think I'll go pay Miss Ella a visit. Who knows, after our talk, she may even donate some supplies to the cause. But first I've got to warn the Cajun restaurants. It would be hard to pull off the New Orleans brunch on Sunday if this witch buys up all the crawfish west of the Mississippi," Heaven said as she pulled Mona out the door with her.

"Don't think I've forgotten our unfinished business, even though I don't have time to talk now. You haven't explained yourself," Heaven said in a sharp tone.

Mona bravely faced her accuser. "I called up the detective and told her everything."

"I bet that was fun. Well, get ready to repeat your story to me later," Heaven snarled as she marched across the street two steps ahead of Mona, intent on her next chore. Halfway across the street she stopped, looking sheepishly at Mona. "I'm going to ask you for a favor but that doesn't mean you don't have to tell me everything," Heaven said.

"And the favor is?"

"Take these photos and have them blown up and laminated with the rest," Heaven said, handing Mona the two photographs from Evelyn's office and turning away before she could ask questions.

The rest of the group straggled out, too, all except for Murray, who sat deep in thought until the gentleman in Sal's chair had paid and gone. Sal, who walked stiffly from a lifetime on his feet, came over and sat down by Murray.

"I don't remember you ever taking the load off during office hours, Sal," Murray teased.

"If I get down, I have trouble getting back up," Sal said with an honesty that made Murray think he must be in some pain today. "So, Murray," he went on, "what can I do to help? These two, Heaven and Mona, have got themselves in a fix. We can't have them the laughing stock of the town."

Murray sighed. "I think it's time for your City Hall connections, Sal. Here's the deal."

Detective Bonnie Weber was furious. She marched through City Hall, ignoring the receptionist guarding the mayor's quarters. She did, however, turn her head and growl "Tell Nolan I'm coming" to the young woman as she passed through the door marked PRIVATE. Bonnie saw Nolan stick his head out of his office as she neared the end of the hall and the mayor's office. She made her hand into a gun and pointed it at Nolan and pulled the trigger.

Nolan looked up and down the hall to see if anyone else had noticed. "What's up, Detective? I've got a room full of people. We're meeting about the land under the Nelson-Atkins Museum of Art. The Nelson wants control, even though technically the land belongs to the city. The Parks and Recreation Department also wants control," Nolan babbled on.

"So, no thanks to you, I find out you were talking to Evelyn Edwards when she died."

"What do you mean?" Nolan asked weakly as he checked out the hall again. This wasn't a good place to have this conversation, but his office was out of the question at the moment. Maybe he could promise to come to her office later.

"There was a cell phone in her briefcase, Nolan," Bonnie said in a low voice. "I checked the redial."

Relief flooded the tall man's face. "Then where did you get the crazy idea that I was talking to her?"

"You're right, ol' buddy, she was leaving a nasty message for the florist who ratted her out to the gala committee. The florist is still blushing from the colorful language she used. That was the last call she made. But someone could have called her. So that got me to thinking about phones, and I asked the phone company for the records of the pay phones in the lobby of the Ruby Theater, and of course I asked the cell phone company for her records. Do you know what I found?''

Nolan knew. "A call from the phone in the lobby to Evelyn Edwards's cell phone. I was angry, I've never denied it. I gave her a chance and she was screwing with me and everyone else."

"So why didn't you just walk into the auditorium and tell her off?"

"I didn't know where she was."

Bonnie shook her head. "Most of the other folks at that meeting knew she was working on the lights."

"I guess I left before they started talking about what she was doing. Believe me, I was so angry . . ." Nolan paused, knowing he shouldn't admit to being "so angry." It was too late. ". . . that I would have gone to confront her face-to-face if I'd known. I had her cell phone number, so I used that."

"And then you kept her on the phone until she fried, didn't you, you stupid bastard."

"No. I hung up before . . . you know."

Bonnie didn't let him finish. "You know what I think, Nolan? I think you were talking to her when she was electrocuted, you ran into the theater and saw what had happened, then you disconnected the phone and put it away in her briefcase because you were afraid it would connect you to her. Then you ran away."

"And no one saw me do all this? How could that be, Detective? What you just described takes time," Nolan said, a last remnant of bravado in his voice.

"The lights had gone out. Everyone was concerned with that problem."

"I'm sure Evelyn Edwards put her phone away herself, *after* our conversation," Nolan insisted.

"I hope you're right, because that phone is at the lab right now, and if it has your fingerprints on it you better tell me now."

Nolan was silent.

Bonnie hooked her fingers on the lapel of his fancy double-breasted suit and gave him a jerk. "If your fingerprints are on that phone, you're looking very good for this death. This is your only warning. Now, go back to the art gallery crowd," she said, and walked swiftly down the hall, leaving Nolan to his fears.

He stood watching her for a minute, then went back inside his office.

The door to Miss Ella's Soul Food was propped open and delivery trucks were lined up outside. Heaven saw cases of foodstuffs being delivered and she walked a little faster. Those were rightfully the gala's crates of greens and sweet potatoes, not Miss Ella's.

Inside the storefront cafe, the bustle that accompanied opening a restaurant was in full swing. Miss Ella was in the center of the swirl, clipboard in hand. Today's outfit was circa 1939, a gorgeous black-and-white crepe dress with big padded shoulders and magnolias painted on the skirt. Her hair was done in an elaborate chignon decorated with crossed chopsticks. She smiled when she saw Heaven charging in the door. "Heh, girlfriend," she called cheerfully.

"Don't girlfriend me, you produce thief," Heaven snarled. "So, what's your game? If you can't get your way and do the gala food by yourself, then no one can do it, is that it?"

"Now, simmer down before you say something you can't take back," Ella said with a little fire in her eyes. "I just assumed you could handle doing this funky ol' meal yourself, since no one else wants to bother with it."

"So you bought up all the menu items you could to make my life miserable. And you still call me girlfriend? Well, I have news for you. I'm not catering the gala Friday night. A group of women who have historic ties in the community are. Many of them are older and they are worried sick that they will let down the whole Eighteenth and Vine revival because they can't find any decent ham hocks. So instead of embarrassing one white girl who could handle it, you're humiliating a whole group of black women who can't."

Miss Ella gave that great big laugh of hers. She loved a good fight. "Heaven, honey, I don't know what you're talking about. Last time I looked, it was a free country and I could buy any damn thing I had the money to buy. I'm expecting a big weekend, sugar. I had to stock up."

"Bullshit. You were seen buying black-eyed peas in a grocery store. No one in the restaurant business goes to a grocery store unless it's for an emergency head of lettuce. You're trying to ruin Kansas City's big celebration. And I might remind you, this is the same town that is letting you move in and do business."

Miss Ella moved close to Heaven. It felt as if she were taking up all the air in the room. Heaven gulped but didn't back away. Ella put the long red nails of one hand on the side of Heaven's face and scraped them down toward Heaven's neck lightly. They left red marks. She hadn't really scratched Heaven, but she was toying with her, that was for sure. Cat and mouse. Heaven didn't move. "This little hick town is lucky to have Miss Ella," the big black woman said. "And don't you forget it, sugar. You're not the only food queen anymore. No sir."

Heaven slipped one hand around to the back of Miss Ella's head and jerked the chopsticks out of her chignon, using the other hand to pull Miss Ella's head back and hold it there. Then she poked Miss Ella's stomach with a chopstick to the rhythm of her speech. "You have to play nice or I'll make sure everyone knows how you're sabotaging the Eighteenth and Vine dedication. And if that happens, you'll find out what a loyal town this is while you sit in here all by your lonesome. I know you don't want that because I bet you have plans to open a few more of these cafes, then take your company public and make a big pile of money. So, don't fuck with Kansas City, girlfriend. I also think Detective

Weber will be very interested in the fact that you called Evelyn Edwards 'Tulsa trailer trash.' If you'd only talked to the woman on the phone, how did you know where she came from?''

Heaven dropped the chopsticks, released Miss Ella, and hurried toward the door without waiting for a reaction. She could imagine Miss Ella giving her a good right hook, but she couldn't imagine the woman sticking a knife in her back. Showing her back side was safer than exposing her front.

All of a sudden, that big laugh erupted from behind her. ''I like your style, girlfriend,'' Miss Ella yelled as Heaven stormed out the door. On her way out, two gentlemen in three-piece suits and sad faces were coming in, briefcases in hand. Heaven paused at the door for a second, long enough to hear them thank Ella Jackson for her consideration to a stranger. At the curb in the midst of all the food delivery trucks was a hearse that said ''The Jones Brothers Funeral Chapel'' on the side. The cheerful guys going to see Miss Ella must be the Jones brothers. The only person Heaven could think of who had died lately was Evelyn Edwards. Why would Ella have anything to do with her burial? But then Ella was a stranger in Kansas City. Who else could she have any remote connection to that had died?

Heaven was so busy rubbernecking that she plowed right into the arms of Jim Dittmar, who was walking along Eighteenth Street in the unlikely company of Bob Daultman, Louis Armstrong Vangirov, and Louis's father.

''Whoa, Heaven. Where're you going in such a hurry?'' Jim asked as he pulled her close and nuzzled her hair the way he had the other night at the cafe. She pulled away, but grinned in spite of herself.

''I've got a meeting with the Cajun cookers who are doing the food for Sunday, the day of the Negro Leagues Baseball Museum dedication,'' Heaven said. ''What about you four? What are you plotting?''

For just a beat too long there was silence. Heaven's internal trouble alarm went off. Then Mr. Vangirov threw his arm around Jim. "Jim is being a good friend. He offered to show Louis where the stage will be on Saturday, so Louis will not feel, how you say . . ."

"Stage fright?" Heaven said with a swift look at Jim. "Well, that's very sweet," she said, and then patted Jim on the cheek. "And you, Mr. Daultman?"

Bob Daultman waved his hands expressively. "I am here soaking up the vibes. It is so . . . so evocative, yes? I can just see the ghost of Charlie Parker walking down Vine Street."

Jim Dittmar smiled wryly. "Yes, it was right on that corner over there the big man pissed on his own shoes because he was so nodded out on heroin. This is famous territory all right."

Heaven put her hands over Louis's ears for a second and looked crossly at Jim. "Stop that. Even if he can't understand what you said, Louis is too young to hear such tawdry tales. Louis, what do you think? Here you are where all the big boys played."

Louis let out a string of excited speech in his native tongue. His father laughed and ruffled his son's hair with a big, rough hand. "Louis is very thrilled. He can't believe he will be playing where Count Basie once played."

Louis knitted his brow in concentration. "I stand . . . where history . . . was . . . made," he managed to say. His eyes were bright and his smile looked about to split his face open.

Heaven nodded her head. "And we're going to make more history this weekend. I better go over to the Ruby and take my meeting. I pray that the Cajun cookers will act better than the others. See you, guys."

As Heaven walked across the street, Bob Daultman gave Jim Dittmar a look. "You better be able to control her," he said in a low, angry voice.

"I can handle her," Jim said with a smile. "What would

she suspect us of, a conspiracy to play in the wrong key? We're a couple of jazz musicians, a filmmaker, and a kindly father."

"An unsuspecting team," Bob Daultman said briskly. "Just the way we like it."

"Just like Berlin and that Greek island," Louis said in English as they walked toward the jazz museum. "Artists are always welcome, aren't they, Dad?" The men and the boy laughed.

Bob Daultman led the way into an entry hall where workers were giving the exhibit finishing touches. Reproductions of old photographs of musicians were being mounted on the walls. Three painters were working frantically on a mural. An empty case stood ready to receive the famous Charlie Parker sax. The history of jazz was coming alive. A harried-looking guard frowned and came their way. From the other side of the foyer, Pam Whiteside rushed toward the group. "Yoo-hoo. Over here," she called. She turned to the guard and waved her hand dismissively. "It's okay. Mr. Daultman is going to film our opening weekend. He needs to see where to shoot."

Jim smiled beguilingly at Pam. "And I was showing our new star musician around. You remember Louis from Cafe Heaven? We tagged along," he said, and put a brotherly arm around Louis.

"Well, isn't this great. Come on, let me show you everything," Pam said.

Bob Daultman twirled around and waved his hands in the air. "Yes, yes. We want to see absolutely everything. I can feel the aura of greatness, even now. I see the ghosts of Eighteenth and Vine coming to life right before my eyes"

"Heaven, it's your daughter," the bartender yelled. Heaven picked up the wall phone. It was early evening, and the pace in the kitchen was still slow.

"Hi, honey, what's up?"

"You'll never believe it, Mom."

"Oh, yes I will. Is this something about you or about Jim Dittmar?"

"You were on the trail, Mom, just like always. But there's no real proof," Iris said, ignoring her mom's question.

"No proof of what?"

"Dad asked around and found out that Jim Dittmar played in all the good jazz clubs."

Heaven couldn't help feeling disappointed. "Yeah, I figured he wasn't lying about that."

Iris returned the ball with gusto. "But he also played a lot of private parties—you know, for people like Dad, mansions with counts and dukes and stuff. And at some of these private parties there were jewel heists. Some old countess would wake up after a late night of dining and dancing and find her emeralds gone."

"And Jim was suspected?"

"No," Iris said reluctantly. "Not Jim personally. But Dad says that sometimes musicians and caterers and other service people who have access get paid lots of money to draw maps of the houses and give information about where all the babes with good stuff are sleeping. He says some of these weekend parties are very formal, with everyone wearing all their best shit, jewelry wise."

"That all makes perfect sense. Musicians would make good inside men. Besides, they always need more money," Heaven said excitedly. "But no one around Kansas City has lots of fancy gems, or if they do they don't take them out of the bank vault very often."

"Will people dress up for this gala?" Iris asked.

"Oh, I don't think so. Just getting the white folks to go to Eighteenth and Vine is going to be enough of a chore. I doubt they'll be wearing the family jewels when they get there. But, Iris, this is very helpful information. It's going to be useful, I just don't know how yet. Thanks, honey." Heaven could see the dinner tickets lining up on the wheel.

"Dad said to tell you we would run your European investigating office."

"Tell him thanks. I'll let you know what happens when we talk on Sunday," Heaven said as she hung up the phone.

She was already three orders of risotto behind.

It was late and Heaven had just finished calling in all the orders for the weekend to the answering machines of the various vendors. It was one of the more amazing things about the food business that chefs, could order their meat and produce and fish late at night and it would actually show up the next day. Lots of nights Sara Baxter did the phone work, but tonight she cleaned up Heaven's station while Heaven made the calls. As she was writing notes on the prep list for the next day, the bartender called out. "Heaven, one of your friends needs to see you."

She looked out, expecting to see Jim Dittmar, but it was Bonnie Weber instead, giving her a tired little wave from a bar stool. Heaven was irritated at her disappointment. But it could be worse. Bonnie was the second-best person to have a nightcap with tonight. Heaven took off her chef's jacket and slipped out of her clogs and into a pair of high heels. The heels might look silly with her black-and-white-checkered tights and her tee-shirt, but they made her feel better. She slipped out of the kitchen into the darkness of the almost-empty dining room. There were two deuces, both couples obviously on dates. Three four-tops were still occupied, one with a trio of gay men, the second with two older couples who had spent a bundle on good bottles of wine and were now talking about where they were going on holidays this summer, and the last with four women who were talking up a storm and drinking margaritas. Tom Waits was on the sound system.

Heaven slipped onto the bar stool next to her friend.

"How did the Cajun cooks behave?" Bonnie Weber asked as she took a slug of beer from the bottle.

"How can you remember all my meetings and yours, too?" Heaven asked. "Tony, how about a glass of California sparkling? What's open?"

"Roederer Estate, Anderson Valley," the bartender replied.

"Perfect," Heaven said. "The Cajun cooks—by the way, only one of them is actually a Cajun—were angels. They flipped a coin to see who would do the jambalaya, who would do the gumbo, the etouffee. No bickering at all. They'll also deep-fry some turkeys and bring in some oysters that we decided to throw on the grill instead of serving raw. 'This here's Kansas City. We don' want to scare the folks, no' was the quote of the day from the one real Cajun."

"I think they call them barbecue oysters that way, don't they? With hot sauce and butter? Yum." Bonnie held her bottle up to Heaven's glass and clinked. "Thanks for the tip earlier. I feel like an utter fool. I should have checked her cell phone, there's no way I should have missed that. I looked at the list of her personals and it just didn't register. And thanks to the stage manager at the Ruby for not telling me about the phone fight Evelyn was having."

"I hope you didn't yell at him. After being around a horrible death, lots of people can't remember a thing until later. You know that. Plus he was scared out of his mind because he thought that it was an accident that could have happened to him. Or not an accident that could have happened to him," Heaven added.

Bonnie nodded. "The sabotage theory. Someone is killing all the Eighteenth and Vine principals, a racist scheme perhaps, or a classical music lover gone mad. That theory took a hit today, thanks to you."

"What does that mean?"

Bonnie wagged her empty beer bottle at Tony and he delivered another. "It means that I checked those pay phones at the Ruby, where Mona spotted Nolan talking and Nolan spotted Mona going in to the auditorium. A call went from one of them to Evelyn Edward's cell phone."

"What did he—"

"He admitted he talked to her, but said he didn't keep her on the line until she was electrocuted. But I think he was still talking to her at the time of the power surge and he probably heard some horrible squeal or something. Then he ran into the stage area and panicked when she was dead, hung up the phone and put it in her briefcase, and ran away. I guess all that could have given him a half-ass heart attack."

Heaven was skeptical. "I know you probably hear this in every case, but I don't see Nolan as a killer."

Bonnie grinned at her friend. "You, who had to fight for your life in the basement of the house of a cute little old lady, should know things aren't what they look like."

"So, are you saying you think he rigged poor Evelyn's accident?" Heaven knew she should tell Bonnie about Nolan's sleeping with Evelyn, but Bonnie was a good detective. She'd probably found out by now and wasn't tipping her hand to Heaven.

Bonnie shook her head. "God knows, it would be much simpler if Nolan was the perp, instead of some nut who could make this weekend really unpleasant. I guess I've been watching too much television, but this project just seems ripe for some whacko who has a hard-on for Kansas City, or jazz—or both."

"Speaking of making this weekend unpleasant, our new best friend Ella Jackson has been very bad," Heaven said. "And I have the feeling that she knew Evelyn Edwards before."

"Bad? Before? What are you keeping from me?"

"Well, I don't have any proof that would stand up in court, but—"

"But that's never stopped you before," Bonnie pointed out.

"Last night one of ladies from the social clubs called and said they had all been having trouble finding the food they

144

needed for Friday night, simple things like sweet potatoes, collard greens, ham hocks. They were afraid they wouldn't have enough food for five hundred people. Someone has been buying up the ingredients we need for this party.''

"And you think it's Miss Ella?''

Heaven nodded. "My crew did a little investigative work, and Miss Ella and her boys were spotted all over town scooping up pork chops. She as much as admitted it when I went to talk to her about it.''

Bonnie put her head on the bar counter and banged it a couple of times. "You not only let your Thirty-ninth Street gang loose on the city, but I bet you went over and made a scene at Miss Ella's. And where did you get the idea Evelyn and Ella were in cahoots?''

"Well, maybe not cahoots, but the first night that Ella was in town, the night that Evelyn died, she called Evelyn 'Tulsa trailer trash.' How would she know where Evelyn came from and where she lived, if she did live in a trailer, which I don't know. That's a personal kind of insult.''

"Yes, I see your point, but it could be that Miss Ella calls everyone Tulsa trailer trash and this time it fit, at least the Tulsa part. But Miss Ella is definitely a suspect for something or other. She's trouble with a capital T.''

"I'd check it out, Bonnie. She's sure making my life miserable right now. I'd love it if she was the mastermind who's vowed to ruin Eighteenth and Vine forever!''

"I will check it out if you promise to stop being so damn dramatic. Now, you came through the first soul food crisis like a champ. What are you going to do this time?'' Bonnie asked.

"I guess I could send someone to Saint Louis for neck bones,'' Heaven said doubtfully. "I'll come up with some creative solution, I hope. By the way, you might check out whether Ella Jackson is paying for Evelyn Edwards's funeral.''

"Now what aren't you telling me?''

"I'm telling you. When I was leaving Ella's, these two undertaker suits came in and thanked Ella for her consideration. There was a hearse outside. What else could it mean?"

"I hate it when I get more information from you than I get from my own stellar police work. By the way, Mona called me up and spilled her guts. She has certainly done a good job of putting herself on the suspect list," Bonnie said.

Heaven was relieved but wasn't going to ask exactly what Mona had spilled. "Well, that must prove something. Mona wouldn't have told on herself if she'd actually done anything. Not that I thought for a minute she had."

"It happens all the time. A wiseass will think he can trick the dumb cops by acting honest. They won't suspect me if I tell them I didn't like Uncle Henry, who had his brains beat out with my favorite golf club," Bonnie said darkly.

"It sure must be hard, not being able to trust anyone," Heaven said.

Bonnie didn't answer. They drank in silence.

Banana Pudding Trifle

1⅓ cups sugar
¾ cups flour
¼ tsp. salt
4 cups milk
8 egg yolks, beaten
1 T. vanilla extract
2 boxes vanilla wafers
rum
6–8 bananas
6–8 Heath Bars or some real English toffee covered with
    chocolate, or toffee bars without chocolate and 1 cup
    good-quality semisweet chocolate, shaved.
2 cups whipping cream
⅓ cup sugar
1 tsp. vanilla extract.

Make a large double boiler with a large saucepan half full
of water and a stainless steel mixing bowl that will sit on the
rim of the pan. While the water is heating in the saucepan,
combine the dry ingredients, then add the beaten egg yolks,
then the milk gradually, whisking as you go to make a
smooth mix. Put this in the bowl over the simmering water,
stir occasionally, and let cook until it thickens and the
pudding coats a wooden spoon. Remove from heat and add
vanilla. Cool to room temperature.

Whip the cream to soft peaks, adding the vanilla and sugar when it starts to stiffen.

Smash the candy with the flat side of a Chinese cleaver or a hammer while still in the candy wrappers, then unwrap the pieces. Slice the bananas as you need them.

Now you have all the parts to layer your trifle: bananas, rum, vanilla wafers, pudding, toffee and chocolate bits, whipped cream. Using a clear glass bowl for effect, build your trifle by lining the bottom and sides of the bowl with vanilla wafers. Splash them with a little rum. Add a layer of pudding, bananas, then candy, then whipped cream. Start over with wafers, rum, pudding, bananas, candy, and whipped cream until you reach the top of your bowl. I usually like to end with the whipped cream and throw some candy on the very top. Chill at least 2 hours—but not overnight, as the bananas will start to turn.

This is a great party dessert; it requires no fancy plating. It also eliminates the hard part of a true southern banana pudding, baking the meringue on the top, which many times turns the banana slices brown.

Ten

So, Murray called last night and said I should ask you about City Hall first thing this morning. What's that all about?" Heaven asked Sal.

Sal was giving a twelve-year-old a crew cut. He transferred the unlit cigar from one side of his mouth to the other. "Murray's worried you and Mona here are gonna end up with egg on your face this weekend."

Mona and Heaven were slumped next to each other in the Naugahyde chairs that lined the barbershop wall, eating bagels spread with an inch of cream cheese. They tried to protest this questioning of their competency but kept eating instead. Neither one could say that it wasn't a possibility. The way things were going, they might be lucky to have only egg on their faces.

"I checked out how this Eighteenth and Vine thing is set up," Sal continued, surprised he didn't at least get a rise out of Heaven. She was usually so easy to bait.

"What do you mean, 'set up'?" Mona asked.

"When they started all the renovation, they had a committee of 'civic leaders' they called 'em, to oversee the project since they had federal money and state money and city money to spend. Plus the mayor knew that if he doled out the construction contracts and such, he'd be accused of favoritism, like usual. So the committee kept a pretty tight rein on the whole thing, money wise. But, now, this dedication weekend is a different matter," Sal said as he pulled the striped cotton cape off the boy. The kid gave Sal a handful of quarters. Sal eyeballed them and threw them into a Mason jar full of change. The kid, who lived around the corner on Bell Street, ran off down the sidewalk. Going to Sal's by yourself for a haircut was a rite of passage in the Thirty-ninth Street neighborhood.

Sal swept up the hair on the floor. "They hit up the big corporations for this dedication," Sal continued.

"We know that because they all have someone on the committee—the Kauffman Foundation, Hallmark, Kansas City Southern Railroad . . ." Mona said. She didn't want Sal to think they were totally out of the loop.

"Even though there's thousands of dollars involved in this dedication," Sal explained, "it's not millions like the renovation, so the mayor's office is taking care of the nuts and bolts of the dedication, leaving the rest up to you bigtime committee members. That's how Evelyn Edwards got the job. There was no bidding process. Nolan just hired her."

"Don't they have to have bids if they spend over a hundred dollars or something?" Heaven asked.

"If it's the city's money, yes," Sal explained. "But this was private donations. No bids necessary. Nolan probably hired her and told the other honchos about it later. If it meant less work for them they didn't squawk."

"So that's why she just appeared one day," Mona said. "But it doesn't explain why Nolan hired her instead of someone who has lived here longer than a few months. Maybe she gave Nolan a kickback to get the job, knowing she'd make up for it when she started squeezing all of the vendors herself."

"Or maybe she has something on him," Sal mused.

"Had something on him. She doesn't have anything on anybody anymore," Mona said cynically.

Heaven didn't like that tone in Mona's voice. She wanted to tell Sal and Mona about Evelyn and Nolan and too many margaritas at the convention, but she didn't want to be the one to leak the story. Maybe the whole world, and specifically Nolan's wife, wouldn't have to know about how Evelyn got her big job. "I better go to work; it's already nine. Thanks for the information, Sal. Now, if you could just find us some ham hocks," Heaven said as they left the barbershop.

"Heaven, what are you going to do about the food?" Mona asked. "Have you talked to Julia and the rest of the social club ladies?"

Heaven and Mona headed across thirty-ninth Street. "No," Heaven said, "and I need your help. Will you call all the clubs and tell them to cook what they can find? Make as much as they can, not to worry about feeding five hundred."

"And what will you be doing? Calling two or three hundred people and telling them to stay home?"

"Well, I will be making phone calls, but it won't be to ask people to stay home. Mona, if this works, tomorrow night will be great, even better than it would have been two plans ago."

"I guess you're not going to tell me what plan C is," Mona whined.

"Not until I see if it works," Heaven said. "Wish me luck."

"Wish me luck, too," Mona said. "I left a note at the hotel for Sam Scott and asked her to have a drink with me tonight. I figured it would be best to get this out of the way. Then, if we do make up, I'll enjoy myself more. And if she won't accept my apology, then I won't have to fret about what I'm going to say to her all weekend." Mona waved good-bye to Heaven and unlocked the door to her shop. Heaven walked around to the kitchen door of the restaurant.

Everyone seemed to be working quietly and there were no major crises, so she slipped into the office and started her calls.

An hour later, Heaven hung up the phone and let out a whoop. She went directly next door to the cat store and danced around, still whooping. "This is going to be so cool," she said, doing a little jig. Two women buying Siamese cat posters and statues stared at her as if she were a large dog. They took their packages and departed quickly.

Mona couldn't help but laugh at her friend, who now was wearing a fish-shaped cat food dish on her head like a chic, surrealistic hat as she spun around. "What has gotten into you, H?"

"I've solved the food shortage problem."

"How?"

Heaven laughed and put the fish dish back on the counter. "It's a surprise. And we can still have banana pudding. Luckily, Ella couldn't corner the market on bananas. I requested the recipe that has crunchy toffee in it, not exactly traditional southern, but what the hell. I had it once in New Orleans, and it was so good."

"Heaven, you're positively giddy. Calm down. Do you want to go to the walk-through together?"

"No, we each need a car in case Sam Scott wants to meet with you tonight. Besides, I have another errand to do," she said without volunteering any further information.

"You sure are secretive," Mona observed.

"Isn't it great? Usually I tell everything I know. See you later," Heaven said, and took off out the door.

Heaven pulled into the Jones Brothers Funeral Chapel parking lot and looked around. "Now what are you going to do?" she asked herself out loud.

Surely funeral homes had a code of ethics. Just because she was curious about who was paying for Evelyn Edwards's burial costs didn't mean they would pop with that information. And it would be pretty hard to pass herself off as a relative. She got out of the car and entered the door marked VISITATION. If Evelyn hadn't been shipped back to Oklahoma for burial, Heaven guessed she'd be in one of those viewing rooms that were such a part of death in the Midwest. Having been born an O'Malley, even a Presbyterian O'Malley, she'd been going to look at dead people in their caskets all her life.

Heaven doubted there would be an official visitation for Evelyn Edwards, so she was surprised to see the name up on the directory—"Edwards, Parlor C"—with an arrow pointing discreetly down one hallway. She found parlor C, a small room intended for someone who didn't die surrounded by dozens of loved ones and friends. Six people would have filled up the space around the casket, an elegant wooden one gleaming with brass fittings—and thankfully closed. This was definitely not just a plain pine box. There were also two tall flower stands, each holding a dozen calla lilies, no other flowers around. The whole deal was quite tasteful.

Heaven realized that for all the deaths she had been around in the last few years, grieving had not been her role. Tasha Arnold, who had died in Cafe Heaven, had been buried back in New York. Heaven did attend the funeral of Pigpen Hopkins, one of the local barbecue champs, but that was more circus than solemn. None of the others had been friends that she had felt a responsibility to see through to their resting places. The finality of seeing this container that now held Evelyn gave her pause. She had been good at distancing herself from the gruesome scene on the stage, but being in this little visitation room brought it all back. She didn't hear the footsteps.

"Well, sugar, what brings you here?" Suddenly Ella Jackson was standing beside her.

Heaven started, then jumped back into the present. "Ella, did you pay for this woman's, you know, arrangements?"

"Heaven, you are the nosiest piece of work. What business is it of yours?"

"None, other than the bond that comes between people who find someone dead. We have that bond, both of us. Did that, or something else, prompt you to pay for this beautiful casket?"

Ella looked away. "That detective friend of yours was giving me the twenty questions for the second time the other day. She said they hadn't located any family, that this one here was still being held in the morgue." Ella glanced over at the casket. "I have never known my daddy, and my momma, bless her heart, died four years ago. I don't know where my no-good brother is, and I don't have children. I've been successful, yes, but if I died, Heaven sugar, there would be no one except one of my managers to take care of my cold body, lay it to rest. This one here didn't have no retinue, no busboys to see after her. I can afford it. Tomorrow they'll send her back to Oklahoma. The funeral home found out where her momma is buried. Even a bitch like Evelyn deserves this little bit of respect."

"Very well put," a voice behind them said. Detective Bonnie Weber stood, filling up the doorway.

Heaven smiled guiltily. "What are you doing here?"

"Oh, you know, H, you've seen those cop shows on TV. The detective always checks out the crowd at the funeral for suspicious behavior. This is as close as I'll get to that," Bonnie said, giving Ella a look.

Heaven knew she'd been caught. "Gosh, I've got to go. I'm due at the Ruby for the walk-through." She tried to scoot past Bonnie as quickly as possible without making eye contact. "Bye now," she said as she hurried down the hall, wishing she could be a mouse in the corner of that room to hear the conversation between Ella and Bonnie. Just when Heaven had her all softened up, Bonnie would come in for the kill. Bonnie would probably want to thank her for that later.

"All the road managers, up on the stage," the stage manager yelled.

"And all the volunteer ushers down here," Mona yelled, and held up a flashlight so her crew could see her.

The Ruby Theater was filling up slowly. Most of the musicians had come into town the day before the big concert. These weren't traveling musicians, like the rock 'n' roll boys who go out with a crew of eighty and have to work every night in a row to pay for all the fancy lights and sound equipment. Jazz artists usually had an easier pace—and lots less money to take home.

This Friday night concert was billed as the Voices of Jazz. The Ruby Theater was reputed to have good acoustics for singers and they'd gotten some big names: Sam Scott, Nancy Wilson, Shirley Horn, Tony Bennett, Ray Charles, and Harry Connick, Jr. Boots Turner's Big Band was playing both Friday night in the Ruby and Saturday on the outdoor stage.

Also unlike the rock 'n' roll boys, these musicians didn't hide in their hotel rooms until it was time to go onstage. Tony Bennett was standing talking to the drummer from the Turner band. Nancy Wilson and her manager, the famous Sparky Jones, who had also managed Nat King Cole, were talking intently to the stage manager. Of course, this was a unique gig. Everyone was curious about the Ruby and the jazz museum. It was a festival atmosphere.

Mona saw Heaven walk in and waved her over. "Isn't this exciting? Do you think anyone will, rehearse?"

Heaven shook her head. "I wouldn't think so. Sound check will be tomorrow. This was just so the stage manager could walk through the program and find everyone a place backstage, which couldn't have been easy. Imagine six star singers needing six star dressing rooms at the same gig."

"You know all about this from Iris's dad, don't you?"

Mona said. She and Heaven hadn't known each other during Heaven's rock 'n' roll phase.

"Well, yes, from Dennis and his band, and later I was a rock 'n' roll lawyer, representing bands. I've spent lots of time backstage."

"I forget about your lawyer days," Mona said uncertainly. She always felt uncomfortable bringing up that period of Heaven's life.

Heaven smiled. "Yes, it was rock 'n' roll that also ended my career as an attorney, when I did that tiny little drug deal for my band. Rock 'n' roll giveth rock 'n' roll taketh away."

Mona was counting her volunteers as they came down to the side of the stage. "Well, it could have been worse. You could have been incarcerated. I've realized lately that we all make some mistakes, and boy can they be doozies."

Heaven wondered if Mona was talking about Heaven or Mona's former friend Sam Scott or Mona's run-in with Evelyn Edwards.

But Mona was preoccupied with her assignment. "I'm missing only two ushers. I think I'll start my little speech . . . you know, bring your own flashlight, know where the bathrooms are, and all that."

"I'm going outside to check on the buffet area for tomorrow night. I ordered trash cans and set up tables, and I want to make sure they're in the right place." Heaven felt guilty whenever she discussed her old run-in with the law. It had happened over ten years ago, and she still couldn't believe how she'd shot herself in the foot and put her daughter at risk. What if she'd gone to jail and Iris had gone to live in England as an adolescent? The thought made Heaven's skin clammy. As she was walking up the aisle of the Ruby, lost in the past, shouting burst out on the stage.

Two old black gentlemen were doing the yelling. Between them stood Sam Scott, elegantly dressed in a suit that looked like an Armani, her short silver hair perfectly cropped. Heaven reached up unconsciously to touch her own unruly red locks.

"Don't put my dressing room next to hers, oh no," one of the old men was saying.

"You still a damn fool, cutting off your nose to spite your face. And there's no cause to be rude to Sam, no cause at all," the other man was saying in somewhat calmer, but no less forceful, tones.

"Come on, Lefty," Sam Scott was saying, her famous voice soaring to the back of the theater as she pulled his arm. The acoustics were swell in here, Heaven thought. "Boots, don't you start no shit and there won't be no shit, you hear me?" she said with her beautiful, long fingers pointed right in Boots Turner's face. "You keep that bitterness to yourself, that old, tired bullshit that you been carrying with you all these years."

Now it was Lefty's turn to pull on Sam's arm. "Come on, honey. Let it go."

Every person in the theater was watching this scene playing out on the stage. You could hear a pin drop.

Nolan Wilkins saved the day. He marched into the fray. "This is all my fault," he said bravely. "I'm Nolan Wilkins, the mayor's liaison for the Eighteenth and Vine district. I'm the one who suggested that Boots and Sam have dressing rooms next to each other. I didn't know you two were on the outs. I remember, Ms. Scott, when you sang with Boots Turner, so I thought it would be nice . . . well, obviously I was wrong and I want to apologize."

A sigh of relief went through the crowd. Heaven was impressed with the way Nolan had handled the situation.

She looked over at her friend Mona Kirk. Mona was frozen, staring at the stage; her face was pale, her eyes huge and round. Heaven was fearful for her friend. Not that she believed that Mona would hurt a flea, no, of course not. But she had been so angry with Evelyn, and her death could have been a terrible accident, maybe one that Mona didn't even know she was responsible for. Now she had to deal with an old emotional hurt. Heaven hoped Sam Scott would agree to meet with Mona. Whether they were able to resume their friendship or not, Mona needed the chance to say her piece.

All of a sudden a familiar line of handsome young men moved past Heaven down the aisle of the theater toward the stage. Each carried a platter or large bowl of food in his arms, wafting steam and good smells through the air. Behind the food procession came, of course, Miss Ella, resplendent in another fabulous outfit, a brown gabardine suit from the World War II era. A jaunty brown pillbox with a shock of veiling was perfectly placed on top of another good hairdo. Heaven wondered if Ella traveled with her own hair stylist. As Ella walked past Heaven she gave her a wink and then a swift and perfectly targeted kick to Heaven's shin with a vintage platform high heel. Heaven instinctively grabbed her leg, holding on to a theater seat for balance. "Hello to you, too," she called after Ella.

Miss Ella took charge. Behind her were two or three young women bearing paper plates and plastic eating utensils, napkins, and big pitchers of tea and lemonade. "I thought you all might need a bite to eat while you get situated," Miss Ella said grandly. "I see my friend Nancy Wilson, who comes to my restaurant in New York." She waved up at the stage. "And lord-a-mercy, there's Tony Bennett. You all must be starved." The boys set the food on the edge of the stage, in front of the lights, and everyone gathered around, grabbing plates and giving air kisses to Miss Ella. Then, just as the atmosphere had taken a decided turn for the better, Ella Jackson pointed her arm dramatically toward the stage and said loudly, "Oh, and there's that famous Boots Turner, one of those traveling musicians that we all hear about. Boots, honey, have you left a girl in every port? How about a family in every port?"

Boots Turner was staring intently at Ella Jackson, as if he were trying to place her. Had they met before?

Ella hurried on, not giving the crowd a chance to start talking. "It's too bad you didn't make it here last week, Boots. You could have met someone you left behind. Yes, a little girl that was your daughter. Her name was Evelyn Edwards, and now she's dead. Now it's too late, Mr. Traveling Musician."

If the fight between Lefty and Boots had stopped the room, this positively froze it. Boots Turner, shaking his head, walked slowly toward the edge of the stage. Ella Jackson was standing below, looking up at him, her hands on her hips, daring him to deny her claim. Everyone else looked away, shifting uncomfortably and stuffing food into their mouths. But there was no opportunity to hear what Boots Turner had to say to her accusation.

Two security guards came running into the theater with stricken looks on their faces. "Everyone stay right where they are. No one goes in or out. Someone robbed the jazz museum! The Charlie Parker sax is gone!"

An hour later, they were finally released from the Ruby. Thanks to Ella's food, if not her big mouth, the wait hadn't been totally wasted. Eating and trying to figure out her words to Boots Turner kept Heaven busy. She had watched them both like a hawk, but every time Boots Turner tried to talk to Ella, she would turn away with some comment like "You know what I'm talking about, old man!" Heaven was dumbfounded. Boots Turner looked genuinely puzzled. The name Evelyn Edwards didn't seem to bring any recognition to his face. And if Ella had any proof she wasn't going to give it up now.

Just when Heaven's opinion of Miss Ella had softened, what with her buying such a nice casket for Evelyn, she'd twisted the knife in this old man. Not that musicians weren't dogs. A trail of children across the country has been the calling card of more than one player. Suddenly, Heaven remembered the photos she had discovered in Evelyn's office.

Two different families with the same man. Now, maybe that was the clue to this puzzle.

No one else seemed to be very interested, or maybe they were just respecting Boots Turner's feelings. Even those who had appeared happy to see Ella initially were avoiding her as they waited unhappily.

The minute the security guard said that no one could leave, everyone wanted to leave, had a perfectly good reason why he should be able to leave, absolutely must leave. As search teams went methodically through all the gear that had been hauled in, singers who were not youngsters anymore sat in the theater and fussed at their road managers to get them out of there. Mona was busy tending to her volunteers, who all had families to feed at home or something equally compelling to do. Sam Scott and Lefty kept to themselves, sharing a plate of food at the back of the room. Nolan Wilkins, with another disaster on his hands, ran back and forth between the theater and the museum, trying to assure all this high-priced talent that everything would be all right soon.

Now that they could leave, Heaven looked around for Mona. She didn't see her friend anywhere, so she took off and drove toward fifth Street before her better judgment led her back to the cafe. As she drove she let her mind rest on the most disquieting part of a disquieting evening. She kept recalling her conversation with her daughter about the jewel thefts that occurred where Jim Dittmar played. Another coincidence? Jim Dittmar was around when rich ladies lost their jewels in Europe, now he was around when Kansas City lost the jewel of its new museum.

Heaven wanted to call Jim at his parents', but it was after ten and she was afraid it was too late if he wasn't home. She didn't know what checking up on him would prove anyway. So she called the restaurant to make sure they were okay, then she called Hank.

Tonight's drama was too big not to share with someone,

and it was a good excuse to call. "First, the old guys were going at it on the stage of the Ruby," she explained in rapid-fire delivery, "the two men who have been fighting over the singer Sam Scott for years, one's a jazz pianist and one's a baseball player. The piano player didn't want his dressing room next to hers—Sam Scott's, that is. Her husband, the baseball player—of course, he's been retired for years—took umbrage. Then Miss Ella crashes the party with enough catfish and collard greens to feed the homeless for a week. Then the most important piece of jazz memorabilia, certainly the most expensive one, is swiped before the museum is even open."

Hank wasn't quite up to speed on the sax. "I know who Charlie Parker is. Did he leave his favorite sax to the city?" he asked.

"Oh, no. Kansas City bought it at an auction in London. And it cost a bundle, $119,000, I think I remember reading. And when the mayor bought it, there was a big uproar, of course. Not everyone in the city thought it was a good use of city funds."

"How was it stolen?" Hank asked.

"Very easily, it seemed to me," Heaven said. "Because they were still working in the museum, the alarm system wasn't on, but the exhibits were already in place. They had a team of security working both in the building and outside because they were setting up stages and there was all kinds of expensive rented equipment. I think they felt safe. The thief cut the glass of the showcase with a glass cutter and those little suction cups, and just took the sax out. They found the glass on the floor. I don't know how he or she got the actual sax out of the area, though. There were lots of people around."

"Heaven . . ."

"I know what you're going to say next," Heaven said, secretly glad Hank was always so concerned.

"Heaven, please be careful. This is the second incident

concerning this jazz museum, and I have a feeling it's not the last bad thing that will happen before the dedication is completed. I love you and I don't want anything to happen to you."

"I don't want anything to happen to me, either," Heaven said. "I miss you."

"I miss you, too, but I'm so busy . . . if I took this course in Kansas City, which I couldn't do, I wouldn't see you for days at a time anyway."

"Have you met any cute girls?" Heaven teased, knowing Hank would hate her asking.

"Heaven, stop trying to drive me away. If you want to end our relationship, just say so. Don't try to make a triangle where there is none."

Heaven thought for just a minute about Jim Dittmar. Was she trying to create a triangle? She laughed nervously. "What if I did say so? Don't tell me you'd just disappear in the sunset?"

Hank was losing patience. "How can I reassure you over the phone? You're trying to pick a fight. If you told me to go away, I'd show you the error of your ways. Not talk you out of it, show you."

Heaven felt foolish, as always. "Good answer."

"Here's the story, and who knows if it's true. These things become part of jazz lore," Jim Dittmar explained. He was sitting in a diner, the Town Topic, in downtown Kansas City with Bob Daultman, Louis Vangirov, and Louis's father. Louis was having his first bowl of Town Topic chili, a frightening concoction that Jim Dittmar insisted was a musician's rite of passage. "Parker was playing a gig in Toronto in 1953, the Quintet of the Year, they called it."

Louis perked up. He'd been crumbling lots of saltine crackers on top of the chili, just like Jim told him to. The crackers had turned a bright orange color from the layer of grease on top of the chili. Louis poked the orange crackers under the surface of the meat and beans. "Who was the quintet?"

"Dizzy Gillespie on trumpet, Bud Powell on keyboards, Mingus on bass, and Max Roach on drums. And Parker on alto sax."

"I love Bud Powell," Louis said.

"Me, too," Jim said. "The problem was, Parker was really strung out; he was always hocking his horns. He went to one of those school instrument stores and bought a cheap plastic sax that kids use when they're not sure if they really want to play the saxophone or the bass drum. His wife ended up with it when Parker died, and she auctioned it off."

"And Kansas City bought it for their new jazz museum," Bob said between bites of an omelette. "Fabulous. You just don't find this kind of drama in fictional screenplays. I'm so lucky that I happened to come down with the film crew for the walk-through. The footage of all those jazz stars' belongings being searched was priceless, absolutely priceless."

"Oh, there's a price, all right," Jim said with a smile. "And we know what it is. Four million bucks."

Ella Jackson was a little drunk and talking to a photograph in her hotel room. She poured herself another splash of Wild Turkey and paced up and down the corridor between the bed and the dresser console. Howard Stern was on mute on the TV. The phone was ringing—ten, twelve times in a row, then a pause while the caller dialed again, then another ten or twelve rings. Ella wasn't picking up.

"That you, Boots, baby? You sure were surprised, ol' man."

The photograph was an 8×10 glossy publicity shot of Boots Turner. He was sitting at a piano with a big smile on his face. The photo was in a cheap black frame and had brown age spots. Boots was in a white dinner jacket that had rounded lapels, vintage early fifties.

Ella stumbled a little, then sat down on the bed and pulled all the pillows behind her back, waving her glass around for emphasis. "I tell you one thing. I'll be glad to get this over with and get back to God's country. These backwards Kansas City folk could screw up a wet dream. Here I have Tiny Bennett and Ray Charles, no, it's Tony Bennett"—Ella giggled—"eating my food. My boys were ready to take the photos"—she took another gulp of whiskey—"and I had you on the hot seat in front of all of 'em. Damn if these Eighteenth and Vine fools didn't lose their star attraction, some plastic-assed saxophone, something you wouldn't have allowed on your stage, no way." Ella giggled and played a pretend sax in the air, still holding her glass. "Serves these hicks right, Daddy. They'll get theirs. It's already started."

Then Ella Jackson passed out, lights and television still on, holding her empty glass in her hand.

Kansas City Chili

2 lbs. lean ground beef or ground chuck
1 large onion, peeled and diced
1 28 oz. can tomatoes
1 large can Campbell's tomato soup, or 2 regular size cans
1 can pinto or red beans
1 can kidney beans
1 small can green chilies, chopped
1 fresh jalapeño pepper, seeded and chopped
1 T. ground cumin
2 T. ground New Mexico red chili or chili powder
kosher salt

Don't worry, this chili will not have orange grease floating on the top like the chili that Louis ate at the diner. This is the typical style of chili every midwestern mom makes, probably without the real jalapeño. It has a mild heat. If you want more, add another jalapeño, some hot sauce, or some cayenne.

In a large, heavy pot, sauté onions and meat together until the meat is browned, adding a little neutral oil, such as canola, if the meat is too lean. Add all the ingredients except the beans and simmer for 1 hour. Add the beans and simmer another 20 minutes. Remove from heat and refrigerate overnight before serving; this marries the flavors better, and you can remove any fat that has accumulated on the top of the chili. When you reheat, adjust the seasonings and be very careful to reheat over a low flame as the tomatoes have a high sugar content and can burn.

This chili is great served with cornbread, rice, and toppings such as sour cream, chopped onions, and grated cheddar or fresh Mexican cheese.

Eleven

"Boy, this is really getting good," Joe Long said as the whole group passed the morning newspaper around Sal's. Sal had just finished his first haircut of the day and was sweeping around the chair. His customer got a bargain this morning, a trim and two first-person accounts of the biggest news in town: the theft of the Charlie Parker sax. Not that Heaven or Mona were eyewitnesses to the actual heist, but being right across the street in the Ruby counted.

"Yeah. Just when I was sure that someone had it in for Evelyn personally, this happens. Now it makes much more sense that someone is trying to ruin the whole opening," Heaven said irritably.

"Look," Murray said, pointing at a photograph of the empty display case. The photographer had gotten some priceless shots of all the music celebs milling around Eighteenth and Vine, just like the old days. "There's Louis," Murray said proudly. And sure enough, there was Louis and his father standing next to Boots Turner. Louis was gazing adoringly at the older piano man.

"It's too bad the photographer didn't know who Louis

was," Heaven said. "He could have gotten a great lead, something about the torch being passed."

Sal leaned over toward the newspaper to see who they were talking about. "That's the kid that played at your joint Monday night."

Everyone turned toward Sal with awe. He had been at the Monday night open mike only once, when the whole show was dedicated to him on his sixty-fifth birthday last year. When Sal left his barbershop, he liked to go home to North Kansas City and put his feet up, relax.

"Now, how do you know that?" Heaven asked.

"He and the other guy in the bad suit went into your place in the afternoon Monday, you walked 'em out a while later, then they came right over here in front of the shop and the kid says something about how he hopes you like him or liked it or something," Sal explained. "I figured they must have auditioned for the open mike. The kid play keyboards?"

Everyone was looking at Sal with various degrees of disbelief. "You are a Sherlock Holmes all right," Murray said. "Except for one thing. Louis doesn't speak English. He's from Minsk, in Belorussia."

"I don't care if he's from the Amazon; he speaks English just fine. He had an accent, yes, but he speaks English as good as my grandmother ever did. How else would I know what he said?"

"Are you sure, Sal?" Heaven asked. "Maybe the father said that to the kid, and you just—"

Sal was belligerent. "Just what? Got mixed up? Mistook the kid talking for the father talking? Right. I'll bet my reputation on the fact that the kid can speak English and if his old man told you different, it's a scam. Now, who wants to bet?"

No one did.

* * *

"I hate to put you in this position," Bonnie Weber said, without looking or sounding like she hated it at all. Bonnie and Heaven were catching a quick lunch together at Winstead's, the Kansas City burger palace. "But I won't bust your chops for nosing around at the funeral home if you just—"

Heaven cut in, impatient to tell her version of last night. "I understand. I was there. You weren't. You want to know who was in visual range, and to answer your first question, if Nolan was in the building, he was," Heaven said as she bit into an onion ring. "Nolan did a great job of simmering down a real doozy of a fight between Sam Scott, Lefty Stuart, and Boots Turner. He was still up on the stage when Ella delivered her food and her big speech about Boots Turner."

"I wish someone in Burglary had been savvy enough to give me a call. After all, I'm working a case . . . shit, what am I saying? I don't have time to cross-reference my cases with anybody, why should they? I just feel behind the eight ball. What big speech did Ella Jackson make?" Bonnie asked as she took a drink of a thick chocolate malt. "And what was the fight about? Was it Sam Scott and Boots Turner? She's one of my favorite singers, behind Aretha, of course."

"Not the same deal; you can like both Aretha and Sam. Well, I haven't got a chance to tell you any of this but Sam Scott was Boots Turner's girlfriend when she sang with his band. Then she met the baseball player, Lefty, and she and Lefty fell madly in love, and Boots has never forgiven either of them." With that juicy flourish of gossip Heaven popped the last bite of a double cheeseburger into her mouth.

Bonnie Weber slapped her forehead with the palm of her hand. "Great! A feud between three famous people who just happen to be involved with the dedication of Eighteenth and Vine, which is turning to shit in front of our eyes."

"Aren't you going to ask me how I know so much?" Heaven said with bravado.

"I was just about to get to that, but I'm afraid."

"Mona told me. She and Sam went to high school together. But they don't speak anymore, either."

Bonnie Weber put her head down on top of her crossed arms on the table and moaned.

"And Miss Ella accused Boots Turner of being the long lost father of Evelyn Edwards, and I think . . . ." Heaven was going to say something about the two photos, but then she'd have to admit she stole them out of a dead woman's office. She'd wait on that one, since it was highly speculative at best.

Bonnie Weber jerked her head up. "And what did Boots say to that?"

"He didn't get a chance to say anything. Security came running in saying the sax had been stolen and the moment was lost. I saw him try to talk to Ella while we were trapped in the Ruby, but she'd make a smart crack and walk away from him every time. I think she was upset that her big moment ended so fast when a bigger disaster came along."

"How did everyone else react to Ella and Boots and to Sam and Lefty and Boots? Boy, that Boots was in a heap of trouble," Bonnie observed.

"I think everyone was embarrassed for Boots. Most of them definitely didn't know who Evelyn Edwards was or that she'd died almost where Boots was standing. But I think everyone pretty much knows about the rift between Sam and Boots. The sax being stolen was the thing that got everyone going, mainly because they couldn't leave the Ruby. I think Tony Bennett missed his dinner reservations at the American Restaurant."

"Any ideas on the stolen sax? Not that I have time to solve someone else's cases," Bonnie said as she ate her last French fries.

Heaven knew she should tell Bonnie about the heists in Europe where Jim Dittmar had gigs, and probably about the fact that little Mr. Louis Armstrong Vangirov had been less than honest, but why bother her? None of these were real solid leads yet. Heaven would relieve Bonnie of the burden of these details until she checked them out. "No one confessed, if that's any help. I'm telling you, the stars at the Ruby were so antsy at being told they had to have their stuff searched, they didn't even start a jam session while they waited. That's bad. I think they might have been worried about pot and other drugs. There was lots of shuffling of bags."

"Ray Charles's smoking pot is the least of our worries," Bonnie said.

"Bonnie, can you tell me what happened at the funeral home, what you and Ella talked about after I left?"

"Well, you'll have to agree that Ella has gone up in the standing as a suspect since she starting throwing money around for Evelyn's burial. Being generous to a stranger doesn't seem like Ella's style. And now that you tell me she accused Boots Turner of being Evelyn's father, well, you don't know that kind of detail about a stranger, now, do you?"

"Not one you supposedly have only talked to over the phone a couple of times," Heaven admitted.

"I wish I could just shut down the whole dedication weekend until I could sort this out," Bonnie said.

"Time waits for no homicide detective, girlfriend. We learned that in evidence class many years ago," Heaven said as they threw down their money on the table and got ready to leave.

Mona Kirk looked around the hotel dining room nervously. To her dismay she was five minutes late. She had changed clothes five times, finally settling on the first thing she had put on, a black sheath with no cats on it anywhere. She did have on cat earrings, but they were small. She was trying to look sophisticated for her old friend. She spotted Sam Scott at the corner table by a window overlooking the Plaza shopping area, a faux-Spanish complex that had been built in the 1930s. A table at the Ritz-Carlton overlooking the Plaza. This was as glamorous as it got in Kansas City.

She hurried over to the table. "Thank you for agreeing to see me," she said, immediately regretting the gracelessness of her opening line. Then she sat down and managed to tangle her purse in the chair legs. All this seemed to amuse Sam Scott.

"We almost have the same haircut," Sam said with the hint of a smile, looking at Mona's short gray hair.

"We both have short hair and we don't dye it. That's about where the resemblance ends. I get mine cut at a barbershop across from my store. You probably get yours cut by some famous stylist." Mona knew she was babbling but she couldn't stop.

"What kind of store do you have?" Sam asked politely.

"A cat store. It's named the City Cat. But I don't actually sell cats, although sometimes I do give them away. People leave off cats they don't want and I have a deal with a vet who gives them their shots and then," Mona wished someone would stop her mouth, "I give them away to good homes."

"If you don't sell cats, what do you sell?"

"Gift items for cat lovers. Almost any thing you can think of is made in the shape of a cat, plus tee-shirts, earrings"— she pointed at her ear like a QVC host—"and then actual things for cats, like jeweled collars, fancy food dishes. Cat lovers are very loyal. Do you have a pet?"

"No, I'm still on the road too much. Lefty usually goes with me. Then there are his speaking engagements. It seems Lefty has become very popular on the sports dinner circuit. The whole country is finding out what I've known for years: My husband is the best."

"I hope I get to meet him," Mona said. When there was silence from Sam she felt her cheeks flush. "Maybe we should order."

Just at that awkward moment the waiter appeared. In Mona's opinion, it was the first good thing that had happened since she arrived at the restaurant. She pointed at something under the entree salad heading and asked for iced tea. Sam ordered a steak, rare, a green salad, no dressing, and a baked potato, no butter or sour cream. Milk to drink. "I won't eat again until after the concert. I have to have that protein and calcium," she explained.

When the waiter was gone Sam took control of the conversation. "I thought long and hard about your letter, Mona. In the long run, I wanted to be fair. If I didn't let you say your piece, I'd be just as bad as . . ." She paused.

"As I was all those years ago?" Mona finished the sentence for her. "When all that ruckus happened last night, I was afraid that would be a good excuse for you to not talk to me. Boots and Lefty and the saxophone and all. But instead you suggested lunch and I have to tell you, I didn't sleep a wink last night, thinking about everything."

"Someone stole Charlie Parker's saxophone. If we weren't on the national news before, we will be now." Sam chuckled. "By the way, how did you find my agent?"

"Easy. Called your record company and asked for your publicist. Told the publicist I worked for Steven Spielberg and he wanted you for a small part in his next film, and so I needed your agent's name and number. Called up your agent and asked the receptionist for the address of the agent's office. It was probably a little more elaborate than necessary, but it was fun."

The waiter brought their food, too fast for Mona's taste. She was afraid this would all be over before she even got her bearings.

"I appreciate all the trouble you went to," Sam said, "and it was considerate of you to give me a heads-up about your part in this weekend. I'm afraid I have my hands full with Lefty and Boots. I didn't need any surprises."

"Like I said in the note, I want to apologize for hurting you with my stupidity and ruining our friendship," Mona said simply.

"Well, Mona, there's been a lot of water under the bridge

since then. I wish I could say it was forgotten long ago. But things that happen to you when you're a kid, they stick in your head."

"The other thing that I need to say is I was wrong. Not only did I hurt you, for which I am sorry, not only did I mess up our friendship, but it all happened because I did something that was wrong."

Sam looked sad. "I hear what you're saying, baby, but you have to understand where I'm comin' from. Intellectually, I know we were just kids, and I know a part of your concern back then was that I'd be treated badly by folks in Saint Joseph. And, God knows, Boots Turner was not the right man for me. But Lefty Stuart is. And he happens to be a black man, too. Now, I'm not saying that we haven't had some tough times. And I know the world we live in, the music world, the sports world, has accepted racially mixed couples much better than in a small town. We are blessed in that respect."

"But? I hear a but in your voice," Mona asked.

"But when I saw you last night at the Ruby, my eyes just filled up with tears. I was that hurt kid again, who found out her friend didn't have unconditional love for her. I wanted to hear, you know, 'Whoever you want, Sam; I'll be there for you, Sam.' I don't know how I'd ever shake that pain, Mona."

"It can't be fixed, can it?"

"Do I blame you? No, honey, I do not. But do I think we can start talking on the phone every week, going on little trips together? No, I don't think that is in the cards for us. I've always missed you, Mona, I truly have."

This was what Mona had feared all these years. It was the reason she had put this conversation off for so long. Some words, once said, just cannot be taken back. A John Hiatt song lyric flooded her mind: "From the tip of my tongue to the end of the line." "And I've missed you, too," she said, and her voice cracked just a tiny bit. She waved the waiter over and gave him a credit card. Sam didn't argue with her paying for lunch. Thank goodness she let her do a little monetary penance, at least.

Sam changed the subject. "How is your husband?"

"Carl. He died seven years ago. It was a freak accident with a forklift at the General Motors plant. He worked there twenty-two years."

"I'm sorry."

"So am I. That's when I opened the shop. It keeps me occupied." The receipt was back, and Mona signed it and added a tip. Her hand was trembling ever so slightly. She got up. "Good luck tonight. I know you'll knock 'em dead."

Sam stood as well. Her lunch was untouched. "You'll be there, won't you?"

Mona felt her eyes filling up. "I'm in charge of the volunteer ushers."

"So I'll catch you there," Sam said, sitting back down. She picked up her knife and fork and stared down at her plate, trying not to follow her old friend with her eyes.

For Mona, the trip to the door of the restaurant took forever. She didn't let the tears fall until she was back in her car.

Heaven was busy being creative, artfully arranging the laminated vintage photos of the social clubs in the center of the tables. It was mindless activity, and she was a million miles away when Nolan Wilkins appeared beside her. She jumped. "Jesus, Nolan, you startled me."

"Sorry. With my luck lately, you'll die right here of shock because I said hello," Nolan said.

Heaven rolled her eyes. "Do I detect an attack of self-pity? Is the universe picking on you, poor little thing?"

"I admit I had trouble getting out of bed this morning, and it wasn't because of my ticker. After all these months, no, years of working on this. Now we've had a death, the Parker saxophone has been stolen, and I had to break up a fight between three of our principal guests, not to mention the one Ella insulted. I can't even enjoy the fruits of all my work."

"Get over it," Heaven said firmly. "Look at what you've accomplished instead of dwelling on what you can't change. The fact that Kansas City got this project done at all is amazing. Hopefully, the police will find the saxophone today."

"Today is almost over, Heaven." Nolan looked at his watch. "It's almost five o'clock."

Heaven stopped fiddling with her table decorations. She poked a finger in Nolan's stomach. "Then it's time to stop feeling sorry for yourself and make sure tonight goes smoothly. You can't bring back Evelyn Edwards, no matter how much you might want to."

"No, I can't," Nolan said mournfully.

"You can't change what happened between Sam Scott and Lefty and Boots years ago."

"No."

"And you can't make the Parker horn magically appear, unless you took it. If you did take it," she said with a grin, "put it back right now."

Nolan smiled. "Well, there is one good thing about the missing sax. We have all kinds of national press coming this weekend—*20/20, 48 Hours,* CNN, everybody will be here either tonight or tomorrow. Pam Whiteside is frantic."

"Pam can handle it, and so can you. Come back later to eat," Heaven, said, pushing Nolan in the direction of the Ruby Theater.

"Wait. Heaven, what did you do about the food?"

"I solved the problem, I hope. Now, go."

Nolan put his arm around Heaven and clung to her a minute. "Thank you. I've got a lot to do and you're right, I don't have time to feel sorry for myself." He headed off across the street just as Julia Marcus came around the corner with her hands full.

Heaven grabbed the big aluminum pans from Julia's arms. "Did you get my message about where to park?"

"Yes, child, I felt like a celebrity. They had my name on

a clipboard. I just hope they don't ride me out of town on a rail when we run out of food."

Another woman was heading their way, her arms full of platters. "Julia, this is my friend Mary Garcia. She lives around the corner from my restaurant, and she is the best tamale maker in Kansas City."

Julia's eyes were wide. "Tamales?"

Heaven reached under the buffet table and pulled out a sign. It said WORLD SOUL FOOD: THE FOOD OF THE NEIGHBORHOODS OF KANSAS CITY. "We needed a way to trick Miss Ella, or whoever was buying up all the ingredients that we needed for this dinner. So I thought of all the other ethnic groups in Kansas City. Every culture has its comfort food, the very soul of who its people are."

"I know what you mean. Black people aren't the only ones with soul food," Julia agreed.

"So I called Mary for tamales, and my Hmong friends, the Laotians who cook at the Nelson Museum. They're bringing summer rolls and spring rolls and they're dressing in their native costumes. I told everyone who had native dress to wear their outfits. I also called the Jewish Community Center. Its ladies are bringing blintzes and chopped liver, and the Russian Jewish community is bringing pirogi. And my friend Charlene Welling is bringing a very fancy version of banana pudding."

By this time a small crowd of women with food had gathered. "Good thinking, Heaven," Julia said. "Won't Miss Ella be sorry that she didn't spoil this night. How are we going to serve all this?"

"Julia, how much food do you think you and your social clubs have?"

"We guess for about half the folks you're expecting, about two hundred and fifty, maybe three hundred."

"Then I think we should offer traditional soul food on each end of the street and at each dessert station," Heaven said. "But let's not try to do everything at both serving stations. Let's have the chicken and dumplings at one end, the smothered pork chops at the other. A church group is also bringing beans, rice, chips, and salsa. And the Thai community group is going to grill satay of pork and chicken and have big vats of Pad Thai noodles. I loaded the grills with charcoal this afternoon. I'll light them in a minute. Both the noodles and the beans and rice are good fillers, so we'll put them on both buffet lines."

"It sounds like a plan," Julia said with a smile on her face and a sneaky look in her eyes. "I just hope I get to see the face of that New Yorker. Will she be disappointed!"

Heaven smiled, too. She reached under the table again and came out with an enlargement of a photograph of Julia and her club. At the bottom someone had written "A Night in the Orient, Twin Citians Club, 1942." Each woman looked more beautiful than the next; they wore brocade Chinese jackets and had fresh flowers in their elaborate hairdos. "I recognized you right away; look at you with those gardenias in your hair," Heaven said as she handed the laminated blow-up to Julia. "Put this up tonight by your club's food station, then be sure and take it home. I had it blown up big for you, to thank you for your help. We have to spread the money around a little more now, but at least we'll have enough food for everyone."

Julia's eyes clouded over as she gazed at her image. She giggled like a schoolgirl. "I met my husband that very night. Thank you. And we're glad to share the food money with these other groups. They've saved us from a disaster. And I like what you did, Heaven. You'll make folks think about how Kansas City is really a melting pot. That's good."

Heaven guided Julia over to the other buffet table. "Come for a minute and look at the other photos. See if you spot more people who will be here tonight. I want everyone to get their pictures."

Julia started right in naming names. "Oh, good God, what a dress that Gladys had on that night. And Sally Thomas, oh, she'll die to see this." She stopped and picked up a photo with a puzzled look in her eye. "What's this one of Boots Turner doing in here?"

Heaven's heart started racing. She grabbed the other blow-up of the photos from Evelyn's office. "How about this one. Is that Boots, too? I didn't recognize him, not in his stage clothes and young and all."

"Why, surely it is, but I don't recall the lady in either of these." Julia studied the two pictures and shook her head. "Someone must have known Boots back then and these got mixed up with the social club photos."

"Well, based on my own photo drawers, that could happen easily," Heaven said smoothly. "I guess we better get this show on the road." She clapped her hands and whistled to get everyone's attention.

Heaven looked at her watch. "It's five-thirty, so listen up a minute, ladies. The chafing dishes are lined up. You all need to get the water heated in them. I left Igloo coolers filled with water at the end of each buffet line. I left a propane fireplace lighter, too. Behind each food line there's a tent. In that tent are tables and a rolling heater. Put your pans in the heater until just before seven, when the party starts. I'm trying to avoid foodborne illness tonight, so let's keep everything nice and hot until it's time to go. There should be chairs, too, so you can sit down once in a while."

"Thanks for thinking of these old bones. You go start your grills now or the coals won't be ready in time," Julia said, pushing Heaven away.

Heaven went around the corner on Vine Street where she had set up the grills and the propane burners for the chicken livers and Sunday's deep-fried turkeys. She almost fell over one of the grills. It was lying on its side, with the charcoal spilled out on the ground. Miss Ella Jackson was busy working on the next one, upending a huge grill. She had on her usual vintage attire, plus a great old flowered apron with a bib. There was black soot from the charcoal on her cheek. She gave the last grill a push, then wiped her hands with a flourish on her apron. Then she had a big laugh. "Well, land-a-mercy, Heaven, these flimsy little ol' grills must have been caught by the wind. I guess you'll have to load them up all over again. See ya," she said with a jaunty wave as she walked back across the street to her cafe.

Heaven had started counting to ten as soon as she saw what Ella was doing. A mud wrestling match was next if Heaven went for the bait. She tried to focus on what had to be done to get this party rolling. She could deal with Ella later.

"Now what are you going to do?" a voice with laughter in it asked. Heaven whirled around and saw Jim Dittmar standing in the entrance to an alley, leaning up against the brick wall as if he were watching a sports event.

"Gee, thanks for stopping her," Heaven snapped.

"She seems dangerous to me, Counselor. I don't want to tangle with Miss Ella Jackson, no sir," Jim said as he sauntered toward Heaven. "But I'll help you pick up the pieces if you want."

Heaven sputtered. "What I want," she said as she pointed her finger at Jim, "is for you to tell me the truth. Did you steal the Charlie Parker sax?"

Jim looked genuinely surprised. "What in the world are you talking about? I'm a piano player, for God's sake. I wouldn't risk these hands breaking and entering."

"Well, that's not what I hear from Europe. My ex-husband tells me you always happen to be gigging where diamond tiaras disappear."

Jim's look of amusement turned serious. He clucked his tongue. "Heaven, why in the world would your ex-husband tell you anything about me? Unless you're snooping and you asked him." He walked up and took Heaven's chin in his hand. She jerked away.

"All I know is that since you've been home, this whole project has gone to hell. Now I have to go get some help. I don't want to get all black from charcoal dust. But don't think I didn't notice you haven't answered my question. We'll talk about this later."

"Curiosity killed the cat, Counselor," Jim called as Heaven flounced away.

Mona was checking in the ushers in front of the Ruby Theater, crossing their names off a clipboard. Heaven caught the sad look in her eyes. "I have an emergency, then I want to know why you look like you just lost your best friend. Oh dear, that was the wrong trite phrase, wasn't it?" Heaven grabbed her friend and gave her a big hug. The grill emergency could wait a minute. "So," she said, holding her friend at arm's length, "I guess lunch didn't go so well."

Mona shook her head. "No, I guess it didn't," she answered, her voice quivering. "Please give me a good crisis to think about. We don't have time to talk about this now. Besides, if I do I might cry, and I sure don't want to do that."

"Do you still have the volunteers from the Boys Club?"

"Yes, they're here until dark, then they come back again tomorrow. What do you need?"

"The darling Miss Ella just dumped over all the grills. I need ten kids for fifteen minutes to scoop up the charcoal, especially some big boys, 'cause I can't right the Big John grills by myself."

Mona took her walkie-talkie out of its holder on her belt. "What has gotten into that woman? She was fun that first night. Heaven, get back to the grills. The kids will be there by the time you are."

"I have one more stop to make," Heaven said as she walked toward the security guard station. "Hi, I'm Heaven Lee," she said, extending her hand toward one of the two uniformed guards behind the stand. They were pointing and gesturing for Boots Turner, who had obviously asked for some directions. One of the guards shook her hand limply and eyed her suspiciously. She nodded at Boots. "Mr.

Turner," she said, before looking back at the guards. "I'm in charge of the food tonight and I have a big problem. Miss Ella, from Miss Ella's Soul Food, is terrorizing the poor women that volunteered to make the food. She just wrecked the grill area."

The two men looked at each other and one of them said, "I'll go over there and talk with her. He was wantin' to know where her place was anyhow," he added, jerking his head toward Boots.

"No, don't talk to her," Heaven said. "I'm afraid it will just enrage her further. Let's try to get through the night without another incident. Will you please assign a guard to each of the food tables, and if she comes anywhere near them, then they could escort her back across the street? Please? And Mr. Turner, after how Ella acted last night, I would think you'd want to steer clear of her."

Boots Turner looked across the street to Miss Ella's Soul Food. "The girl has mistaken me for someone else. I couldn't sleep last night because of it, and I won't be able to play tonight until I straighten her out."

"Good luck with that one," Heaven called as the big man walked away. She didn't think Ella had mistaken him for someone else. It looked like Ella knew exactly who he was.

The food was a smashing success. The city council members in districts with Hispanic and Jewish and Asian constituents were tickled pink to have the ethnic cuisines of their voters included. The black members of the city council couldn't be mad about the world soul food theme when they saw that the ladies of the black social clubs got to be the stars of the show.

"The only thing missing, Heaven, is Italian food," the mayor said as he shook her hand.

Heaven agreed. "Italian food is the most popular food in the universe, and I'm sure it's the most popular cuisine here in Kansas City. However, the Italian festival is next weekend in Columbus Park, so the women of Holy Rosary were already busy working on that. Next year we'll plan it so they can be a part of this," she said insincerely, knowing she sure wouldn't head this project again. Next year maybe the social clubs could run the whole thing.

Promptly at eight-thirty Heaven shut down the food lines and tried to shoo the patrons to the Ruby for the big concert. The vendor who had the city contract for beverages for this weekend kept the bars open, and there was still a party atmosphere in the blocked-off streets.

Heaven had arranged with Harvester's, the local food bank, to come at eight forty-five to pick up the leftovers in their truck. But there was precious little for them to collect.

"They almost picked us dry, Heaven," Julia Marcus chuckled. "But I like that you have the leftovers going to the homeless. That's real thoughtful."

Heaven had found an end piece of cornbread that had fallen behind one of the bread baskets, and she was munching away. She had also smuggled a couple of bottles of wine in with her boxes of supplies, so she was having a white Italian wine, a Coppo Gavi, in a paper cup over ice. "When you work in restaurants and see all the waste, Julia, you start wanting to do something about it. I freeze leftovers at the restaurant and Harvester's comes and picks them up once a week."

Although the Ruby concert was sold out, Heaven had arranged for everyone who had contributed food to have a standing room pass. She glanced over at the theater. "Julia, you better go. I think Ray Charles is the lead-off singer, so you don't want to be late."

Julia was clutching her vintage photo. "You are right about that. I don't want to miss ol' Ray." She shook hands solemnly with Heaven. "You sure know how to throw a party, child. And I'll be back on Sunday for the baseball museum dedication. I want to get Lefty Stuart's autograph."

"He's a cutey, isn't he?" Heaven said honestly. Sam Scott's husband had real charm. Heaven felt a pang of sympathy again for Mona—for Sam Scott, too. Heaven hugged Julia and watched the social club women walking over to the concert, friends who didn't need many words to communicate anymore. Laughter followed them, warming the May night.

Heaven sat waiting for the rental company team. They were coming at nine, after the crowd was inside, to break down this set-up for the gala and replace it with the screened-in booths that the health department insisted on for public outdoor events where food was sold.

She could hear the sounds of the Boots Turner Big Band starting the show. She wondered how his talk with Ella had gone, thought about the photos of Boots, then just let it all go out of her mind for a minute, all the puzzles fading into the beautiful harmonies of the horns. This was how she liked to hear concerts, from backstage. It just happened this time the backstage extended to the front street. She could hear the crowd cheer for the first time in many years in the Ruby Theater. She sat on the edge of a table drinking wine out of a paper cup as the warm breezes carried the music outside in waves. If she squinted her eyes just right, those ghosts of Eighteenth and Vine appeared, snapping their fingers to the beat of the music.

Right on time, the rental crew showed up and started breaking down the buffet tables. Heaven fished around in her bag for the diagram of the location of the barbecue stands. She wanted everything to go perfectly tomorrow, without hurt feelings among the barbecue restaurants. Now that the hardest meal to organize had gone so smoothly, she had hope the rest of the weekend could go the same way. She was cautiously proud of herself: one meal down, two more days to go.

An hour later, the change was almost complete. Heaven supervised and sipped wine.

It was fun to be out almost alone in the night. The street was dramatically lit, with potted palms creating backdrops at the barricaded ends of the street. It was like a movie set. And of course Bob Daultman, the resident movie maker, had been in rare form tonight, insisting on getting shots of all the food and having the women of the various nationalities explain what they had made. Yes, Heaven could see why Bob Daultman was a prizewinner. He could draw people out, make the story seem bigger than life. He had interviewed Heaven about her inspiration for the world soul food theme and had stimulated her imagination with his flattery. Heaven was now sure the whole gala meal was the most brilliant thing she'd ever done, instead of just a desperate solution to a problem.

"Do you keep the grills and the propane tanks and big pots?" the rental foreman asked, reading off a list.

"Yes, we keep them all the way through Sunday." Although the barbecue people weren't technically going to grill—they slow-cooked their meat in smokers—a couple of them were going to do sausage and hot dogs, and more than one said they might use the grills to warm up their ribs or chickens. On Sunday, they would deep-fry the turkey in the big stockpots over propane flames on tall stands, just like they did in New Orleans during Mardi Gras. They would also use the grills for the oysters.

Heaven watched the rental crew leaving and decided maybe she should check to make sure that all the coals were out. The Thai cooks who did the satay were in the Ruby listening to the music and she hadn't checked back there since they stopped serving. It would be just her luck if she burned down the historic Eighteenth and Vine district on its first night of its second life.

She was laughing at the thought when she stepped around the corner. Suddenly she saw a stockpot flying through the air, a silver blur in the night. She was hit hard and fell. Then everything went black.

* * *

The first thing Heaven saw when she came to was a flashing blue light. The second thing she saw was Detective Bonnie Weber. The detective did not look happy.

Heaven tried to get up and was greeted with a breathtaking pain in her right temple. "Boy, does that hurt," she gasped.

"I bet," Bonnie Weber said seriously. "It looks like someone took a swing at you with that stockpot. If it makes you feel any better, the pot has a dent, too, although I think it might have come from the brick wall and not your head."

"I bet it was that bitch across the street, Ella Jackson," Heaven said as she tried a second time to sit up.

"Yeah, it looks like you two had it out."

"Not really," Heaven said, trying to put all the events of the evening in order. They were slipping around in her head in their own stream of consciousness; the mayor and the social clubs and all the guests were coming in and out of focus. "She pushed over the grills and made a mess with charcoal but I just called security."

"Heaven," Bonnie Weber said, shaking her slightly, "whatever happened here wasn't just turning over some grills, and Ella Jackson definitely got the worst end of it."

This time Heaven grabbed Bonnie's sleeve and pulled herself up. The horizon line was spinning, her stomach was churning. She saw the faces of Mona, Nolan, and others blur before her.

Then she saw Miss Ella Jackson being wheeled away on a stretcher. She had an oxygen mask over her face and blood all over her pretty clothes. She looked worse than Heaven felt.

Sweet Potato Pecan Pie

enough pastry dough for a one-crust pie, or a frozen pie
  crust
2 cups cooked, mashed sweet potatoes
1 cup sugar
3 eggs
6 T. melted butter
1 T. vanilla flavoring
½ cup orange juice

Topping

6 T. softened butter
½ tsp. cinnamon
½ cup brown sugar
½ cup flour
½ cup pecan halves

Beat sugar and eggs until lemony. Add sweet potatoes, butter, vanilla, and orange juice. Turn into your pie shell.

Combine all the topping ingredients and cover the sweet potato mixture with it.

Bake at 350 degrees for 1 hour, give or take 10 minutes for the real temperature of your oven. The top will be browned and sizzling and the potato mixture should be set in the middle.

Twelve

Okay, we can go now," Bonnie Weber said.

Heaven opened one eye. "I don't know why I had to stay in this stupid emergency room all night," she said crossly.

"Because you have a concussion and they wanted to make sure your brains didn't start running out your ears," Bonnie Weber said just as crossly.

Heaven dangled her feet over the edge of the examining table. The blow to the side of her head was now an ugly, swollen, purple knot. She gingerly felt it. "Ow."

"Here, let me help you down," Bonnie said. "Here are your clothes. Let's go get breakfast."

In a few minutes, Heaven emerged from her cubicle, squinting in the bad lighting of the ER waiting room. Mona was huddled over the morning newspaper. When she saw her, she flipped the front page around.

The headline, THE CURSE OF EIGHTEENTH AND VINE, was only upstaged by a particularly gruesome photo of Heaven sitting on the sidewalk, blood caked on her face, being checked out by the medics as Ella Jackson was being hustled away on a stretcher.

"Nice. Very appealing. Would you want to eat a meal cooked by this woman?" Heaven moaned.

"Ella? No, I can't say that I would," Mona said in an attempt to coax Heaven back to her usual sarcastic self.

"Mona, what are you doing here? And how is Ella?" Heaven asked as they walked out to Bonnie Weber's car.

"I'm here because I was worried about you, of course. And Ella's still asleep," Mona said delicately.

"In a coma?" Heaven asked.

"No, she woke up once, but she's hurt pretty bad, H, and they have to do CAT scans and stuff today," Bonnie said seriously.

"Have I already talked to you about this? Did we talk to each other during the night?" Heaven asked.

"A couple of times," Mona replied, looking at Bonnie Weber for support.

Bonnie opened her passenger door and helped Heaven sit. Mona got in the back. "Is the Corner Restaurant okay with everybody?" Bonnie asked.

"Of course," Heaven said. "I need some of those good fried potatoes to help me recover. I'm sure you've told me, but what happened to us, Ella and me?"

"You know you got hit with a stockpot? Well, Ella got it with a full propane tank. And whoever whacked her was using the thing like a sliding fast ball."

"Do the cops think I did it?" Heaven asked with a little catch in her voice, as if she had just thought of that possibility.

Bonnie looked over at her as she turned the car south on Broadway, toward Westport Road. "Hello! What am I? Chopped liver? In case that blow to the head has caused amnesia, I AM the cops."

"No, not you," Heaven tried to explain. "I'm assuming you know I didn't do it. But other cops, your superiors. Am I in trouble?"

"Yes," Mona and Bonnie answered more or less at the

same time. "Come on, Heaven, let's go in and eat. You're in no shape to be arrested just yet," Bonnie said as she parked the car.

As the women entered the crowded diner almost every pair of eyes in the place followed them. Most tables had a morning paper open, and Heaven saw her own photo looking back at her all over the room. A part of her wanted to go home and hide in bed, but she knew she needed to eat. The big dedication was just hours away. She ordered her favorite, a Porker, which involved sausages, potatoes, onions, green peppers, eggs and a couple of kinds of cheese. Mona ordered bacon and eggs over easy, with fried potatoes. Bonnie ordered scrambled eggs and chili.

"And I think we need an order of pancakes for the table, those corn cakes with the bananas," Heaven added.

The other two women looked at her in mild alarm. "A blow to the head sure made you hungry," Mona observed.

"I didn't really eat last night at the big party, just nibbled. Can I ask you a silly question?"

"Of course," Bonnie said while filling her coffee with enough sugar and cream to make a cake.

"Did I talk to Hank last night or was it my imagination?"

"You talked to him. He was worried sick," Mona said.

"Which one of you ratted me out and told him what had happened to me?" Heaven asked.

"Guilty," Bonnie admitted. "When we got to the medical center, I asked Hank's buddies in the ER if they had his number in Houston. I have an agreement with Hank to let him know when you get wounded in the line of duty."

"Line of duty. Ha. I don't exactly remember what was said, but I know it made me feel better to talk to him. Thank you, although I feel like the kid at camp who almost drowned in the lake and the counselors called my dad and told on me," Heaven said as she dove into her food.

When the eating frenzy had subsided, Heaven looked across the table. "Well?"

"In my professional opinion, the possibilities are, Bonnie said, number one, "you and Ella got into a knock-down fight and your club was bigger than hers."

"Now, wait a minute. What did I do?" Heaven asked, all fired up. "Knock her in the head with a propane tank, then knock myself out?"

"Shut up a minute and let me talk. You and Ella have had two run-ins in the last two days. Her employees said you pulled her hair yesterday and—"

Heaven cut in. "I grabbed her by the chignon. I didn't pull her hair."

Bonnie calmly went on. "*And* you had the security force watching her every move last night. Even Mona would have to testify that you accused Ella of vandalizing the grills in the very spot you two were found."

"But the grills really were turned over," Mona hurried to say. "I went back there to see for myself—not that I didn't believe you, H."

"And a good prosecutor would say that Heaven could have turned those grills over herself to make Ella look bad. Did anyone but you actually see her in the act?" Bonnie asked, looking sternly at Heaven.

Heaven, who was in the throes of a terrible headache, was beginning to realize how serious the situation was. "Jim Dittmar saw Ella do it, I think." Of course, Heaven realized she had accused Jim of stealing the Charlie Parker sax, which might not put him in the best mood for corroborating her story. She'd just have to deal with that later if she needed proof of Ella's misdeed. "Can we go to possibility number two now? I hate possibility number one."

"Possibility number two," Bonnie recited, "is that you interrupted some standard street violence. Perhaps Ella was being robbed, and you just happened to come around the corner at the wrong time. Possibility number three is that someone knocked out Ella with the intention of actually killing her and knocked you out to implicate you by making it look like a fight. Or vise versa. Possibility number four is the curse of Eighteenth and Vine, as the *Star* called it this morning. That is, that someone has rigged the accident at the Ruby either to kill Evelyn specifically or anyone in general, stolen the saxophone, and attacked you and Ella, all to ruin this weekend and the chances of the district's being a successful tourist draw.''

"Boy, that was a mouthful, Bonnie," Mona murmured. "Which do you think is what really happened?''

"Oh, probably some combination of all the above. Sometimes detecting is like geometry," Bonnie said.

"And what about Boots Turner? I hate to blame him for this, but Ella did make a pretty nasty accusation about him in public," Heaven said.

Bonnie got up. "I thought about that. I should have had him as possibility number five, but this attack took some real strength. It wasn't just a case of pulling a trigger, and he is in his seventies. But I know better than to rule someone out because he seems too weak. If Evelyn were his daughter, and that's a big if, he might have been angry enough at Ella for outing him to whack her good. Then you came around the corner at the wrong time and he wanted to make sure you didn't see anything. What's the last time you remember? Did you happen to check your watch right before you got hit?''

"No, but it had to be around ten-thirty. The rental guys came at nine and they'd just left.''

"Well, Boots had the first set, from nine to nine-thirty. So, it's possible.''

Heaven still was sitting down, not quite up to standing like Mona and Bonnie were doing. "Wait, one more thing. What if whoever stole the sax . . . what if Ella were part of that scam. She did bring all that food into the Ruby just at the right time to create a diversion, when the sax was getting ripped off. What if she asked for a bigger cut or whatever . . .''

"A falling-out among thieves, possibility number six," Mona said, looking at Bonnie for confirmation.

"Yes, that's a possibility, I suppose," Bonnie said with a weary smile. "Now, can we go?"

Heaven got up unsteadily. "Where's my van? And has anyone called Murray and the kitchen crew?"

"Back at Eighteenth and Vine, and yes," Mona answered. "Murray had interviews set with some of the jazz stars for an article for his column this morning or he would have been at the hospital. I called and talked to Pauline, and she said everything was fine and they had a good night last night."

"At least I'd already covered myself on the schedule this weekend, so I haven't put more work on my crew with this fiasco than they already had."

"Mona, I'll drop you at your car at the hospital. I know you have volunteers to coordinate," Bonnie said.

Mona nodded. "And since I have to go to Eighteenth and Vine anyway, I'll take Heaven to her car."

Bonnie patted Heaven's hand. "Heaven, can you go home and rest for a couple of hours? You look like hell."

"I'm on my way. It's only nine in the morning. The barbecue booths won't be open until eleven. At least I can get a shower."

Bonnie Weber parked her car near Mona's in the emergency room parking area. "I'm going back in to check on Ella's condition. Please be careful, both of you. If we do have a nut who's psychotic at the whole idea of Eighteenth and Vine, something else bad will happen."

Heaven turned to her friend. "Just for the record, I did not hit Ella Jackson, ever."

"I believe you," Bonnie said, "but not everyone knows you like I do."

Jim Dittmar jumped into the equipment van that Bob Daultman's crew was using. It resembled a television sports producer's van. Bob had multiple video cameras circulating around the various events. He or his assistant sat in the van and made notations of especially good snips and pieces of business on camera 1, 2, or 3, notes to be used later in the editing room.

Bob Daultman turned toward the door when Jim came in. "Look at this footage from last night. Isn't this priceless?" he said as he turned back to the monitor showing Ella and Heaven receiving first aid as the evidence technicians were working on the crime scene.

"I'm getting the willies. I think we should send the kid right now," Jim said as he watched his injured friend on the screen. "This is not our usual MO. There's a lot of violence going on, in case you haven't noticed. Every cop in town is working one of these cases. And the paper is tying all of this together, this soul food restaurant owner, the sax, Heaven, and the woman who died last week."

Bob Daultman waved his arm dismissively. "And so your idea is for the kid to disappear two days early. They'd be all over that like a cheap suit. Those two wouldn't get to the Colorado border."

"This is not a western movie. They don't have to ride horses as fast as they can for the state line. They'll be in Paris before anyone misses them."

"No," Bob said firmly. "They stay. Your redheaded friend has made a star out of Louis and has been talking him up all week, since her little cabaret on Monday. And speaking of her, didn't you say she and Ella had a big row and Ella tipped over her grills last night? It sure looks like Heaven took the payback to Ella and got carried away. I love a good cat fight."

"Yeah, and I also told you Heaven has been asking questions about us in Europe. She came right out and asked me if I stole the damn sax."

"So what?" Bob asked. "She's in more trouble than we are by far, someone saw to that. We play out our hand. I've never seen you lose your cool. Just simmer down and enjoy yourself."

"Bob, you didn't hire some goon to clip the wings of those two women, did you?"

"No, but it certainly deflected some of the heat off the stolen sax, now, didn't it. Besides, what if I had? When did you get so squeamish? You've bound and gagged a couple of little old rich ladies yourself."

"I told you. I'm through with all that. I wanted to retire. That's why I came back here."

Bob laughed a short little nasty laugh. "But you just couldn't keep your hands off the diamonds, could you, Jimmy? And this hasn't been so hard, now, has it? You didn't have to go off to some nasty mansion in Switzerland to do a job. The job came to you. I'm looking forward to you and Louis playing together this afternoon, Jim. Break a leg," he said as a dismissal.

Jim stepped out of the van and went over to the stage. It was another pretty May day in Kansas City.

There was a knock on the door. Lefty Stuart went to open it with a big smile on his face. "Did you forget your key, baby?" It was Murray Steinblatz and Heaven Lee, not Sam Scott, standing there looking expectantly at Lefty.

"I'm Murray . . ."

Lefty Stuart nodded as if he'd just remembered something. "The fella from the *New York Times*, yes, yes. We have an appointment. Sam should be back soon. She's out taking her walk. Come in."

Murray and Heaven came in, and Murray said shyly, "I am from the *Times*, but I live here in Kansas City. I write a column called 'Letters from the Interior' about what happens around here, in the Midwest."

"Would you like some coffee?" Lefty asked politely, and he turned toward Heaven.

"Yes, please. I'm Heaven Lee, Mr. Stuart. I came along with Murray to ask a favor of you and Ms. Scott."

Lefty poured coffee for both Murray and Heaven. "Call me Lefty. Aren't you the young lady who was attacked last night, you and the restaurant owner from New York?"

"Yes, that was me."

Lefty put his hand up on the lump on the side of Heaven's head. His touch was very gentle. Heaven wanted to grab his hand and make it stay on her wound, it felt so good. "That's an ugly bump, Heaven. You should be in bed."

"I know, I know, but the Eighteenth and Vine neighborhood only gets dedicated once. I promise everyone I'll stay in bed all next week and nurse my wounds," Heaven said with a laugh.

Murray sat down and brought out a reporter's notebook and a tape recorder and placed them on the table. "While we're waiting for your wife . . . Wasn't Kansas City where you two met?"

Lefty Stuart's eyes lit up. He sipped his coffee. "That's right. Sam and I did meet here in Kansas City. I had already retired from baseball and I was here to throw out the first ball at the opening day for the old Athletics. As it turned out, Sam and some of the boys in the band had come to the game that afternoon. Then that night, the Boots Turner band was playing at a club in one of the hotels downtown and I went to see them. I wouldn't be surprised if it was the Muelbach."

Murray had started writing as fast as he could. "You have a good memory, Mr. . . . I mean, Lefty."

"Well, when your life changes with one look, you kinda remember where you were when it happened," Lefty said simply.

The door opened and Sam Scott came in. "I'm so sorry I'm late. I started window-shopping. This Plaza is just beautiful."

Murray got to his feet quickly. "Ms. Scott, I'm Murray Steinblatz. And my friend Heaven Lee came along. She has something she really needs your help with. She practically called me from the hospital and asked me to bring her along."

Heaven started fishing around in her purse. "This won't

take long. Then you and Lefty and Murray can visit," she said as she brought out the two photos of Boots Turner.

Sam looked at Heaven with concern. "That's a very ugly head wound, child. This must be important. By the way, how's that other woman, the one who showed up at the Ruby the other night?"

"That's why I'm here, because of what Ella said the other night," Heaven said.

"You were there?" Lefty asked, thinking about his own scene with Boots.

Heaven nodded. "I'm the volunteer in charge of the food for the weekend, so I was there and heard what Ella said to Boots." She held out the photos toward Sam Scott. "These are photos that Evelyn Edwards had in her office"—she glanced at Murray as if to say, Save the lecture for later— "I think the man in both pictures is Boots."

Sam Scott took the two laminated photographs and studied them. "Yes, it's Boots, it sure is."

"Do you know any of the other people, either of the women or the kids?" Heaven asked hopefully. "Was Boots married?"

"Not to these women, honey." Sam Scott handed the pictures back to Heaven. "Those shots are from the fifties or early sixties, by the look of the clothes. Boots hadn't been married at all until after . . ." She looked over at Lefty.

"Until that day in Kansas City when he lost you," Lefty said quietly.

Heaven looked down at the shots with disappointment. "I know this is a hard question, but do you think Ella Jackson could have been telling the truth, that the woman who died here last week could have been Boots's daughter, one maybe he didn't know about?"

Sam Scott shifted and looked away from Heaven's eyes. "I don't think that's possible."

Lefty put his arms around Sam Scott and hugged her. "Now, honey, I know you know Boots and I don't, but I do know men, and I know what it's like when you're on the road. There are lots of temptations out there, lots of pretty women who want to sleep with a famous musician."

Sam Scott broke into a grin and elbowed her husband in the ribs. "Or a famous baseball player, I might add."

Heaven and Murray laughed along with Sam and Lefty. Heaven knew Sam Scott wasn't telling everything she knew, but it was time for her to leave for the dedication. She slipped her arm through Murray's. "You two are a real inspiration. Thank you for all the help. I'm just going to have Murray walk me to the door and then he's all yours. Promise me you'll finish that story about the day you met, Lefty."

"It's one of my favorites," Lefty said.

Heaven walked to the door quickly and headed out into the hall. "My brain is mush," she whispered. "What's Boots's room number again?"

"Heaven, you're in no shape to be up. Please go home," Murray said.

"Murray, we already went through this. What's his number?"

"1724. At least wait for me and we'll go together. What if he's the one who attacked you and Ella last night?"

"We're at the Ritz-Carlton, for God's sake. What's he gonna do, pop me with a gun because I ask him about his offspring? Now, go back in there and finish your interview." Heaven closed the door and headed for the elevator.

Boots Turner opened the door and looked at Heaven quizzically, the same way he had looked at Ella the other night, like he was trying to place her.

"Boots, I'm Heaven Lee. I'm the volunteer in charge of food for the Eighteenth and Vine gala. We met last night at the guard station when you were asking how to find Ella Jackson."

"I know who you are. I 'spect everyone does after that picture in the newspaper this morning."

Heaven slipped in before Boots had a chance to ask her

what she wanted. She didn't go far, though, just stood a few steps from the door. Boots glanced out in the hall.

"If you're looking for Murray Steinblatz, the reporter, he's on his way. Murray's a friend of mine."

Boots took a large white hankie out of his pocket and mopped his brow. "Lord knows who I'm looking for. Maybe the cops, again. I'm surprised to see you here, miss. I thought you'd still be in the hospital, along with Ella."

"Did the police come and ques . . . talk to you about last night?"

Boots sat down in one of the room's fancy chairs and gestured toward the other one. Heaven perched on the edge.

"They did more than that. They took me down to the station. Since Miss Ella said her piece the other night, I guess I'm suspected of killing this Evelyn person, then trying to do the same to the both of you."

Heaven didn't want to beat around the bush. She had a pounding headache and still had to deal with the barbecue crew. "I know it's about time to go to the dedication, so I'll just—"

"I don't think I can go," Boots said as he mopped his brow again.

"What's the matter?"

"My heart. It's pounding like a conga player on cocaine. I had heart surgery last year, and this whole police thing has got me real upset."

"Boots, you've got a couple of hours. You better just lie down and relax. But first will you take a look at these two photos, please?" Heaven gave him the photos.

Boots grinned. "Nadine Edwards. Barbara Jackson. Lord, I haven't thought of them in years. I was still skinny back then."

"Maybe that's the problem, you haven't thought of them. Boots, I found those two photos in Evelyn Edwards's office." She didn't give Boots a chance to ask her how. "Evelyn is the dead woman. I think she thought you were her father. If one of these women is Barbara Jackson, the child with her could be Ella Jackson. Are these two little girls your children?"

Boots had tears in his eyes. "No, they are not. I talked to Ella for a minute last night before the concert. I know she's convinced that I'm her daddy that she never knew. And from what she tells me, Evelyn thought the same."

"Did you have a relationship with the mothers?"

"I did. And with Nadine, I continued to keep in touch long after the physical was gone. I met both of these ladies when they already had these little girls. Sweet little things."

"Would you be willing to take a DNA test to put this story to rest?"

Boots sighed. "Oh, I'll be tested if it's necessary. Heaven, I'm not sure how you fit into this problem, except, of course, that someone attacked you. But I'm gonna tell you this right now, just in case something happens to me today and my heart just gives up on this old, fat man. I wish I could be the father of these girls. I can't have children. I had the mumps go down on me when I was a child."

"So there's no way?"

Boots shook his head. "No way."

Heaven got up. "I'm so sorry you had to tell me something so personal. But if you haven't told the police, I suggest you do after the concert. They probably haven't seen these photos yet, unless Ella had copies, too. But you're already in trouble with them, and your offer to be tested should help." Heaven headed toward the door. "My friend Murray Steinblatz will be here soon. Will you tell him I've already gone to the dedication? He's a good guy, Murray is, and if you don't feel better, ask him to take you to the hospital to get checked out." Heaven patted the the big man's arm. She felt sorry for him. "We need you," Heaven said.

* * *

"How did Boots seem to you? Is he going to be okay?" Heaven asked eagerly, cutting into a piece of sweet potato pie. She and Murray were sitting at a table in the middle of Eighteenth Street. The celebration was in full swing around them. The mayor had proclaimed. The city council had pontificated. Jim Dittmar and Louis had both played to much applause. Now the Boots Turner Big Band was wowing the crowd.

"He seems like a fine, old gentleman. You shook him up with those photographs."

"Did he tell you?"

"Not for publication, but yeah, he said he couldn't have kids."

"And the police shook him up before I got to him. Even if he's lying like a dog, if he's the father of both Evelyn and Ella, I don't think he's in good-enough shape to knock us out. This is great sweet potato pie. I like the pecans on top," Heaven said.

Murray took a bite of pie off Heaven's fork. "I don't think he's the father of Evelyn and Ella. Nowadays, most men won't try the old 'I can't have children' routine if it's not true. The new testing is just too good. But I'm more interested in the shape you're in."

Heaven gave Murray a hug, stealing a rib that was on his plate in the process. She stripped the rib clean of meat, eating like she hadn't in a week, and tossed it on her own plate, where several other bare rib bones were piled next to the pie. "Bad shape, Murray. If this were not a once-in-a-lifetime event I would be home in bed. I feel like shit. Now, what have you heard about my accident last night?"

"Bonnie and Mona kept me up-to-date," Murray said, touching the knot on Heaven's forehead. "That's an ugly lump."

Heaven brushed his hand away impatiently. "No, not what you heard through official channels. What's the word on the street? You've been around here all day, interviewing people for your story. What do people think happened between me and Miss Ella?"

Murray shrugged. "I've got a great story for my column, of course. You and Miss Ella are the icing on the cake. We've got an event planner dead, a valuable jazz memento stolen, and a prominent New York restaurateur attacked. Oh, and a prominent Kansas City restaurateur attacked. You do the math. You can mix 'em and you can match 'em. There are hundreds of theories."

"Murray, what do *you* think?"

"This is a tough one, H. It's hard to imagine the three incidents aren't related somehow."

Heaven nodded. "When you throw in how upset the food community was about Ella opening a restaurant in Kansas City, it really gets hard to settle on a motive. And how is Ella related to the saxophone?"

"Maybe she had something to do with stealing it—you know, she was the one who cased the joint or something. And then her partner. . . ."

"I thought of that," Heaven said with a wry chuckle. "And if they, the sax stealers, were trying to shut her up, she could still be in danger, as soon as she's able to open her big mouth, that is."

"I was going to say it wouldn't make sense to kill someone over their cut of what you could get for a plastic saxophone, but I should know better by now," Murray said.

"Maybe it wasn't over the money. Maybe someone didn't want Ella telling anyone they were involved, maybe a security guard who got paid off to look the other way."

"Or the guy who drives the rental truck who got paid to slip the sax out while we weren't looking," Murray said. "Honey, there are lots of variables. I don't think we can solve the curse of Eighteenth and Vine during lunch. Anyhow, this crowd doesn't seem to care about the curse. They're having a ball."

The smells and sounds and sights were pretty great. Black

children and white yuppies mingled. Gorgeous black women in African dress, leather boys with tattoos and art school girls with nose rings all stood grooving to the big band sounds of Boots Turner. The aroma of smoky meats wafted from the barbecue stands. An ice cream truck sold Popsicles and Fudgsicles. Lemonade and ice tea stands stood at both ends of the street. The committee had decided not to sell beer or any other alcohol so the dedication could be a family event.

Several thousand people clustered around the stage, while another thousand sat at the tables or in lawn chairs they had brought from home. Hundreds of others were touring the jazz museum and the Ruby Theater. The music sounded like the sound track of a movie—and, of course, Bob Daultman's video cameramen were everywhere, so it was the sound track of a potential movie. It wasn't big, by Chicago or New York festival standards, but for lots of Kansas City people, it was the first time they'd ever seen Eighteenth and Vine, even though it was such a big part of Kansas City history.

Murray, famous for his lack of rhythm, was tapping his toe with something resembling a beat. "I do have to confess that today I had delusions of solving all three crimes . . . Evelyn, the stolen sax, and you and Ella getting attacked. I thought it would make a really great ending for my column."

Heaven laughed and then winced from the pain that came with moving any skin on her face. "Murray, be my guest. I'm sure Bonnie Weber would love you forever. 'Letters from the Interior' is going pretty well, isn't it? New Yorkers like hearing about the heartland."

"So far, so good. I've even started to get fan mail."

Heaven's eyes narrowed. "During the break, can we go up to the stage?"

"So much for just enjoying the music. You flipped right back to investigator to the stars. What's up?"

"Sal said that Louis can speak English. He and his dad

told us he can't speak English. Let's test him. You say something to his father, and I'll watch his reaction."

"Like what?"

"Oh, for God's sake, Murray, I don't know. Say something about his piano playing. If you're talking about something dear to his heart, and he understands, I should be able to see a reaction."

"Heaven, I hate to be a party pooper, but he could understand English and still not be able to speak English."

Heaven glared at Murray. "This is just the first step. Boots should take a break in another ten minutes or so. I see Louis waiting at the side of the stage. Get ready," she barked.

Jim Dittmar appeared out of the crowd and sat down at the table with Murray and Heaven. He carefully touched the ugly knot on Heaven's head. "I'm so sorry this happened to you. I came out of the Ruby right as they were taking you and Ella away last night. Then I had to be here early this morning to meet with the tech guys."

"Don't apologize. Mona and the good detective baby-sat me. I'm grateful you whipped the entertainment into shape. You and Louis are quite a pair."

"Thanks. He's a good kid." Jim traced the outline of Heaven's hand with his own finger, touching her softly.

Murray blushed and got up. "I'm going to congratulate Louis," he said. "Good job, Jim."

"I'll meet you up there in a minute," Heaven said as they watched Murray trudge toward the stage.

"So where were we? Oh, yes, you'd just asked me if I'd stolen the sax, said your ex-husband had told you bad things happen when I play a house party."

"Well?"

"I don't mean to talk down to you, Heaven, but have you ever been to a big country house in England, besides Mick Jagger's and the ones owned by your ex and his buddies?"

"What's your point?"

"My point is that there are about thirty service personnel for every guest. Yes, I have been around when things have been stolen. But so have dozens of other people, and most of them don't make a quarter of the money I make, so they would make much better suspects than I would. There are caterers, waiters, hairdressers, florists, amusing but broke guests who have much more access to the upper floors of these big houses than I ever would. For instance, the hostess will sometimes provide a hairdresser and makeup person for the weekend. That lucky lady or fag can go in and out of the bedrooms much easier than a piano player. Besides, they usually carry big cases that would be easy to hide a tiny diamond necklace in. And that's just one of many scenarios I could paint for you, my dear. I'm kinda hurt your ex-husband would say such a thing, being a musician himself.''

"I don't think you're the thief anymore," Heaven said.

"Good," Jim said as he reached down and picked up Heaven's hand and started kissing her knuckles. She let him kiss three before she drew her hand away, slowly.

"I think Louis and his father did it. I'm pretty sure Louis is fooling us.''

Jim pulled back and sat up straight. "What do you mean, fooling us? You think he has a tape recorder in his pocket? Jazz isn't like pop music. He can't pull a Milli Vanilli.''

"He acts as if he can't speak English, but Sal . . . you know, at the barbershop across from my cafe . . . is positive he heard Louis speaking English to his father.''

"How?''

"Oh, I guess putting a subject and a verb together. I don't know how.''

"No, Heaven, how did Sal think he heard him speaking English?''

"They came out of the cafe, stopped in front of his barbershop, and the kid said something to his dad in English. Now, why would the Vangirovs lie about Louis's ability to speak English unless it meant something?''

Jim shrugged, nodding wisely. "Plenty of foreigners do that. They pretend they can't speak the language so they can avoid answering a lot of silly questions and people will talk in front of them, say things they wouldn't if they thought they were understood. I did it myself in France, played dumb. But I've never seen any evidence the kid understands a thing. And even if he did, it doesn't mean he stole the sax, for heaven's sake."

"Well, we'll see, won't we," Heaven said as she stood up.

"Heaven, I don't like the sound of that. Please leave the poor kid alone."

"Jim, this is your town and this is a district dedicated to the kind of music you play. This so-called curse of Eighteenth and Vine won't exactly make people want to come down here, even though they showed up today, thank goodness. Now, I know I'm a little sensitive because of that photo in the paper this morning and I know the New York papers will pick it up because of Ella, but just about everything that could go wrong has, and I'm surprised that you're not more upset about it. What if Louis and his father are some kind of decoy?"

"For what?"

"I don't know—yet," Heaven said with emphasis on the "yet." She got up and walked toward the stage without waiting for Jim or looking back. He thought about running to catch her but he couldn't move. The gloom that had settled over him the day before was tightening its grip.

By the time Heaven reached the stage, Boots Turner's set was over and Louis had run out to sit by the big man for a photo op. Heaven saw Murray talking to Mr. Vangirov behind the piano. She smiled broadly at both of them, a signal for Murray to do something.

"So, Mr. Vangirov, I thought Louis dropped the beat a wee bit on that first sixteen bars of the Jay McShann piece," Murray said like a true jazz geek.

It didn't take a detective to notice Louis's reaction. He whipped around to see the idiot who had doubted his tempo. His little eyes were full of hurt pride for a second.

When he caught himself, he smiled at Murray sweetly. "Louis has trouble with that piece," Mr. Vangirov admitted. "Was it noticeable?"

"Gosh, no," Murray said, not wanting to hurt the kid's feelings if he could understand. He wasn't sure Heaven was on target about this.

Boots Turner looked up and saw Heaven. "We meet again. How's your head?"

"Sore. I see you've met Louis Armstrong Vangirov. Isn't he amazing?"

"Boy has licks," Boots said. Mr. Vangirov made the pretense of translating. Louis smiled beatifically.

"Have you ever played in Russia, Boots?" Heaven asked. Murray rolled his eyes.

Boots nodded in the affirmative. "All around the world, especially in the sixties. That was when the State Department would send us overseas to be their secret weapon."

"Musicians?"

"Yeah. Old Congressman Adam Clayton Powell sent Dizzy, me, Louis. It was the Cold War, you know. We were fighting the Commies for the third-world countries." Boots chuckled.

"I saw Louis Armstrong in Minsk in 1961," Mr. Vangirov threw in proudly.

"They called 'em goodwill tours," Boots mused. "We went to Africa, Asia, you name it. They loved us in Africa, baby. 'Course, that whole goodwill stuff was a crock."

"What was a crock?" Murray asked.

"They had goodwill for us when we were in other countries, but back home, we were still sitting in the back of the bus.

"Louis Armstrong was going to Africa and he canceled, bless his heart. Said as long as that Faubus was keepin' children out of school in Arkansas, the government could go to hell." Boots chuckled. "The FBI opened one of their files on him and tried to catch him doing something they didn't like till the day he died."

208

"Did you ever feel that you were being investigated?" Murray asked, completely sucked into this little wrinkle in history he'd never considered before.

"Oh, sure, baby," Boots said, softly playing "All of Me" and letting Louis join in. "We had an integrated band, and to some, that was out of line. That group was as American as you could get: black, white, male, female, Jews, and Baptists. I remember a cracker spitting on Sam Scott in Atlanta, calling her a nigger lover." With the mention of Sam Scott, Boots looked melancholy.

Jim Dittmar appeared beside Heaven. "Boots, are you stealing my duet partner?" he joked. "Louis, vamoose, we've got a show to put on." The quartet playing next had joined the group around the piano and was waiting respectfully for Boots to get his butt off the stage. As Boots walked off, Heaven pulled Jim to the side.

Jim looked tolerant but condescending. "Well, Agatha Christie, did you trick the kid into an English phrase?"

"Listen to me," Heaven said excitedly. "Boots was talking about how all the bands toured the world, sent by the State Department in the 1960s. And we know the Vangirovs had black market jazz records. That's how Louis learned to play. So, what if someone back home in Minsk, or wherever, fell in love with jazz when those bands were going over there and now is willing to pay big bucks for Charlie Parker's saxophone? I bet Louis and his dad took it and we have to get it back before they leave here. It's a cultural icon! And yes, he understood when Murray criticized his tempo."

Jim shook his head. "You have a wild imagination, Counselor. I can guarantee you that Louis did not steal the sax."

"You cannot guarantee something like that," Heaven said with a stomp of her high-heeled foot.

"Heaven, I've been thinking about what you said, about our city pride and all that shit. You're going to have to trust me for a few hours. The Charlie Parker sax will not leave the city, if I play my cards right."

"Tell me!" Heaven demanded.

"No. We have to get off the stage now. Come on."

Heaven agreed only because she saw Detective Bonnie Weber moving through the crowd. She grabbed Jim's arm. "Please, promise you'll call me at the restaurant later."

"I promise. Now, let me introduce this group," Jim said tensely.

Heaven stopped for a word with Bonnie before heading for the cafe. She had to work the sauté station tonight.

Bonnie Weber had visited the Rosedale Barbecue stand and was digging into a beef on a bun.

Heaven, always bossy about food, corrected her choice. "At Rosedale, you order chicken. They have the best chicken. And someone around here has the best sweet potato pie. Murray got me a piece."

"You know I hate chicken," Bonnie Weber reminded her friend. "Unless I see its little head cut off right in front of me, I won't be comfortable eating chicken. I only like home-grown chickens, not mass-produced ones."

"And they are mass-produced," Heaven agreed. "Their little claws never touch the ground. They live their lives in cages."

Bonnie took a bite out of her barbecue beef and eyed her friends. "How's your wound?"

"It hurts like hell. How's Ella?"

"She's groggy still, but they don't have to do brain surgery or anything. I talked to her about an hour ago, and the doc was right on my ass so I couldn't really do a proper job of questioning, but Ella said basically the same thing that you did: she didn't see anyone before she went down."

Heaven decided she better trot out her new pet theory. "Okay, forget about that for a minute. I think Louis can really speak English and he's been acting like he can't and I know you don't have time to solve the robbery too but the cases seem to be related so maybe if he's lying about the English he might be lying about other things."

"That bump on the head has addled your brain," Bonnie said sarcastically.

"Okay, then, I'm leaving if you don't want my input. I've got to go to work," Heaven said. She dreaded working the line tonight. Her skin was drawn across her head wound so tightly she thought it was going to burst.

"Don't go away mad," Bonnie said with a humorless laugh.

"What are you going to do?"

"Shake the trees a little, then go home and have dinner with my family. I'm bushed. Your little escapade last night wasn't the most restful."

"For me, either. If I get through this evening without biting someone's head off, I'll be doing good," Heaven said as she marched resolutely away. She knew she should give Bonnie the photographs and tell her about Boots and the girls but she didn't have the stomach for the trouble she'd be in. She had to get through the night first.

Bonnie Weber walked across the street to the open door of the new jazz museum. She could see Nolan Wilkins escorting a group of local businessmen from the big band area to the bebop department, where an empty wall case, the one that had held the famous saxophone, had been covered up.

Nolan spotted Bonnie Weber and quickly walked toward her. Nothing she had to say could be something the businessmen needed to hear. "Detective, terrible about last night. I thought the worst had happened already, what with Evelyn and the theft of our prize exhibit."

"I thought you guys over at City Hall knew what we know at the police department: Things can always get worse. It doesn't seem to have kept the crowd away."

Some relief showed on Nolan's worried face. "The crowds have been great. We were sold out last night for the concert, and today the families really seem to be enjoying themselves."

"Just so you know, there were no fingerprints on Evelyn Edwards's cell phone."

"Good. I mean, I'm glad that's over."

Bonnie Weber pulled on Nolan's tie, straightening it a bit. "It's not over. The phone didn't levitate up to her ear. Even *her* fingerprints weren't on it. That means someone wiped it. A very bad sign. Now, go back to your sugar daddies." Bonnie walked away, ready to take the night off if the bad guys would let her.

Heaven was exhausted. It was almost eleven-thirty and somehow she had made it through the night in the hellishly hot kitchen. She had waited as long as she could but had finally taken a swig of the Tylenol Three elixir the emergency room had given her. The tight band of pain around her head was diminishing. She stepped out in the dining room, released from cleanup by Sara Baxter. Murray came over to her and took her arm. "You don't look so good, boss."

She smiled. "We were busy. This Eighteenth and Vine weekend brought in some business."

"Yeah, that was something, to have Tony Bennett and Sam Scott in the joint at the same time," Murray admitted.

"Did it go okay? Did they enjoy their evening?"

"Heaven, telephone," the bartender yelled.

"Yes, everyone enjoyed their evening. Go get the phone. It's probably Hank," Murray said. "He called earlier but I told him you couldn't talk. He just wanted to make sure you were up and at 'em."

It wasn't Hank. "Meet me at Lincoln," the familiar voice said.

"Please, don't make me," Heaven pleaded. "I just spent seven hours at the sauté station and my head is killing me."

"You've got to," the voice said, and hung up.

Heaven took off her chef's jacket and walked back to the kitchen, grabbed her jean jacket, switched from kitchen clogs to high heels, and gave a weak wave to the kitchen crew. She was halfway there when she realized she hadn't told anyone where she was going.

* * *

When Heaven had been an entertainment lawyer, one of her little tricks was to bring new clients to Lincoln Cemetery. There, she would lead them to Charlie Parker's grave and they would ooh and aah and say how cool it was, almost as cool as Jim Morrison's grave in Paris. Then Heaven would tell them this was a great example of why a musician had to have his affairs in order, because if there was one thing Charlie Parker had not wanted, it was to be buried in Kansas City. He had said it for the record dozens of times, yet here he was, planted in a town that "Bird" always felt didn't really understand him or his music. And remember, she would scold, he had been a young man when he passed, so it was their duty to assign those royalty rights and make those wills, matters no young person likes to think about, especially musicians, who are not known for long-range planning.

So driving toward Lincoln Cemetary at midnight, while not what Heaven wanted to be doing, was bringing back memories. For once, maybe because she was so tired, she was enjoying the snatches of scenes that she had played out at Charlie Parker's grave without thinking about what might have been if she hadn't lost her license to practice law. The tour and lecture had always involved drinking a bottle of champagne; she remembered that part fondly.

The gates to the cemetery were closed, so she parked her car on the street. This particular cemetery had beautiful old headstones, and high school kids with guns, when not shooting each other, loved to blast the top off a sandstone cross or riddle the fine old photographs that were part of some headstones with bullet holes. But it wasn't hard to get into the cemetery as the low stone walls on the side streets were built long before you had to protect the dead from the living. Heaven slipped over the wall and stood for a moment getting her bearings in the dark. The pain reliever was making all the edges of the scene soft and out of focus, surreal.

Long before her eyes adjusted to the dark, her ears picked up a melody. Even if she hadn't been to the Parker grave before, all she'd have to do tonight was follow the wail of an alto saxophone playing a bluesy rendition of "Take the A Train."

Heaven found Jim Dittmar sitting on the ground, leaning on the Parker headstone with a bottle of Dom Pérignon champagne wedged between his legs and the stolen sax in his hands.

Heaven sat down beside him. "I forgot you can play the sax," she said. "Too bad you can't afford anything but this plastic number."

Jim laughed ruefully and poured some champagne into a plastic cup. "This here is a four-million-dollar baby, Heaven. Cheers," he said, and clicked his plastic glass against hers.

"Are you going to tell me how this happened?"

"Here's the story," Jim said. "Take it or leave it. You got a call, a mysterious call, telling you to come out to Lincoln Cemetery and there, on Charlie Parker's grave, the caller said you would find something very important. You made the trip, found the sax, and get to be the hero."

"No questions asked or answered?"

Jim reached over and touched Heaven's face. "I will volunteer one piece of information."

"I'm ready."

"I didn't hurt you, nor do I know who did. Please believe that."

Heaven took another gulp of champagne. "I do believe that. But why don't you play the hero? Since we're making this up, the sax could fall into your hands just as easily as mine."

"Trust me, Heaven, it's better this way. I'm in enough trouble already; I don't need a front-page story."

Heaven desperately wanted to grill Jim until he told her the truth. But she was off her form. The head injury, the day and night on her feet, and the Tylenol elixir were taking their toll. She was more than willing to take the saxophone and run with it. In a minute. "When you say trouble, are you going to be arrested by INTERPOL or something? Do they still have INTERPOL?"

Jim chuckled. "No, I'm not talking about that kind of trouble. You know how it goes, Heaven. Sometimes it's easier said than done."

"What's easier said than done?"

Jim hadn't really told Heaven the story of his second career. Maybe later, in a month or two. Maybe not ever. "Leaving our past behind. Do you want this or not?" he said, waving the sax.

"Yes, hand it over. I thank you; the city thanks you," Heaven said as she jumped up and gave Jim a hand to get to his feet. He offered her the champagne bottle and she took a swig. She liked the way champagne straight from the bottle tickled your nose. She lowered the bottle and turned to Jim, pulling his head to hers. He had always been a great kisser. After a few seconds in an awkward but passionate kiss, awkward because their hands were full, she put down the champagne and took the saxophone.

"You coming?" Heaven asked.

"Nah. I think I'll stick around and kill the Dom, talk to the Bird a little, tell him my troubles. You know, you're the first person I visited this historical site with, Counselor."

"I was thinking about that on my way over here. Get your affairs in order was the lesson, as I remember. How are you doing on that one?"

"Better now," Jim said quietly. "I almost made a big mistake."

"Someone's going to be dissapointed. Is it those Russians?"

Jim laughed and shook his head. "You never stop, do you? No, it's not the Russians I'm worried about."

Heaven kissed him again, this time on the cheek, and turned toward the street and her van, waving the sax in the air. "Isn't it great when we get a second chance?" she called over her shoulder.

* * *

The hospital room was dark. Ella Jackson lifted the sheet and checked her watch one more time. The watch's face glowed if you pressed a button on the side. It was almost two in the morning. Surely she could get out of here soon. She had all of her clothes on, except her shoes. She'd done that a little at a time, putting on her underwear, then ducking back under the covers, then pulling on a pair of jeans and a sweatshirt she kept at the restaurant for dirty jobs. She'd insisted when two of her staff had come to visit that they go back and get those clothes, a pair of sneakers, and her purse, and bring them to the hospital. They'd tried to talk her out of it, said they'd bring them on Sunday, said she wasn't going anyplace until sometime next week, said they'd bring her a nice vintage outfit to leave the hospital in. She told them that if they knew what was good for them they'd go get the jeans and sweatshirt. They went.

Ella was in no condition to escape. The side of her face looked like raw hamburger and glistened with an anti bacterial gel. She had a crack in her skull, and the doctor had made her queasy with a description of how her brain was traumatized and swollen, pushing against the skull plate. Her hair had been shaved around the wound; the rest of her hair was matted and tangled. She would shave her whole head as soon as she could, go for the ethnic, hip-hop look.

Ella's vision was still fuzzy around the edges. There was some talk that a retina had been knocked loose. And the headache, the headache was throbbing throughout her body. Maybe it was a toothache; she could feel the sharp edges of a broken molar.

None of this had the least effect on Ella's decision to leave the hospital. She was determined.

Suddenly, a nurse stuck her head in the door. Ella moaned lightly and turned over on her side. The nurse tip-toed over to the bed and took Ella's pulse. Luckily, Ella had still been holding her watch in her hand. She had the covers up around her neck with her hand sticking out. She'd been able to pull up the sweatshirt sleeve when she'd turned over. She couldn't do anything about her racing pulse, though. The nurse didn't seem to be alarmed and left the room as quietly as she had come in. Ella stayed as still as she could, listening to the drumbeat of pain going through her body. She fell asleep for a short while and woke up with a start, feeling around in the bed for her watch. She grabbed it and pressed the button. Two-forty.

She slipped her feet over the side of the bed and padded over to the closet. The sneakers were there. She sat in the one chair in her room and put them on, having real difficulty with the tying part. Then she slipped her purse out of the bedside drawer and looked around the room once more. "I better get while the getting is good," she whispered, and peeked out the door. Luckily she was at the end of the hall, just across from a stairway Exit sign. In a minute, she was gone.

Duck and Sausage Gumbo

2 ducks
1 onion, quartered with skins
2 carrots
1 bunch parsley
celery, the leafy tops and the bottom
2 bay leaves
a few sprigs fresh herbs, oregano, thyme, savory
1 lb. smoked sausage, andouille if available, or Polish
½ lb. tasso or other spicy ham
½ cup medium dark roux
½ cup each diced onion, celery, green pepper
6–8 cloves garlic, minced
1 lb. okra sliced or 2 T. file gumbo powder
6 tomatoes, diced, or 1 28 oz. can whole tomatoes
Tabasco or other Louisiana hot sauce
1 T. soy sauce
½ tsp. cayenne
kosher salt and ground black pepper
Other Options: 1 lb. large shelled shrimp, oysters, rabbit,
    chicken

Making gumbo is a creative process with just a few rules to guide you. Rule #1. The Holy Trinity: onions, celery, and green pepper are the mirepoix of Cajun cooking, one of the basics. Rule #2. You need either file, which is ground sassafras roots, or okra to thicken your gumbo, not both. If you can't handle okra, use the file powder that is available at most good food stores. If you use okra, put it in the gumbo pot early, as the stringiness stops after cooking for a while and is the ingredient in okra that helps thicken the gumbo. Rule #3. You must use roux, but I'm passing on the easy oven method of making roux that comes from John Martin Taylor. No standing and stirring for hours with this one.

Stock

Make the stock for your gumbo with the ducks, onion, celery, carrots, bay leaves, and herbs in your largest stockpot full of cold water. Bring to a boil, then reduce to a simmer and cook until the meat is falling off the duck bones. Strain the meat and aromatics out of the stock. Cool the duck meat and separate from the bones and coarsely chop. As the stock cools, the duck fat will rise to the top and you can skim it off. You can do this step a day or two ahead of when you make your gumbo. Any extra stock can be frozen.

Roux

Mix equal parts melted fat and flour—the fat can be vegetable oil, lard, or duck fat. In other words, 1, 2, or 3 cups each of flour and fat, depending on how much roux you want to make. Spread the fat/flour mixture on a baking sheet with a rim. Bake at 350 degrees until the desired color is reached, in the case of the duck gumbo we want a color between caramel and mahogany. Stir every 15 minutes. Freeze in ½ cup quantities in plastic bags.

Gumbo

In your heaviest pot, sauté the trinity in the roux. When the onions are soft, add the garlic and the diced ham, then in

5 minutes or so, add the okra or file powder, the tomatoes, then about a gallon of duck stock. Simmer 30 minutes or so. Add the sausage, the duck meat, and more stock as needed, as well as the seasonings. Simmer another 30 minutes while you make long-grained white rice to serve your gumbo on.

Thirteen

How dare you!" Bob Daultman yelled. "You make a decision that affects the whole team, you cost us big bucks, you better have a damn good explanation."

"I only know what I read in the newspaper. Someone called Heaven Lee, told her to search at the grave of Charlie Parker, she found the sax, the city is saved from total humiliation, case closed." Jim Dittmar was unmoved by the filmmaker's hysteria. After he made up his mind the day before he'd never looked back.

Louis Armstrong Vangirov was eating Rice Krispies from room service in Bob Daultman's suite at the Ritz, a vast improvement over the Motel 6 that he and his father had been relegated to. Next job, he would insist on better accommodations. After all, he was an important part of the team. He glanced down at the front-page photo of Heaven walking into the police station with the sax. "Nice picture of Heaven. She got a nasty bump on her head."

"Who will pay us?" Mr. Vangirov whimpered. "And what about the customer in Japan? He prepaid, didn't he?"

"Four million bucks!" Bob Daultman screeched. "What in the fuck are we going to do about that, Mr. Dittmar?"

"You're the treasurer. Give it back," Jim said as he walked over to the round postal mailer he had brought with him and left propped by the door. He pulled out a rolled-up canvas and flung it out on the floor.

Bob Daultman perked right up.

Louis looked up from his breakfast cereal. "A nice Jasper Johns."

"Very nice indeed. Early sixties, one of the flag series. Well, well, well," Bob said as he walked around the painting.

Jim started rolling up the canvas "I called a few galleries before I liberated this baby. These are selling in the 5–10 million-dollar range now, depending on how many flags. Even if we have to dump it we can get 2 or 3 million. I don't want a penny, unless you get full price. That should pay all the overhead for this fiasco, give you three some change. I'm assuming you can return the sax money, that you didn't spend the client's millions before we delivered the goods."

In his mind Bob was already holding an auction for the painting. "Of course not," he snapped. "I learned my lesson about pre-spending from that unfortunate diamond-and-sapphire affair in Venice. How were we to know the old bird had sold the real diamonds years ago and was wearing paste?" He turned the edge of the canvas over and inspected the back. "Johns is still alive, but he's been out of this period for thirty years. There'll never be more of the flags. I think there's a collector in Brazil who would just love this."

"Don't forget the old clothes designer in Paris," Louis added, his face behind the Sunday funny papers.

Bob pointed at him as if he were the star pupil. "Good idea. Louis, you and your father can take this back with you tonight. You brought the suitcase with the fake bottom, didn't you?"

"Of course," Mr. Vangirov said.

Jim grabbed a piece of toast off the room service cart, smeared it with jam, and ate. "And, just to show you I'm sorry I reneged on this deal, I won't retire this year. I'll do Cannes," he said with his mouth full.

Bob Daultman and Mr. Vangirov smiled at each other, dollar signs flashing in their eyes.

Louis looked up from reading Snoopy. "How about Prague, too? The old broad and the emeralds? We've already spent time on her, getting to be her favorite piano players."

Jim shrugged. "Okay, I'll do the emeralds, too. Bob, look for a gig in Cannes in August, when all the rich folk from Paris throw their jewels around. Then we'll go to Prague. But I'm staying in Kansas City with my son until then."

Bob Daultman patted Jim on the back. "Our little family, back together again."

Louis beamed and turned the pages to find Doonesbury.

Heaven sat in the dark in the Negro Leagues Baseball Museum. They were previewing the Black Baseball History film for all the volunteers. Tears were running down Heaven's cheeks. Of course, she was a notorious softie, but the fifteen-minute piece was very effective, showing how the separate but unequal worked in sports. Heaven wondered what it would be like to travel around the country and not be able to find a place to eat or spend the night, to have people be afraid to drink from the same water fountain you drank from.

The film ended and applause filled the room. The lights went up. She looked at Mona, who sat beside her. "Well, if that wasn't something."

Mona wiped an errant tear from Heaven's face. "You better run into the bathroom and splash your face. You're the star of the day, so you can't be a crybaby."

Heaven tried a smile. "You know how easily I cry on a good day. I don't know if I can make it, Mona. I still have a headache and a lump. I stood on my feet for sixteen hours yesterday, then spent most of the night sitting at the police station, answering stupid questions."

"Well, you don't expect anyone to believe that story about the mystery man and the call and someone just leaving the sax on the grave, do you?" Mona asked as kindly as she could.

"That *is* the story, Mona. I promise. Not even Sal or Murray will get me to change it. It's a miracle, so why not just leave it at that." Heaven got up and they walked out into the sunshine.

"You should have done yourself a favor and insisted they call Bonnie and wake her up. You could have been home by two if you'd done that," Mona fussed.

"Bonnie—and you, too, I might add—was up all the night before at the emergency room with me. She needed her rest."

"So did you. What time did you have to get down here to meet the Cajun cookers?"

"I was home at three-thirty, and down here at nine-thirty. But from four to eight-thirty, I was dead to the world. Iris called and I didn't even hear the phone ring. And Hank, he called, too. I've got to call them back this evening, when this whole thing is finally over."

"If Hank were here, you'd be grounded, young lady, for not taking care of yourself," Mona asserted.

"What was I going to say when I got this mystery phone call? No, I can't come pick up the dumb sax because my head hurts?"

"Well, you could have told Murray where you were going. You don't need me to lecture you about that. I know Murray called you this morning as soon as he saw the paper and gave you hell. It was dangerous, young lady."

"I'm only six or seven years younger than you, you can't call me young lady," Heaven said.

"But you did make the front page of the paper two days in a row, a record even for you."

"Yes, and that was such an attractive shot of me going

into the police station at one in the morning, zonked out on painkillers and champagne, with a knot and a big purple bruise on my head, and the plastic sax in tow. There's never been a newspaper photographer just hanging out in front of the police station before. I guess this curse of Eighteenth and Vine has changed that."

"You had on cute high heels," Mona said.

"Thank God."

It was almost time for Lefty Stuart to speak. Then a huge gospel choir was scheduled to perform. The choir included Ray Charles, the Mighty Clouds of Joy, and most of the Staple Singers.

Secretly, the gospel was Heaven's favorite program of music of the whole weekend. She loved the jazz songbirds and that's what she played in her restaurant. The instrumental jazz bands that played on Saturday appealed to her mind. But the gospel music made the hairs stand up on her arms; it was goose pimple music, pure emotion.

Maybe it was so appealing because Heaven had been raised as a Presbyterian, belonging to a group not known for its rousing hymns. Maybe it was because she didn't have the kind of strong faith that gospel music celebrated. On this Sunday, Heaven was hoping for a little healing from the music. She was beat up physically, and even though she was thrilled about recovering the sax, the uneasy feeling that had been with her since Evelyn died hadn't gone away.

"How's the food?" Mona asked. Heaven was staring blankly at all the different choir robes and singers onstage, like a baby in a crib stares at a colorful mobile.

"Just great," Heaven said, and focused back on her friend. She'd have to watch herself today; she had just spaced out completely. "They've got the turkeys in the oil. It's time to light the grills for the oysters," she said, heading toward the grills, which for today had been rolled out in full view on Eighteenth Street. No one wanted to be hidden out of sight, even in broad daylight.

Today's dedication was an invitation only affair, but with

the baseball officials, the city fathers, and the corporate sponsors who were paying for the whole weekend, at least five hundred people would be eating lunch. At the last minute, the Cajuns had decided they should cook some crawfish, too, just in case. So there were three huge stockpots frying turkeys, two chock-full of crayfish and corn on the cob and new potatoes, big pans of jambalaya, soup tureens full of gumbo and etouffeé, and thousands of oysters to throw on the grill. It was a feast. Beer and wine and sparkling water were being poured at two drink stations, along with the drinks of the weekend, ice tea and lemonade.

The mayor called everyone to attention and introduced Nolan Wilkins, explaining how Nolan was the one who had pushed for the Negro Leagues Baseball Museum. Nolan got to introduce Lefty Stuart, noting that he was the fourth player from the Negro Leagues to go to the majors; one of eleven from the Negro Leagues to be inducted into Cooperstown, in the Baseball Hall of Fame; the first black coach in the majors. Mona was watching her friend, Sam Scott, and saw how much love and pride shone in her eyes as she looked at her husband.

"Bullet Joe Rogan, Smokey Joe Williams, Turkey Stearnes, Mule Suttles, Biz Mackey, Willie Wells," Lefty began his speech. "These are just a few of the players who should have a place in the Hall of Fame. These are players who made the Negro Leagues so popular that our annual all-star game at Comiskey Park often out drew the white all-star game, with fifty thousand folks in attendance.

"But these good men aren't in Cooperstown, so it's with special thanks, that I come to Kansas City to dedicate this museum to honor the history of the Negro Leagues. Because of you, these fine players will have a place for their story to be told. Thank you for giving us our place in history," Lefty said to a great round of applause.

"You in Kansas City can be proud of the man who owned your Kansas City Monarchs, J. L. Wilkerson," he continued. "Wilkie invented night baseball by rigging tall decks of lights five years before the white majors had night baseball, and he never got any credit for it when the white leagues adopted his technology. This is just one of the many stories you will hear when you go through the museum. It is full of the tales of professional men, going back to 1884, when Moses Fleetwood Walker played in the big leagues, before they decided they didn't want black players. You'll learn about Andrew "Rube" Foster, who established the Negro National League in 1920 and paid the price for his hard work, dying in a mental hospital in 1930." The sadness in his voice was real.

"I could go on and on, telling you about these good men. When Jackie Robinson was asked to join the white major leagues, their stories faded. Now, here in Kansas City, they will be honored. They will be remembered." Lefty bowed to the audience, signaling the end of his speech. There couldn't have been many dry eyes at that moment. Heaven noticed one of the most hardhearted bankers in town wiping a tear as he cheered. The applause was deafening.

The choir went right into an up-tempo gospel song, and for just a minute, Heaven understood why people went to church. She let the beat carry her for a minute, her eyes closed. When Bonnie Weber came up and goosed her, she jumped.

"Congratulations on your amazing discovery. You made my buddies over in the burglary department very happy—very puzzled, but happy. Are you going to tell me what really happened?"

"No," Heaven said with a grin. "But I do have to tell you something about Evelyn and Ella."

"And I have to tell you something about Ella first. She walked out of Saint Luke's Hospital during the night. I don't have the foggiest idea where she is. I've checked her hotel room and the cafe. I'm out of ideas."

Heaven looked down, not wanting to make eye contact with her friend while she confessed another infraction. "I went up to Evelyn's office—after you'd been there, of

course—and someone had already trashed the place looking for something. I think it was Ella."

"Keep going."

"And this mirror was broken on the floor and I picked
it up and said, 'Someone is going to have seven years of bad
luck.' That's another reason I think it's Ella. Then these two
photographs fell out of the back of the broken mirror. They
were both of the same man, but in each photo he was with
a different woman and little girl."

"And you didn't give them to me?"

Heaven shook her head, trying to think of a good defense. Finally, she just moved on with her story. "I had the
photos blown up, hoping someone would recognize the
people. Julia Marcus did. Well, not everyone; she recognized
the man. It was Boots Turner in both pics. She didn't know
either woman or child. But I think one was Evelyn and one
was Ella."

"Is that all?" Bonnie was steaming like Heaven knew she
would be.

"Well, almost. I showed the photos to Boots."

Finally, Bonnie blew up. "You did what? You went to confront a suspect by yourself?"

"Murray was right behind me. Well, actually Murray was
in the same hotel. No one's going to hurt you at the Ritz,
for God's sake. Let me tell you the rest. And I'll take a
tongue-lashing, but does it have to be today? I'm on my last
leg."

"Please continue."

"Boots says that he can't be the father of either of the
little girls because he can't have children, something about
the mumps when he was little. And Murray says that men
don't lie about stuff like that anymore because of the good
DNA testing."

"Did Boots say he knew the mothers?"

"Yes, he said he had a relationship with them both, but
the girls were already born. They were small, though, so if
Boots were around, he might be their first memory."

"But if they thought Boots was their daddy, and he'd never been around since, they must have cooked up some way to confront him this weekend. Together."

"I guess that eliminates Ella as a suspect in Evelyn's death," Heaven said with a hint of disappointment.

Bonnie shook her head. "I don't think so. It sounds like a plan that could go bad in a minute—sibling jealousy, revenge, and some kind of a scam. Every one of those can lead to murder."

"Bonnie, I'm sorry I didn't tell you about this sooner, I really am. Now I'm going to grill about a thousand oysters. I promised the Cajun cookers," Heaven said, and headed across the street. Bonnie turned around and around. She didn't know where to start.

Boots stood at the side of the bed, bent down and gently shook the arm of the woman sleeping in his bed. "Ella, it's past noon, time to get up. How you feelin'?"

Ella Jackson moaned and raised herself up. "I feel like I been rode hard and put away wet." She'd slept in the clothes she walked away from the hospital in. Now she got up and looked at the mirror. "Now, this is a scary-lookin' child. I'm gonna need some time in that shower to make things right."

Boots led her gently into the living room of his suite. "First you're gonna have a nice breakfast. I didn't know what you liked, so I got a little of everything—French toast, an omelette, bacon, and orange juice and coffee. I'm going to jump into the shower while you eat, then you can have the bathroom."

"Thanks, Pops," Ella said sourly.

"I'm not your father, Ella. I wish I could solve that mystery for you. I know it must be hard, not knowin'."

"Then why did you let me in here last night, sleepin' on the couch so I could have the bed, and why are you treating me so nice now?"

"Well, child, you must not have felt safe going to your own place. Whoever did this to you may not be done."

Ella didn't answer. She tucked into the French toast silently. Boots started to say something else, but went to take his shower instead. He wanted to help this girl, he surely did. But she had so much anger and sadness.

Ella waited until the water was going full force in the bathroom. Then she got up with a little stagger, grabbed the table for a second, then went over to the suitcases that Boots had stacked in the corner. "Let's just see what the hell we've got here, Pops," Ella said as she threw the cases on the bed and opened them. She had no idea what she was looking for, a scrap of paper with her name on it, a newspaper clipping, a birth certificate. She found a wad of cash and slipped it into her jeans pocket. "Thanks, daddy-o," she murmured as she continued the search.

Then her hand hit the cold metal of the .357 that Boots had stuck into the suitcase. She pulled it out, looked in the side pocket, and found the clips. By the time Boots Turner came out of the bathroom in a clean white tee-shirt and a crisp pair of navy blue pleated trousers, Ella Jackson was standing where he could see her right away. "Smart of you to bring this big old gun, Pops. You never know when some nut will invade your bedroom. Now, get your shoes on. We got to go to the big grand finale down at Eighteenth and Vine."

You either had them or you didn't, and Heaven had them. Waitress ears and eyes, that is. Waitress ears gave you the ability to hold a conversation in front of you and hear way off to the side that someone needed cream for their coffee or wanted to order dessert. Waitress eyes allow you to smile at the table you're serving and see the guy waving for his check practically behind your back. Heaven's waitress eyes snapped on when she saw Boots Turner coming across the street. She was talking to Jim Dittmar at the time, but she kept Boots in her sights so she could try to figure out what he was up to. Heaven, stuck behind the grill, was down to her last two hundred oysters. She put the ones that had popped open on a big platter, then dribbled a little more hot sauce and butter on them before she took them over to the serving table. "Here. These are heavy. Take this one over to the serving area and get me two empty platters. I'm almost finished, thank God."

"Yes, Counselor," Jim Dittmar answered happily, and grabbed the oysters. He had taken Louis and his father to the airport and seen their plane take off. Bob Daultman was still here, of course, but he was busy in the truck and hadn't bothered Jim all afternoon. It was almost as if he had his life back.

Heaven stood as close to Boots Turner as she could get and not leave the grill. He was talking to Nolan Wilkins. "I need your help over at the Ruby, man," Boots said.

Nolan, relieved because the day had gone so well, smiled and held out his hand to shake Boots's. He hadn't noticed the worried look. "Where've you been, Boots? You would have loved hearing Ray Charles sing with the Mighty Clouds of Joy. It was down."

"Today was Lefty's day. I wasn't even going to stop here before I went to the airport," Boots said gruffly, glancing over at Lefty and Sam Scott, who were sitting at a table surrounded by Lefty's fans. "But I had to."

"What do you mean, you had to?" Nolan asked.

"Nolan, man, please just come over to the Ruby with me. I think I left something, and I really need your help."

Heaven could see Nolan's face from where she was standing. She could see him trying to figure out why it was so important to Boots that he, Nolan, helped him instead of a janitor or some other attendant at the theater. Then she heard Nolan, out of politeness to the old guy, say, "Sure, Boots. Let's go, man." The two men took off across the street arm in arm.

Heaven started splashing hot sauce on her last batch of

oysters as fast as she could. When Jim Dittmar came back, his hands full of empty platters, she started barking orders. "Just give these two more minutes, then plate them up. I have to run across the street for just a minute. I'll be right back." She took off running before Jim had a chance to argue.

"Heaven, what's up?" he yelled after her. She didn't look back.

The theater was dark, but the doors were unlocked. Heaven supposed they had left the Ruby open so anyone could poke their head in for a look-see. The crowd was on the other side of the street, filing into the jazz and baseball museums in a steady stream. There was a line to get into the baseball film.

Heaven crept into the Ruby, wondering what in the world Boots and Nolan were up to. She went into the theater and started toward the front. Two spotlights were making pools of light on the stage. Nolan was standing in one, Boots in the other. Heaven waited in the back, in the dark. What was going on?

"I am sorry, man," Boots was saying. "But if I hadn't gone and got you, she would have started shooting outside where all the folks are."

"Shut up, Pops!" a disembodied voice yelled. A gunshot hit the stage near Boots Turner. He jumped, and so did Nolan Wilkins.

"Ella, how did you ever get the idea I was your daddy? I know it didn't come from your mother. She wouldn't lie to you."

"Evelyn had these letters you wrote her momma. You said you were real proud of me, how I'd become important in the food business." Ella fired again, making both men jump. Boots was mopping his forehead. Heaven knew his heart was pounding.

The shots were coming from above the stage.

"Why would you be talking about me to Evelyn's

momma? You asked about Evelyn, too, and there were the photographs," the voice said.

"We were friends. Us old folks still write letters, talk about what's going on with our friends. Did you know your two mommas knew each other when they were young? I met them both at a big dance hall down in Oklahoma somewhere near Salisaw," Boots offered. Heaven could tell he was trying to engage Ella in her past, the real past, not the fantasy that she and Evelyn had created.

"You bastard," Ella screamed. "You left my momma for her momma, or vise versa." Two more shots rang out, this time one landed near Nolan, who had been beginning to ease out of the spotlight. He jumped back into the middle of the pool of light.

Boots looked up, and Heaven tracked where he was looking—the catwalk over the stage. Heaven crept down the side aisle, careful to stay in the dark.

"I did not, Ella," Boots protested. "I met your mother, then six months later, when we were touring in Oklahoma again, she had a boyfriend, a man you must remember because Harry and your mother got married."

"A damn Indian bastard," Ella shouted.

"Yes, well, I know it didn't work out, child. But that was why I met Evelyn's mom. It was innocent."

"Ha!" Ella replied with another shot, which pinged off a stage light. Heaven was afraid one of these wild shots was going to ricochet and actually hit someone. "And you, Nolan, you killed my sister, you bastard."

Nolan Wilkins's face crumbled. "It was an accident."

Heaven started walking faster. Nolan knew better than to confess while he was in the target zone.

"Talk, sucker," Ella yelled.

Nolan tried to look up and another shot whistled across the stage. He put his arms up over his head, trying to protect himself. "She called and told me the florist was coming to the meeting to tell the committee about her kickbacks.

She said she better be able to keep her job if I knew what was good for me. She pushed me up against the wall and grabbed my hand and put it up under her dress," Nolan's voice broke into a sob.

Heaven slipped off her shoes and crept up the steps on the same side of the stage she thought Ella was on. She figured it would be harder for Ella to spot her if she came up behind her. Silently, she searched for the ladder to the catwalk and spotted it downstage. Boots Turner spotted her and she put her finger up to her lips to hush him. Boots turned toward Nolan and away from Heaven. "Son, maybe you shouldn't try to talk about this now," Boots said in a soothing voice.

"Talk," Ella yelled. "Talk or you'll die."

Heaven started up the ladder.

Nolan continued, his voice shaking. "I had to wash my hands. They had her . . . her perfume on them. I grabbed a rag from under the sink. I washed and washed. Then someone called my name out in the lobby. I must have left the water running; the rag was on the edge of the sink. It must have fallen in and the water got stopped up and ran over."

"Ella, it sounds like the boy didn't mean to hurt Evelyn. And that girl, she wasn't your sister. You've got to get over that idea."

"Shut up, Pops. Nolan, tell pops here. No matter that you might have stopped up that sink by accident. You tried to kill me for real, you bastard."

Nolan glanced up and continued. "Ella saw me with Evelyn at the theater, before she died. Ella laughed and said it was worth free rent for her restaurant. I couldn't do that. I told her we had to talk about it in private, away from her restaurant and her crew, on Friday night. We met outside. I just felt so desperate. I grabbed the first thing I saw and slammed her. Then Heaven came around the corner and I hit her. I went back to the theater and, if someone hadn't found them in ten minutes, I swear I would have called 911 myself." Nolan hung his head, knowing how gutless he sounded.

"You bastard. Take this," Ella said, and this time she shot him in the arm. He collapsed, howling with pain and holding his arm. Blood spattered everywhere.

Heaven was on the ladder two steps away from the catwalk, peeking over the top. She looked around desperately for something to hit Ella with. A thick rope was looped around the catwalk. It had a big knot on the end, a knot about the size of a softball. Heaven slipped the rope from the catwalk and dashed up the last two steps. With one hand, she grabbed the ladder for balance. With the other she swung the rope back as hard as she could.

"What do you think you're doing, Ella? It must be thirty feet high up here. Get down right now," Heaven demanded like a schoolteacher. She let go of the rope, and it swung slowly in an arc toward Ella. Ella tried to swat it, but instead of the rope knocking the gun out of her hand, as Heaven had hoped, Ella lost her balance. She just crumpled and slipped over the edge, but managed to hold on to the catwalk with one hand. In the other hand was the gun, which seemed to be discharging automatically. Heaven peeked down. She could see no one. Nolan had obviously crawled out of the spotlight, and Boots had disappeared.

"Boots, go get help," Heaven yelled, hoping he was hiding somewhere. "Ella, drop that gun and hold on with both hands. I can't help you if you're waving that damn gun around."

Ella held the gun high in the air and tried to point it in Heaven's direction. When she pulled the trigger nothing happened.

"Now that you've used all your fucking bullets, drop that stupid gun," Heaven yelled. A second later she heard a clatter on the stage.

Heaven was holding on to the ladder, but she would have to let go to get to Ella. She decided to crawl, so she extended herself, dropped to her knees, and let go, grabbing the catwalk tightly. She started crawling slowly toward Ella, trying not to look down. She could hear Nolan whimpering somewhere on the stage below.

"Ella, say something to me. When you stop yelling I get worried."

Ella's voice sounded scared. She no longer seemed bigger than life. "Heaven, I think I've fucked up, girl. I can't hold on much longer."

Heaven crawled a little faster. "You better hang on; you've got me up here, and I don't have very good balance. If I fall to my death, I'll haunt you forever." Heaven stopped, laid down on the catwalk, grabbed Ella's arm, and peeked over the side. "Jesus, what happened to you? Wait, I know what happened to you. But that shaved patch on your head is a bad look."

"Only you would take this time to insult me, Heaven. I'm going to fall, baby."

"No, you won't fall! Do this. I can't stand and pull you up. You have to swing your legs and then I'll pull your body up. Now swing, damn it!"

Ella threw her leg as high as she could. Heaven heard noise at the entrance to the theater. She hoped it wouldn't spook Ella. "Now, Ella, the other leg. Don't pay any attention to them." Ella threw her other leg and now was hanging upside down, like a kid on a jungle gym. Heaven pulled and tugged on the other woman. "Help! Somebody, help me. I can't do this alone."

Bonnie Weber appeared on the catwalk at the other side of the stage and started crawling toward Heaven. "I'm coming, just hold your horses. Ella, slip your elbows through the scaffolding so you can get some weight off your hands. Heaven, just stay as flat as possible."

Heaven looked down and saw Mona, Sam Scott, Lefty, and of course Jim Dittmar. "The fire department is right outside, Heaven. They're coming in with the big net, just in case you fall," Mona said, trying to be helpful.

By this time, Bonnie had reached the two women. "H, help me haul her butt up here," Bonnie said while she reached down and grabbed Ella's arm, jerking on her like she was a sack of potatoes. The firemen were below, holding a large trampoline-style net they used as a last resort in fires. In a moment it was inflated, and it looked like the kind of mattresses stunt men used. Bonnie Weber looked down. "Okay, on second thought, this will be easier. Bye, Ella." She unwound Ella's fingers from the catwalk scaffolding, and the woman fell like a stone, only to bounce a couple of times below. Heaven and Bonnie looked down. "Last one down buys the wine," Bonnie said.

Heaven looked down and called, "Hey, get her out of the way. We're flying down." Police officers and firemen grabbed Ella. The medics were already working on Nolan.

Bonnie held out her hand. They were just able to touch fingers, so Bonnie scooted closer to Heaven so they could hold hands. She held a thumbs-up and started counting. "On three. One, two, three." The two women rolled off the catwalk and down onto the inflatable mattress.

Everyone applauded.

Jim Dittmar followed Heaven into her darkened home. "Thank you for doing this, but don't think we're going to have sex or anything just because I practically died today," Heaven said as she flipped on the light in the big kitchen.

Jim smiled, ignoring Heaven's wisecracks, and opened the refrigerator. "Not bad for someone in the business. I've observed over the years that the refrigerators of restaurant people are usually empty or just full of booze. We've got a whole turkey breast, minus one or two slices, some Swiss cheese, a head of roasted garlic, some Brie. Any bread to make a sandwich with?"

Heaven opened the freezer and produced a loaf of sourdough. "We can slice this and put it in the toaster oven, but I don't think I have the strength to slice frozen bread."

She let her head fall to one side dramatically, as if she were failing, which she was. "I need champagne, then I need to call my daughter. She's in England, you know."

Jim was busy cutting perfect slices of bread out of the sourdough. "Why don't you go call your daughter, take a quick shower, get into something more comfortable, and I'll be up with champagne and turkey melts in just a few minutes."

Heaven shook a finger at Jim. "Forget about the slip-into-something-more-comfortable routine. I only let you come here because I agreed with you and Bonnie and everyone else that I shouldn't be alone tonight."

"You've had a tough weekend, Counselor, what with saving the city and Ella Jackson," Jim said as he sliced turkey. "Where's the butter?"

Heaven took the butter out of the refrigerator door and handed it to Jim. "It's Plugra. And I knew you wouldn't ask me as many silly questions as Mona or Murray. Bonnie was busy with Nolan and Ella."

"What'll happen to them?"

"For Nolan, it's manslaughter for Evelyn, assault for Ella and me, but he's a good guy who did bad things. He should be able to plead down," Heaven said as she cut a piece of Brie and found some crackers in a cupboard. "Ella, I think if she promised to never come back to Kansas City, she might get off. But I guess she will be prosecuted for kidnapping Boots at gunpoint and shooting Nolan."

Jim shook his head. "I don't think Boots will testify against her."

"I don't either," Heaven said as she ate cheese and crackers and made one for Jim. "One good thing that came out of this disaster was that by the end of the day Mona and Sam Scott were talking to each other and so were Boots and Lefty and Sam. I saw them all hug good-bye. There's just nothing like a good disaster to bring people together."

Jim smiled. "And Bob Daultman was as happy as a pig in you know what. He still had all his crews working when the scene in the Ruby came down, so they covered it from all POVs. I'm sure you'll see yourself falling from that catwalk in slow motion in a screening room near you. He got a little more than just an artsy jazz documentary. He'll take that to Cannes next year and win something."

"What about Louis and his dad? I bet they weren't pleased, leaving empty-handed," Heaven said, trying one more time.

Jim grinned and shook his head. "They left happy, trust me." He put down the knife and took Heaven by the hand. "Go upstairs and call your daughter. I'll behave and I'll feed you, I promise."

"I am kind of hungry," Heaven said as she went up the stairs. "And cranky," she yelled.

Jim smiled, looked for and found a sauté pan big enough to grill two sandwiches at once. He turned on a burner, set the pan on the fire, and dropped in a pat of butter. From above he heard a one-sided conversation.

"Iris, it's your mom. I guess you're not home. I'm sorry I missed your call this morning. It won't be a Sunday without talking to you. You won't believe what happened to me today. Call soon. I'm fine."

Then another. "Hi, Hank. I guess you're off at the emergency room. Well, before you see some silly picture of me in the newspaper, we had another little problem today at the Ruby Theater, but I'm fine now. I'm dead. I mean, I'm alive and well, just tired, so don't call me back tonight. I'll talk to you tomorrow."

Soon he heard the shower go on and then off. Jim found plates, a wine bucket, champagne glasses, and a bottle of Veuve Clicquot, cold in the refrigerator. When he got to Heaven's room with all the loot, he found her curled up with the phone resting on the bed next to her, fast asleep in a big Kansas City Monarchs tee-shirt.

Jim put the tray on a coffee table and leaned down to ruffle Heaven's hair with a hand that then touched her lips. She didn't stir and he plopped down in a big leather club chair and poured himself a glass of champagne then turned on the television. He took the diamond out of his jeans pocket and tossed it up in the air, caught it with one hand, then put it back in his jeans. "Another day, another dollar," he said out loud, and started on his sandwich.

It was great to be back in Kansas City.

Recipe Index